MIDTOWN SOUTH

The hot center of the world's most intense city—New York.

MIDTOWN SOUTH

The place that pulses twenty-four hours a day with all kinds of people—and all kinds of crime.

MIDTOWN SOUTH

The new novel of authentic police action and gripping human interaction by a talent to watch,

CHRISTOPHER NEWMAN

MIDTOWN SOUTH

Christopher Newman

FAWCETT GOLD MEDAL • NEW YORK

A Fawcett Gold Medal Book
Published by Ballantine Books

Library of Congress Catalog Card Number: 86-91175

ISBN 0-449-13064-9

Manufactured in the United States of America

First Edition: September 1986

For Jim Houston and
Page Stegner

ONE

It was hot in the room. Sweltering. Sweat trickled from the Blade's armpits. Fourteen months of crawling through the city's social sewer were about to pay off. The constant testing and ass sniffing. Pissing blood for three days just a month ago, after Mickey and his pack of biker thugs sized him up, with a couple bootprints on his kidneys for good measure. He'd passed all their little tests.

The netherworld of the Lower East Side was crowded with dilapidated dumps like this. Four stories of crumbling brick, designed initially as tenements for emigrant Europeans. Italians, Ukranians, Hungarians, Lithuanians, and the list goes on. As they have, to melt in the pot. But the buildings and a few diehards remain in squalor previously unimagined by even the lowest slumlord. Perfect for an outlaw motorcycle gang. This block was their turf, something the neighbors learned to accept and finally even appreciate. The cops couldn't protect a daughter walking home on that street after dark, but the gang could and did. It was generally understood that they didn't want any trouble here. Those who broke this unwritten law got plenty of time in Intensive Care at Bellevue to think and reconsider. Word got around.

The Blade would have preferred a more neutral site for the transaction. But Mickey had the goods, so Mickey made the rules. The Blade could only go along if he hoped to consummate the deal. His kidneys and his pride had suffered too much indignity to allow turning back. So he carried on through with it, working without a net on a highwire stretched between now and never.

The place stunk of rotting garbage. In one corner, a dented can overflowed. Beer bottles. Styrofoam burger and french-fry containers. Mickey pulled a six-pack of Bud in cans from the refrigerator and offered him one. He accepted, only to let it go flat on the table next to his elbow. It was no time to let the edges of perception fray. Not now.

The wire itched. Outside on the street, Sammy sat in the beat-up Econoline van, getting all of it on tape. It was the first time they'd used this unit picking it up from Intelligence the previous afternoon. It was smaller than the old rig, about the size of a Zippo lighter. And light. Only the pull of adhesive tape against his skin reminded him that he had a death warrant taped to his rib cage.

It seemed uncommonly quiet in the place. Only a few of the customary Harleys were parked at the curb outside. Upstairs somewhere, he could hear a pounding heavy metal riff. Mickey's only backup in the kitchen of this first-floor apartment was a heavy-muscled cretin with oily, swept-back hair and a crowbar-customized set of teeth. Johnny the Ape. The same charmer who had danced the two-step on the Blade's lower back.

Shoulder against the door and looking bored, the Ape

belched and crushed the empty beer can in his hand. At the table, Mickey lifted the first bag out of the leather satchel and grinned.

"Dig it, hotshot. Pure Bolivian blow. You want? Mickey delivers. Now I think you got something to show me."

The biker had been eyeing him with the wariness of a cobra. This skinhead punk in the tight black leather and spikes was part of a new order he didn't want to understand. Weird, vicious, and slippery. The Blade wasn't the first of his kind he'd dealt with. In this case, he'd thought it wise to assert his physical dominance early on. He knew Johnny hurt him. But he was back. With $200,000. Moving with the appearance of fearlessness.

The Blade's shaved head was running rivulets in the heat, the beads of perspiration glistening like dew on a melon. He stooped for his briefcase, wiping the sting of salt from his eye. Setting it on the table, he thumbed the latches. Stacks of closely packed twenties sighed with release.

Mickey selected a bundle of 500 and fingered it.

"Okay, slick," he said. "Do your thing."

The Blade removed a small kit from his hip pocket and uncorked two vials. A little of the powder went into each. Positive. Now came the clincher. Digging from the bag with a carefully cultivated little fingernail, he snorted with gusto. Mickey relaxed visibly.

The hype had been accurate. The tests spoke of extraordinary purity. The Blade's brain was refusing to quibble with science.

"Sold," he grunted, pushing the briefcase at Mickey. "Very nice." A small smile forced its way past the edges of his curled lips.

Outside, a pair of chopped Harley panheads rumbled and coughed to a stop. Boots thudded on the stoop and up the hall outside. The door behind the Ape reverberated with heavy thudding.

"Mickey. It's Mutt. Open up."

Mickey nodded to Johnny. The Ape pushed off from the panel and slid the dead bolt. Two huge, grizzled bikers ambled into the room.

"This here's the Blade." Mickey indicated his guest with a sweep of his grease-stained paw. "Mutt and Ralphie."

The new arrivals eyed the Blade's leathers and shaved head. Acknowledgment was made with head jerks.

"The Blade's just bought himself four elbows of the slick spic."

Mutt absorbed this information. "You toss him?"

Mickey waved him off. "He's passed the test. It's cool, man."

"What's cool?" Mutt pressed. "You let some dude walk in here with a suitcase full of money and you don't toss him?"

"All I want is the blow, man," the Blade told him. "I don't want no trouble."

Mutt whirled on him. "Shut it, fuck face! If you're cool, you won't get no trouble." He nodded to Ralphie.

Without a word, the big biker ambled over to stare the Blade in the eye. In the next instant, he had ahold of the front of his vest and was pinning him to the wall. With his other hand, he groped inside. Around the right side, down low on the ribs, he stopped.

"What you got here, dude?" he snarled. Turning, he glared furiously at Mickey and the Ape. "The fucker's wired, you assholes! The puke is a motherfucking cop!" Whipping back a ham-sized fist, he chopped the Blade hard in the solar plexus. His target doubled up, twisting in an attempt to avoid the knee aimed at his face.

"Get the fuck outta here!" Ralphie hissed to his associates. "Fast. I'll take care of this cunt."

The Blade was already on his way to the floor, fighting

for air every agonizing inch of the way. As the other three bikers moved quickly to gather up their goods and clear out, Ralphie dropped to one knee. His stale breath was hot in the Blade's ear.

"You're dead meat, fuck face!"

He ripped the transmitter and half the sleevless T-shirt off the narc's chest. With a broad sweep of his arm, he smashed it against the wall.

Mickey, Mutt, and Johnny the Ape were halfway to the door when it came down, hardware and all. In its place stood the biggest black man they had ever seen. Six-foot-ten and three hundred pounds of him. He had a Walther P-5 in one hand and three feet of wrapped pipe in the other. Sam "the Man" Scruggs.

"Hit the deck, Joey!" he barked. The Blade, writhing in his struggle for air, didn't have far to go.

Ralphie spun and was bringing a .38 Smith & Wesson up when Sammy's automatic spat. Ralphie was flung like a rag doll. He crashed into the wall and collapsed across the Blade's outstretched legs.

Clawing at the corpse, the Blade struggled to roll left as he dug for the gun holstered at the small of his back. From behind the dented garbage can, he saw the Ape zeroing in on Sammy as Mickey distracted him. His fingers found the butt of the PPK and probed to wrap around it. Once he got a grip, he jerked hard, clearing the obstruction and instinctively thumbing the safety in one motion. He aimed and dispatched two quick rounds into the center of the Ape's chest. In the same instant, Sammy's gun roared, dropping Mickey in his tracks. The spinning bodies of the two bikers collided violently and collapsed in a tangled heap, both now projects for skilled morticians.

Mutt, the only escape being the one his buddies just took, surrendered.

"Christ!" Sammy shook his head, stepping over the

corpses to help the Blade to his feet. "We were supposed to bust 'em, Joey, not execute them. Hanrahan's gonna shit."

Red-and-blue lights flashed, cutting the back alley darkness. The area of Third Street and Avenue B was garbage-strewn and sinister, even under the shroud of darkness. Dante felt a sickness in his heart. He'd been working this human cesspool too long. Places like this. Meeting places hidden away in rotting buildings. Broken plaster. The filth of shooting galleries with their wads of bloody cotton. The stench of urine. Always urine. The low-life crud couldn't even see the way clear to piss out a window.

The hubbub of coroners, uniforms, meat wagons, and radio squelch subsided as Dante pulled the door closed and sat facing Sammy in the backseat of the sedan.

"I've gotta get out, partner."

A long, pregnant silence ensued. The black man's eyes probed his own.

"Whatever you say, Joey. We've been through an awful lot. When the time comes, I believe you're the only one who knows it."

Five long years. Too many for that sort of work. It ate at you. But they'd been good. Maybe too good. Narco had been reclutant to pull them. Ever since the Knapp Commission, they'd been walking on glass. These two were the only real commandos they had anymore.

Dante nodded. "I've reached capacity. It came in there. Full up. Look at me. Four months to Halloween, and I'm already dressed for the parade."

Lieutenant Jim Hanrahan was a man valued by the Narcotics Division for something other than his even temper. Ever since the big cleanup in the seventies, they'd found themselves in need of a stickler. Someone who could still get results, even with the rule change. Hanrahan was a model of efficiency. Wound tight as a clock spring, he drove himself and the men around him to levels of precision previously unknown. As a result, few arrests slipped through his fingers on technicalities. The lieutenant's men did their homework. He demanded it. This case was going to be a feather in his cap, indicating where he could go once he passed the captain's exam. The pricks at One Police Plaza, right up to the commissioner, were going to sit up and take notice of how Jim Hanrahan stomped the bike gangs.

He slid into the front passenger seat of the green Plymouth without so much as a glance at his two cowboys. With a jerk of his head, he ordered the driver to start. A skinny little ferret of a man, he appeared to his troops to be a guy perpetually in motion. Even now, as he struggled to control his anger, his Adam's apple bobbed up and down and the sinews of his jaw danced.

"I'm out, Lou," Dante announced.

"Shut up!" Hanrahan snarled. "Unless you think you could enlighten me as to what the fuck you thought you were pulling in there."

"It came apart, Jim," Sammy said quietly. "There wasn't any choice. In another couple seconds, Joey would'a been dead."

Hanrahan shook his head. "This was going to be the big one. They were gonna owe me after this. I was going to squeeze those bastards until I had the entire setup, source to street. You were supposed to *deliver* them to me. But you gotta be *Starsky* and fucking *Hutch* in there. Instead of giving me a pass, they're gonna want my ass, and I ain't putting it out there."

"I don't think you heard the man," Sammy said evenly. "He said he's out. Finished. Quit."

"What?" Hanrahan snorted, whirling to face them. "Who you kidding, Dante?"

His man sighed and spread his hands. His knees still refused to stop shaking from the firefight. He ached, was still a little high and bone-tired. He didn't want to fight with the ambition of his desk-jockey boss. He wanted to go home and wash the feeling off in a long, hot shower.

"I'm not kidding anyone, Jim. I just can't do this anymore. As of tonight, the Blade is retired. I'll either get the transfer or quit the job. Either way it has to be. I'm out."

Hanrahan shook his head in amazement. "You gotta be kidding, Dante. Who do you think'd take you? You haven't been in a squad in five years. You may think you're some kinda superman, but you just fucked up the big one. By the time I get done with you, the boys upstairs are gonna think you're the walking plague."

"That'd be just like you." Dante sighed. Slouching back in his seat, he idly eyed the city as it passed outside. Since he had gone undercover, it had become a jungle to him. He would never see it the way he once did. Not anymore.

"Save your own neck and feed me to the wolves. What the fuck, Lou? I guess I never expected anything else. It's never really sunk in with you. We work dope. Human scum. You think a guy does this kind of work and then goes home to listen to Barry Manilow at night. You sit there in your nice little cocoon, demanding the impossible. It never rubs off on you."

"I *made* you guys who you are," Hanrahan shot back. "You think I don't know the game?"

"The game? You know the game, all right." Dante nodded. "And it doesn't have anything to do with eleven-year-old kids becoming junkies and dying six years later in the gutter. That's *my* war, *Lieutenant*! I take it home with me. I don't get much sleep some nights because of it. I crawl through it. What I see hurts because thank God I'm still human enough to let it. *My* shit still stinks. Look at me, you asshole!'' Sitting upright, he fingered his disgusting costume. A fire of loathing raged in his eyes. ''I'm tired of living in a world where I can't even flush the toilet.''

TWO

The area Rick chose for his Manhattan hideaway had come up dramatically in the past several years. On the north side of Twenty-second Street between Ninth and Tenth Avenues, it sat at the edge of a reborn Chelsea. A four-story brownstone, uncharacteristic only in that it had a street-level garage. In the late sixties, when the New York real estate market bottomed out, he'd picked it up for a song. An extensive renovation saw the installation of elegant appointments and contemporary convenience. With the garage, he could enter and leave by car, avoiding the prying eyes of his neighbors. Twice he had installed mistresses here, and in the intervening years, dozens of women were entertained. With the passage of time, Rick became more and more the loner. Mistresses and other lengthy associations were forsaken for a stream of one-nighters. Now he hated having even them in the house. He preferred to find his sex in the streets.

The girl had changed his life. She drove him to distraction. Since the day when the simple sight of her had sparked the fire that now consumed him, he was unable to find satisfaction. The girl becoming a woman. An unforeseen beauty being sculpted by invisible hands, reaching out to mold her to the image of absolute perfection. The girl in her all-but-nonexistent swimsuit stepping out into the bright sun of the terrace below his. Golden-tanned. Shaped like the goddess Aphrodite. Strutting in the glory of her chrysalis, unaware of the obsession behind the eyes furtively observing her.

The power inherent in simply holding a woman no longer satisfied him. Now the girl's awe-inspiring passage through puberty redefined womanhood. Sex with any other could only be an outlet. His love had found focus. It burned in his heart like an acetylene flame.

Rick eased the snout of the BMW into its street-level berth. The automatic garage door hummed shut as he climbed a flight of stairs to the kitchen. With the touch of a finger on a pressure dimmer, the bar area beyond a dividing peninsula was flooded with soft, indirect light. He loosened his tie, contemplating the velvety heat of Scotch in his throat.

It had been a long day in the trenches. A couple of film deals out West. A proposed shopping mall ready to break ground in North Carolina. He made the Scotch a double, then paused to admire the Hefner and Guccione babes pasted lovingly in a gallery of pulchritude along the near wall. Tits held invitingly. Twats spread. He had chosen them because, in some way, each reminded him of her.

He carried the drink upstairs to his bedroom; he removed the gray hand-tailored suit and padded barefoot to the door of his wardrobe. Black leather pants and matching jacket had become something of a uniform to be worn on these nights. Against the late July heat, he ran the car's air-conditioning at maximum chill. Tight against him, the leather felt like an impermeable second skin. When the moment of arousal came, it helped to remind him of how much he wanted to be able to reveal his love to the girl.

Because the time was not yet right, the weekly search for a fitting surrogate vessel had become ritual. Out there among the dozens who lined the desolate streets of the far West Side, she awaited him. Someone who, in some crude way, reflected her likeness. With these, the fantasy of fulfillment had been reenacted on countless occasions.

He would let the drama build slowly, searching nights early in the week until he found her. Seeing her up close and talking to her was important. He would never make an invitation that first time. The tension of fantasy needed time to build. He would hold the memory of her carefully, allowing it to mingle with his image of the girl. Only when the two merged did he allow himself to engage the surrogate. The approximation to the pleasure he anticipated was more likely to approach the heat of his fantasy when he practiced such restraint.

Naked, he pondered himself in the full-length mirror. Barrel-chested and thick through the shoulders, he was still physically formidable. With age, a little softness had crept across the gut. Not much. He worked hard at the spa to avoid the deterioration plaguing most men his age.

The mat of chest hair had completely grayed. His legs were veined. Nevertheless, he still had a commanding presence. One read it in his eyes and the ease of his bearing. All in all, he was pleased with where both body and mind had taken him. Once encased in the cool, polished hide, he zipped the fly.

In his jacket, with gold and diamonds on his hands, a mass of heavy chain around his neck, and an I.D. bracelet emblazoned with Rick in heavy Gothic script, he returned downstairs and slid once again behind the wheel of the

BMW. Rick the Dick. Rick the Prick. Rick with the mighty candlestick.

Two nights ago he had seen one who looked enough like the girl to make him sweat. He'd talked to her. The excitement of seeing her again swelled against the tightness of his pants. He licked his lips with the thought of the hunt.

Eleventh Avenue and Twenty-seventh Street. Brian Brennan had chosen this desolate and obscure corner of Manhattan to take a last stab at recovering the thing he had lost. The southern extremity of Hell's Kitchen was an odd place for a man of his stature to do anything. Let alone live. Outside the windows of his warehouse loft, other giant warehouse blocks stood filth-encrusted and paint peeling, windows obscured with dust. The commerce that once gave them breath was dead. A block away, along the Hudson River, the once-bustling piers of the Port of New York lay derelict. Many had burned, blunt pilings and nothing more to evidence the glory days of a seaport unequaled on earth. The rail yards servicing the port, long abandoned, had been bulldozed along with block after block of low, rusting storage sheds. A convention center had risen in an effort to reclaim this wasteland. Concrete and glass to replace a heart and soul condemned to death by the efficiency of container ships and modern transport. The commerce now thrived in places like Brooklyn and Bayonne, New Jersey. What the convention center could not reach to reclaim stood as decrepit monuments to another time. Populated by prostitutes hustling the tunnel traffic to New Jersey, by pimps and a cornucopia of one-horse small businesses. Building supplies. Body shops. Welders. Sheet metal fabricators. Cheap storage. . . . And a sculptor who knew that he had sold out. Fifteen years ago, when the struggle seemed destined to bury him under a weight of pain.

One thing led to another. The decision was an easy enough one to reach at the time. He had been thirty-one years old; starving in a drafty dump on Prince Street. Sweatshops full of sewing machines above him and a ball-bearing manufacturer below. A graduate of the Rhode Island School of Design.

In 1969 disillusionment was running high. The flower was proclaiming some mystic power. Old visions were being given new paint jobs. The artists of the generation were imagining new social orders, dreaming that a civilization might give a damn about what they thought and created. The area south of Houston Street became a hotbed of this new zeal. In a city in the throes of decline, a groundswell of artistic renaissance grew like fungus on a dying branch.

Brian Brennan's early work was strong, if still scattered in its perspective. But encouragement and groceries were nevertheless hard to come by. He scratched by, mooching off friends and doing odd jobs. The output of artistic work was steady, despite the distractions of survival. He had rigged a small, illegal foundry and poured small quantities of molten bronze and aluminum. Then, one night while out with Charlie Fung at the Blue Note in the Village, he found Lisa Garriston.

She'd appeared, edging her way toward a chair two tables away, at the beginning of the second set. Maybe twenty-three or -four. Definitely gorgeous. The woman she joined had the same sort of look about her; rich girls slumming it. The getups were too contrived, as if they'd raided trunks in the attic of a flapper grandmother.

Fung elbowed him in the ribs. "Do you see that?"

Brennan prided himself on his powers of observation. He had indeed seen that. Her glow seemed to fill the room. And it was not just the glow of good looks. It was scrubbed good looks. Thin good looks. Moneyed good looks. He moved to prevent this Chinese mad hatter from getting any ideas.

"The tall one's mine."

"Says who?" Fung snorted.

"Says me." Brennan smiled, pushing himself to his feet.

It had been a tough week. With the rent due, he had taken work demolishing the interior of a brownstone prior to its renovation. The money was enough to carry him for another couple of weeks . . . and buy drinks. He had already downed several and wasn't feeling the least inhibited. Strolling toward the targeted table, he drunkenly considered an opening line. When he reached it, he still hadn't come up with one. Instead, he simply pulled up a chair and sat.

"I beg your pardon?" the other of the two women said, in a tone of irritation.

He ignored her, staring at the object of his desire. "You're beautiful," he said. "I just had to come over here and tell you that."

The woman blushed, while her friend rolled her eyes. The man in front of her was tall, maybe six-two. With an athletic build and not bad-looking if you could forgive what he was wearing. Rope-soled shoes. Faded salt-and-pepper corduroys. Open-necked Indian cotton pullover and rumpled linen jacket.

"Can I buy you a drink?" he asked.

She shook her head. "I think not. Thank you very much for the compliment, but I'm really not interested."

"You don't even know me," he countered.

"And she doesn't want to," her friend said.

Brennan smiled and turned to point at Charlie across the way. "See that Chinese guy over there? That's Charlie

Fung. He's going to be a famous painter some day soon. If you offer to take your clothes off for him, maybe he'll immortalize you."

The woman's eyes bulged; veins stood out on her forehead.

"I'm leaving, Lisa. Are you coming?" She got up, leaving an almost-full drink on the table. Her friend rose to join her. Undaunted, Brennan followed them outside onto the sidewalk.

"Listen," he pleaded, touching the woman named Lisa's arm as the watchdog attempted to hail a cab. "I apologize if I was rude. But how the hell was I going to meet you otherwise? I'm not a bad guy."

"I don't think you're my type."

"How do you know? Where's your sense of adventure?"

That seemed to get under her shell. She was obviously out experimenting with the other side of life and, by the look of it, hadn't gotten too far.

"You're some sort of artist, aren't you?" she asked tentatively.

"Yeah. A sculptor. And I don't bite. Come have coffee with me. I'll behave. I swear."

She looked toward her friend waving her arm in the street.

"I can't just ditch Janie."

"Then don't. Drop her off and come back. See that coffee house over there?" He pointed diagonally across the street. "I'll wait."

She looked undecided as her friend finally flagged a cab and yelled for her to hurry. With little or nothing to lose, Brennan returned to his table, downed another drink, and said good night to Fung.

It was an hour and three espressos later that she pushed into the smoky interior from the street. Standing a lot less assuredly now that she was alone, she surveyed the room.

Brennan watched her. She looked like a fish out of water here. But she was a knockout. He waved.

"I'd just about decided you weren't coming," he said, sliding over on the banquette.

"You were almost right," she returned, joining him with affected nonchalance.

As worldly as she tried to present herself, this was all new and very outrageous behavior for her. They had another coffee and then went for a walk through the Village. By the time they reached Washington Square, she'd told him a little about herself and supplied a last name to go with the first. Garriston. Lisa Garriston. It was another couple of weeks of meeting for drinks and lots of talk before he persuaded her to inspect his sculptor's lair. Above all else, the woman was cautious. But in the end, the sheer power of his life-style drew her out of her suspicions. He was good. Much of his work was exercises in classic form. Emulation of the great achievements in realism; not a lot of this wild, Post-Modernist stuff you saw so much of. And he drew. Detailed anatomical sketches and project studies littered the place. The romantic power of what he embodied dovetailed too perfectly with her own dilettante's passion for art. The Garristons owned a fortune in contemporary paintings and sculpture. Her mother was a trustee of the Whitney Museum. Art and artists may well have been two distinct balls of wax, but if young Lisa was going to rebel in an age of rebellion, what better direction? Three weeks after their first meeting, she slept with him. For a woman like Lisa, this of course meant she was in love.

Within a month Brennan's new lover introduced him to the owners of two Madison Avenue galleries. Both were primarily impressed with his command of the realist aspects of the medium. One, who often brokered commissions for monuments and busts, wondered aloud if perhaps he might be able to handle such a thing. The president of a charitable organization she was affiliated with was retiring. Depending on how a bust of him worked out, there could be more of that sort of thing. Lisa eagerly accepted for him.

The bust was better than just passable. Literal renderings were not difficult for him. Mixed with the right amount of flattery, his craftsmanship pleased both the subject and the commissioner. Within a year he was swamped with similar projects. Lisa became a fixture in his life. With his new affluence, he found he could almost afford her.

While never associated with the serious exploration of the medium, Brennan gained popularity among wealthy collectors. He made investments, guided by members of his new circle of acquaintances. His personal fortune grew. Maintaining the loft in what had now been dubbed SoHo, he moved his residence to Lisa's Fifth Avenue and Eighty-second Street apartment. In seventy-seven, they were married.

Over time, the magic of his meteoric rise to a position of respectability began to wear thin for Brian Brennan. The company Lisa kept generally bored him. They all seemed intent on sucking the life out of everything they touched, armed with their purchasing power. The time finally came when Lisa wanted a baby. Even with the best fertility gynecologist in the East, there was nothing doing. Something about hostile mucus. She became bitter. More and more, the disenchantment they each felt with their lives mingled to create a chemistry too volatile to be tolerated. They fought like cats and dogs for almost four years before Brennan finally decided it was time to quit. Six months ago, he got Lisa to agree to a trial separation. He purchased the building on Twenty-seventh, outfitted a studio and Spartan living quarters on the fourth floor, and moved in. He had not known what to expect. Or where, if there were even a direction, he might go. All he *did* know was that, for the first time in a decade and a half, he could breathe again.

Diana Webster, artist's model and occasional lover, was due at any moment. He moved around the place, hastily trying to kick it into some kind of order. At thirty-two and already an aging punklette, Diana lived the scene on Saint Mark's Place in the East Village. Brennan used her as the subject of dozens of slick renderings. The Webster-inspired nude had become something of a trademark for him. To this day, gum popping, goofy face, and all, she had the most amazing body he'd ever set eyes on. Along the way, she had become one of a number of affairs he slid in and out of behind Lisa's back. But this one, unlike the others, evolved to become something unique. They stayed friends, sleeping together when they found the need arose. But most important, Diana was the one he was able to talk to about the disillusionment filling his life. She was a good listener. And she never really wanted anything from him. Not in the sense that Lisa and the others had. She seemed to just enjoy being around him. He liked that.

When the intercom buzzer squawked, Brennan checked the video monitor to make sure it was her and released the downstairs door.

"Hiya." She grinned her crooked grin, bussing him on the cheek. "God, it's hot out there."

"Air-conditioning's on," he said. "Something cold to drink?"

She asked for a seltzer, dropped her bag onto the sofa, and followed him into the kitchen.

"What's news?"

He shrugged. "Not much. Shipping the big piece to

Connecticut next week for casting. Thinking about spending most of the month up there. Want to come?"

"Next week?" she asked. "Can't. Charlie has me. Week after that maybe."

Brennan had purchased a derelict estate and built a foundry on its waterfront property in Pleasure Beach, west of New London. Every summer he spent at least a month there catching up on the work of committing his models to metal. Throughout the year, he tried to pour on the average of once a month, but it never seemed to be enough to stay ahead of the work load.

"Anything new on the domestic front?" Diana asked.

"Lisa? We're going to a party at the Modern next week. Her therapist insists that seeing me on neutral ground would be constructive. She called me at one in the morning last night."

"To invite you to a party?"

"And to remind me that she gave me the best years of her life. She blames me for her unhappiness."

"And because it was one in the morning, you agreed to go just to get her off the phone, right?"

He handed her the seltzer, it's ice clinking against the sides of the dewy glass. With an iced tea of his own, he touched hers and smiled. "That's right. If I'd hung up, she just would have called me back."

They wandered back into the living room and sat.

"Where are you taking me for dinner?" she asked.

"There's a nice new little French country place on Ninth. Just downtown. Feel like trying it?"

"Only if you promise to take me back here and ravage me afterward." She smiled mischievously. "I've been horny for a week."

"You've got a deal," he said, throwing a cushion at her.

THREE

"Come on, baby," Rick muttered, drumming the streering wheel. The BMW idled at a red on Thirty-fifth Street at Eleventh Avenue. To his left, a low dilapidated diner oozed fluorescence out into the harsh yellow-orange of the street lamps. Three black hookers stood on the corner, jiving with two patrons who had just left the place. Across the avenue, like a perverse crystal, the geometrically ordered slabs of convention-center glass reflected the Midtown skyline. Empire State Building prominent. New and old skyscrapers of the Garment Center. All shimmering like warped, fun house images. And everywhere along the new sterile sidewalks and gray concrete walls loitered whores. Dozens of them. It was hot out and many wore little or nothing. Even in his air-conditioned car, the sight of all that sex made Rick sweat.

He had been on the prowl for forty-five minutes. On three occasions, he thought he'd seen her, only to be disappointed. Her pimp had changed her stroll. The one who reminded him of the girl.

The light changed. Slowly, he crept around the corner and alongside the new construction. The prostitutes smiled, beckoned, revealed their secrets and waved. Still sweating, he rolled slowly south.

At Thirty-third, he saw her. Tall, lanky, straight blonde hair.

"Oh yeah, baby," he breathed. "Here's Daddy."

He caught her attention as he eased to the curb. She pushed off the pay phone she'd been leaning against and wandered over, looking bored. She stooped to peer inside the passenger window as he ran it down.

"Twenty bucks," she said in a flat monotone.

"I'm good for it, baby. You're letting the cool air out."

"Let's see your money."

Impatiently, he drew a roll out from inside his open jacket and flashed it through the wash of streetlight on the seat. The door handle clicked in release. The blonde climbed in.

"Straight blow job, honey. I don't do no extras."

Rick chuckled. They all said it. Don't touch me here. I don't swallow come. But for a price, he always got his way. That's what money was for. Lots of money. They all loved it more than they hated having him touch their tits.

"I got it all tucked away nice and neat in here, baby," he crooned, running his hand across the shiny leather bulge in his crotch.

The whore rolled her eyes, wordlessly saying that she'd seen them all at least once. The quicker you got them off, the quicker you got rid of them. Taking the money with one hand, she slid her other hand across the same straining hide.

"Not yet!" he hissed. "Wait until we stop."

"I was only checking your head of steam, honey. You

ain't kiddin'. You're a stud. Most johns ain't half as hard as you. Pull it over and let me help it get a little fresh air."

Rick knew this area by heart now. Until you got down into the high Twenties, the territory was too exposed. The cops who patrolled the area never busted a whore until she was actually in the car with a customer. Then they busted the john, too.

He turned and leered. "In a second, baby. Couple more blocks down. A man in my position can't afford a run-in with the law."

"Let me out," the whore ordered.

"Whoa," he said calmly, reaching into his jacket to pull out another twenty. "No problem, baby. I know a place. A good place."

She eyed the green skeptically and shrugged. Then she took the money and stuffed it into her top. A few blocks further south, at the corner of Twenty-seventh, he pulled to the curb, scanned the rearview, and backed around the corner into a darkened loading bay.

Even with the extra twenty, the whore had become fidgety. Moving so far south of that night's stroll meant separation from her pimp and his protection. She had done it before, but she never liked to. The john reached to touch her hair.

"Let's get it done, honey," she said. Moving into position, she undid his belt quickly and unzipped him.

"Slowly," he cooed. Another twenty was dangling in front of her face. "Real slowly."

"I suck cock, honey. You want to pay me extra, that's your business. But it don't change nothin'. You pay me, I suck you off. Period."

Rick looked hurt, as if she'd broken a spell he had carefully conjured.

"Please, baby. Easy. You're so beautiful. You shouldn't talk like that to Daddy."

Inside, he was furious. Sixty dollars and she wanted to jerk him off and split. He wasn't used to being treated like this. Not him. After all, he was willing to pay. That's what she was after, wasn't it? Money? What did the rest of it matter?

From out of her bag came a prophylactic. Having freed him from his pants, she ripped the packet with her teeth, spat the wrapper onto the floor mat, and had it on him in one practiced move.

"No, baby," he moaned. "No rubber." There was more money in his hand. "I want you to swallow me." Grasping, he caught her hair to stop her.

"Ow! You fucker. You're hurting me."

"No rubber, baby. Swallow me." He pushed the money at her.

The whore shook her head, jerking free of his grip.

"Sorry, buster. I don't swallow come. Either you play by the rules, or I jet out of here and you can jerk yourself off for all I care."

"Like hell," he hissed, suddenly transformed from his passivity. Grabbing the front of her elastic top, he jerked it to her waist. This couldn't be her. She would never treat him like this. "You want to act like a whore?" he snarled. "Then Daddy's going to treat you like a whore." Reaching for her breasts, he sunk his nails furiously into them. The woman's scream in his ear seemed a thousand miles away.

"You fucking bitch," he ranted. "I'll teach you to respect your father." Her screams were smothered against his shoulder. Her knee slammed up at him time and again, each time missing the mark.

He could feel the flesh of her breasts against his sweating chest as he bear-hugged her to him and fought off the knee. Curiously, there was no pain as it slammed into his thigh. Something was happening. No woman had ever worked so excitedly against him before. Her wild, animal fear fanned the heat of his desire. Squeezing her harder, he rose up with her as she strained against him. Together, they fell back onto the seat, the weight of his bulk crashing into her. The head beneath his shoulder snapped back against the headrest. She went limp with submission. Thrilled with the power in his body and the force of his will, he came into the rubber with great spasms of release.

Gasping for breath, he fell back into his seat. Across from him, the whore lay unconscious. He stared at her bleeding breasts. Only they weren't bleeding any longer. The weight of his frantic lunges must have broken her neck. He was confused by her strange body attitude. He reached over to touch her face. With the contact, her head flopped at an unnatural angle.

"Jesus." He wheezed, breathless. "All you had to do was swallow me, baby." Grabbing at the rubber on his wilting member, he jerked it free. "Just swallow me, goddamm it!"

He pried open her mouth and stuffed the condom into it.

Brennan blew smoke rings and stared up through them at the ceiling. Diana padded barefoot back into the room, carrying a pair of beers, and climbed onto the bed.

"That's a disgusting habit," she said, handing him one of the bottles.

"Sex after dinner?"

"Smoking in bed. I thought you quit last week."

"Everywhere else," he said. "Now I smoke *only* in bed."

She shrugged, propped herself up with pillows, and sat there naked beside him. Dinner had been good. He had been good. She could look past the smoke rings. Sipping the ice-cold Heineken, she dragged the glistening bottle across her upper arms and neck. Getting laid in late July had its price in sweat.

"Are you sure you can't come up with me next week?" he asked. "It'll be a lot cooler up there."

"And stiff your best friend for a week's work?"

"Screw him. Charlie Fung could find another model in a minute. . . ."

She'd turned, frowning at him. "Go ahead, Brennan. Say it. Broads like me are a dime a dozen, right?"

"C'mon," he complained. "You know what I meant. It would be good to get away."

"I've got to pay the rent, Brian. Charlie's paying premium dollar. He's been steady. I'm not going to leave him in the lurch."

Brennan sighed, smoked awhile in silence, and drank. Eventually he held the beer bottle at arm's length and stared at it.

"Do you think I drink too much?"

She shrugged. "I don't know. You're not an alcoholic. You're Irish. It's an hereditary hazard."

"The fight we had last week? I was drunk."

"I know."

The air-conditioner hummed, valiantly trying to influence the temperature. The bedroom door hung open, subverting its effectiveness. Brennan kicked the sheet back off his legs and stood. Belligerent. That's what he got when he drank too much. And he knew it. Lisa's constant bitching had helped to fine-tune the impulse. Diana watched him from the bed.

"You look great like that," he said. "Jay-ass naked with a beer in your hand. Mind if I get my pad?"

"Twenty bucks an hour," she said.

He was already hurrying out of the room.

"Fuck you, Webster," he called over his shoulder.

* * *

Diana read a paperback while Brennan drew. Both of them lost track of the time. An hour and then another passed. Neither was wearing a watch. When Diana finally rose to stretch, she noticed the digital readout on the clock radio.

"Holy shit! It's after one. I've got a singing lesson tomorrow at ten o'clock."

Brennan yawned and put down his pencil. The floor around him was littered with sketches. Stooping, he gathered them up.

"Let me look," she said, coming over. He handed the bunch to her.

"Why don't you just sleep here. I'm not quite ready for bed yet. I'll work in the studio."

She followed him out of the room, heading for the bath. He watched her move past him and across the room. What an incredible ass.

When she found him again, he was sitting on the window ledge, pad on his knee, quickly drawing the scene on the street below. Down on the sidewalk diagonally across the avenue, a pair of prostitutes loitered against a streetlight standard. Brennan had captured them in their bored attitudes and outlandish costuming.

"Where should I put these?" she asked. In her hand were the dozen drawings he'd done of her.

"On the table over there. What did you think?"

"The same thing I always think. That you ought to paint instead of being the Vargas of the sculpture world."

He shrugged. "It pays the rent."

"The rent's paid, and you know it. Kiss me good night, asshole."

Alone in the studio, thinking more about drinking than painting, Brennan continued to draw the street. He wasn't sure he was a nasty drunk, but he did know every real fight he'd ever had saw him soused. Then the bitterness over the wasted years floated up near the surface. Lisa may have given him the best years of her life, but vice versa was also true. The resentment was deep-seated. He'd been as much of a whore as those miserable souls out there on the street. It made him mad. He took it out on people.

Diana seemed to understand in a way Lisa never had. She'd always acted like her whole marriage to him was one ongoing favor. He hated her for it. But Diana looked at life differently. She moved with a coarser crowd, aspiring along with the rest of them to be some sort of avant-garde rock/video artist. He didn't pretend to understand the nuances. Plenty had passed him by while he nested in his comfortable little backwater. But Diana could take it better and knew how to dish it out without having it eat her up inside.

Out on the street, the pair he was drawing began to drift uptown as a small foreign-looking car pulled to the opposite side of Twenty-seventh on the avenue, paused, and backed around the corner. Across the street, the mammoth warehouse building adjacent to him sported a wide, yawning truck bay. By day it was generally jammed with semi tractor-trailers parked halfway out into the street. Now it was deserted. The little car pulled back into the gloom. In another moment, its headlights were extinguished.

Brennan was used to such nocturnal occurrences. A whore and a particularly cautious john. On nights like these, he'd often amuse himself with timing them. The interludes generally ran an average of eighty-five seconds. He picked up his binoculars.

There wasn't much to see, the action hidden in the darkness of the loading bay. The mean of eighty-five seconds elapsed, rolling on toward two, three, and then four minutes. The guy had to be spending a fortune in there. And then, in the ambient light reflected off adjacent glass, the window of the passenger door gleamed dully.

The hooker was getting out of the car. Headlights suddenly came on and the car rocketed out of the space, ran the light at the corner, and squealed off into the night.

But Brennan hardly saw the car. There on the ground, where the woman should have stepped out and walked back to the street, lay a crumpled shape.

"Holy shit!" he muttered to himself. In another breath he was replacing the binoculars and searching for his thongs.

The elevator wouldn't be fast enough. He took the stairs two at a time. On the street, the smothering humidity hit him full-on as he raced to the opposite curb. Dressed only in gym shorts, he looked as if he were out for a late-night run in this soup.

The loading area was easier to see into as he entered it. The amber glow cast by the streetlamps gave everything a vaguely surreal look, like footage from an apocalypse movie.

As he approached the object on the ground, Brennan's worst fears were confirmed. It was a woman. Young; maybe eighteen. Blond. White stockings with frilled panties and matching garter belt. One of those elastic tube-top affairs had been pulled down to her waist. She was sprawled facedown; her head lay at an odd angle. Stooping, he felt the carotid artery for a pulse. She was dead.

It wasn't until after the police arrived that he and two uniformed patrolmen together discovered the condom stuffed between her battered lips.

FOUR

Stuart Sprague met Manhattan District Attorney Harry Ransome every Sunday afternoon at two for tennis. During the season, the date was generally kept at the tycoon's East Hampton estate. Ransome and his wife, Jenny, would drive over from their place in Quogue, and the women would join them for mixed doubles after a couple of warm-up singles sets. Sprague, detained in the city, had helicoptered out early that morning to join his wife at the beach.

"How many times have I said it, Stuart?" Ransome asked, eyeing Penelope's graceful shape as she glided in effortless play against his wife. "What a catch."

Sprague sipped his rum and tonic and smiled. "C'mon, Harry. Look at those two. Penny and Jenny. They're like bookends. We *both* scored, buddy."

Ransome appreciated a guy like Stuart Sprague saying so. They'd come up together. Their families had been dirt poor together. But the similarity ended there. Harry had gone to Columbia Law and Sprague had become a giant. A colossus. Everything he touched turned to gold. Salvatore Abbruzzi aka Stuart Sprague. Off the boat at two-and-a-half. Raised in the squalor of the Lower East Side. And look at him now. Honorary Vice Mayor of Culture. Jacob "Harry" Rantzman didn't want to know everything about his ascendancy. What he admired were the man's loyalty and his will.

Having clawed his way to the top of the heap, the scruffy kid from Avenue C was, at sixty, as big as they came. From the lowly position of runner on the floor of the stock exchange, he'd eventually found his way to a job with a small investment broker. Opportunities arose from insider information. Profiteering off takeover bids. Stock manipulation. Out-and-out securities fraud. The money earned from these enterprises laundered and reinvested through foreign "ghost" companies. The resultant tax advantages. With a world-class bankroll amassed, he moved into more legitimate enterprise. Uranium mining. Bioengineering. Pharmaceuticals. Corporate raiding and leveraged buy-outs. Sal Abbruzzi had become Stuart Sprague, and Sprague had become an internationally recognized tycoon. He moved money by the truckload. Where and how were not Rantzman's concerns.

Harry Rantzman was grateful that his old friend never forgot him. A good word here. A contribution there. Rantzman was a good lawyer. Crackerjack. But there were a lot of good lawyers in New York and only one District Attorney. When Sal was changing his name from Abbruzzi to Sprague, he suggested Harry give the idea some thought. To Harry Ransome, Stuart Sprague had been a real friend.

"Wild one last night," Ransome mentioned, easing back in his chair. "Had me out of bed at dawn."

"How's that?" Sprague asked.

"Those animals over on the West Side. Some sort of

war going on over there. They found a working broad murdered. Real nasty. But get this. Paul Garriston's son-in-law, the sculptor, discovered the body."

"No shit? Where?"

"In his front yard, more or less. I guess he and little Lisa aren't getting on. He's got some bohemian setup in one of those warehouses down by the old Twenty-third Street ferry pier."

Sprague looked surprised. "A guy like that? He must be worth a decent piece of change. Does the nudes, right?"

"Same guy. Always a little bit of an embarrassment for Paul, I think. Imagine a guy like him having a son-in-law who carves nude women. And Lisa was a good-looking girl. She could have done better than that."

Sprague nodded. "Great-looking girl. Real nice set on her. You're keeping this quiet, I hope?"

"Trying. What with the wife dying last year, Garriston doesn't need a thing like this."

"You want me to put my two cents in?"

"It wouldn't hurt," Ransome said. "What good are we if we can't protect our own, huh?"

Inspector Gus Lieberman had expected trouble in assigning Joe Dante. When a man came out from undercover as spectacularly as Dante did, he *had* to have trouble. That bastard Hanrahan had tried to feed him to the wolves.

The operation went badly. Granted. There were bodies to be explained and another deep plant to protect. But Gus knew Hanrahan. The man was a hind-end–sucking son of a bitch. If there were a way to make another man look bad and save his own skin, he'd take it. The operation was his. All the credit would have been his if it had gone well. It stood to reason that he should also take some of the heat. His refusal disgusted a cop like Gus Lieberman. Joe Dante was a good man. There was no excuse for the way he'd been left exposed like that. The papers had a field day, and Dante had been suspended until the duty captain cleared him.

Lieberman reviewed the file in detail. The city of New York had asked the man to become a cowboy. Only an insider could fully appreciate what that meant. It was the most dangerous work he knew. Wearing a wire into a nest of mugs like that spoke of either insanity or uncommon bravery. Lieberman knew Dante well enough to know he was anything but insane. He also knew that the man had volunteered, his rock-solid psychological profile further recommending him. And his record, working in association with Sam Scruggs, spoke for itself. No similar team in memory approached their level of effectiveness.

West Twentieth Street between Seventh and Eighth was jammed with cars; normal for a precinct street. It wasn't a bad block, in a part of town that had done nothing but come up lately. Chelsea.

Gus eased his green Buick Electra up on the sidewalk in front of the Tenth, flipped the vehicle I.D. card onto the dash, and eased his bulk out onto the pavement. A starting linebacker for Rutgers in the old days, he had annexed twenty-seven years of sausage heroes and beer onto an already formidable frame. Diets never interested him as much as they did his wife. She worried about him dropping dead of a coronary and leaving her with two kids in college. As a concession, he'd quit smoking a month back. It made him so ornery that the guys downtown had begged him to start again. He smiled at the memory of it and lit a Carlton. Faggot butts. But you had to trim the fat where you could.

The old precinct house had been given a recent face-lift. Two shades of department blue, both a little bright for his taste. But at least they were new. Little else had changed.

Same woodwork. Same scuffed linoleum. Same dozens of coats of old paint under the new, filling the contours of the moldings and burying hundreds of yards of extinct exposed wire.

The Detective Squad Room had hardly changed. New paint, yes. But the same battered metal desks and sagging green lockers. A large central grouping of half-a-dozen desks made the tiny space seem impossibly crowded and cluttered.

Lieberman picked the Tenth because it was small, because he knew the commander from academy days, and because they had a sticky little problem. With only thirteen detectives assigned there, he thought Dante might have a shot at fitting in.

Sergeant Larry Morris sat with his feet up on his desk. Engrossed in the current *Playboy* gatefold, he failed to notice the big man's arrival.

"You're drooling, Larry," Lieberman said, dropping into a chair. "You guys got drinkable coffee today?"

Morris looked up, turned the foldout Lieberman's way, grinned, and flipped the magazine onto his blotter.

"Ever had anything that looked like that, Gus?"

"There ain't anything that looks like that. Believe me."

"Losada!" Morris hollered. "Get the inspector a cup of Java, huh? Milk, no sugar."

The two eyed each other a moment.

"So how's it, Larry?"

"It's this prostitute thing, right?"

"They're nervous downtown, buddy. This witness you got is Paul Garriston's son-in-law. It seems the poor man lost his wife to cancer last year and contributes heavily to the mayor's campaign fund. They don't want his name dragged into this. There's something ugly going on between this flaky sculptor and the man's daughter. They don't want *that* in the papers either. These people are Harry Ransome's friends. We got to play it very carefully."

Morris shrugged and waved a hand in the air.

"I wouldn't worry too much, Gus. We've already talked to the guy and he didn't see much. No sense in dragging him any further into this. He couldn't even make the car. As far as I'm concerned, this is just another casualty of the Times Square war. A friendly warning, you know?"

"Any idea who?"

"You kidding?" Morris snorted. "That game's got more players than the Yankees. My guess would be that a nasty customer by the name of Willie Davenport has something to do with it. He always seems to."

"Somebody trying to muscle in?"

"Always. It's like being heavyweight champ. Seems like every couple of months, some young Turk wants a shot at the crown."

"Whose girl was this?"

"Some sleaze by the name of Slick Sloan. The man's a two-bit hustler. Two possession convictions and one sales arrest. Heroin. They couldn't pin it on him."

Lieberman shrugged and puffed his cheeks. "Your theory is the guy stepped outta line?"

"What else?"

"And what's *he* say?"

"To us? Nothing. On the street, that he's been unjustly persecuted. None of these assholes is ever *justly* persecuted."

The inspector nodded, pushed himself out of his chair, and stood to stare at the big Manhattan street map. "So what are you doing now?"

"I've got two-thirds of the day shift on it. This thing on the Square is getting a little out of hand. A torched Caddy three nights ago. A Lincoln two nights before that. Add to that the murder of a convention center foreman. Inside revolt as best as we can figure it. The guy was a prick and somebody blew the left half of his head off. Just with homicides my guys are stretched pretty thin. Then there's the three rapes and a knifing victim in ICU over at Saint Vinnie's."

A pretty Hispanic detective—tall, great shape in a linen skirt and white blouse—brought Lieberman coffee in a paper cup.

"Howzit, Rosa?" he asked.

"Crazy," she said, rolling her eyes. "Ask the Sarge. The whole West Side has gone berserk in the past week."

"Hang on to your hat," he said. "You still got the whole of August to get through."

Once she'd withdrawn, Lieberman jerked his head in her direction. "How's she working out, Lar?"

"Losada? There's potential. Real by-the-book, y'know. She'll loosen up some. I don't regret your sending her to me, if that's what you mean."

"I suppose." He nodded. "Excellent patrol record. No lack of initiative either. Still, I've wondered if maybe she wasn't too good-looking to make it in a squad full of animals like you've got."

"They've all tried to make her," Morris said. "What the hell'd you expect? If I were one of 'em, I'd give it a shot myself. Pat Meehan's been the only real problem."

"Figures," Gus grunted.

"I've had to rein him in a couple of times," Morris continued. "The man just doesn't seem to know the limits."

"Never will. Too bad she's not big enough to take him out back."

"I've seen her contemplating it," Morris said.

Together, they eyed the back of her figure appreciatively as she stood at a file across the Squad Room.

"She still stays on the Seventeenth about her parents,"

Lieberman said. "Guy named Grillo's got it. She drives him crazy."

"You would, too, if someone orphaned you like that."

"I'm not blaming her. It's just that it's been seven years. Chances of nailing them now are one in a million."

"It happens. So tell me, Gus. You're not here to admire Detective Losada's ass. What's up?"

Lieberman had to smile. He and Larry Morris had known each other too long.

"This pimp war thing is what's up. The commissioner is trying to figure out what to do with Dante. He's leaning toward you."

"Jesus." Morris shook his head. "Here?"

"Come on." Lieberman grunted, waving him off. "What you've just been telling me only confirms his thinking."

"Then I take it all back."

"He wants him to work this hooker thing, Larry. Dante's an imaginative guy. You keep your other people working the street, but we want Dante underneath."

The idea upset Morris visibly. The pencil he gripped was in danger of being snapped in half.

"What the hell's wrong with Midtown South? They're better equipped to handle a guy like that. He's a renegade, Gus. He's been outside too long. I have enough dead bodies on my hands without having one of my own adding to the pile."

"Dante's gotten a bum rap," Lieberman said. "I know him. I had him in my squad when I commanded the Sixth. He's a good cop. Intelligent. The son of a bitch reads *psychology* in his spare time. I remember that the decision to volunteer for Narcotics came hard at the time."

"The commissioner's not asking me," Morris said evenly.

"He has to have your cooperation, buddy. It won't work without it. We want to give him a pretty free hand, but he's working with *your* net. Extensive contact and support. And the commissioner wants you to assign him Rosa."

"What!?"

"Checks and balances," Lieberman said, smiling. "Like you said, the man's been outside a long time. We hope they'll counterbalance each other. On the other side of it, there's the opportunity for Rosa to learn a lot in a hurry. Dante's a master, Lar. He'll help take some of the starch out of her shirt."

"Probably try to take her tits out of her shirt."

"You got him wrong," the ranking cop said. "He does the job he's given. Ten to one, he's gonna come up with something creative. And you never know. He cracks this thing without our friends from the Fourth Estate walking all over it, it'd be a feather in *your* cap."

Morris sighed. "Send him over," he said. "We'll baby-sit your cowboy. But none of this 'feather in my cap' shit, okay? As far as I'm concerned, somebody owes me one."

Lieberman shrugged and threw a manila envelope onto the commander's desk. "Read the file, buddy."

FIVE

The welcoming committee had other business the morning Joe Dante reported to the Tenth Precinct. The press he'd received in the wake of the biker-bust fiasco stimulated little curiosity on the squad level. Morris had already announced that he was coming aboard to work on this pimp war and the recent murder. Everyone knew that it was only because some bigwig's son-in-law tripped over the stiff that any fuss was being made. Dead whores were a yawn in this neck of the concrete jungle. The fact that the new guy would catch it was fine by the rest of them. No one liked having city hall telling them how to do their job.

Dante was a little surprised when Lieberman called from the commissioner's office to tell him he was being assigned to a squad on Manhattan's West Side. And the Tenth, no less. He felt fortunate not to have been banished to deepest Queens or the Bronx. At least his new assignment was close to home. Dingy and antiquated, it sat in an area he considered something of a nonneighborhood. The territory it covered included a large chunk of what had once been referred to as Hell's Kitchen, an area of tenements and warehouses servicing the old port and rail yards. Now the city was attempting to rescue the area with a giant new convention center. Entire square blocks had been razed to make room for it.

Sergeant Larry Morris sat shoulder-deep in paperwork as Dante rapped on the frame of his open door. He looked up, not immediately recognizing his crew-cut visitor.

"Dante," the guy announced.

He looked different from the expected. Boyish for a man of thirty-eight. Tall; maybe six-two. In good shape. Broad-shouldered and slim-hipped. Good clothes just to the left of preppy. And good-looking. That's what surprised him the most. He'd expected a guinea cowboy, dripping Brooklyn from the ends of his Pancho Villa mustache.

"Come in." He motioned, standing to lean over the mountain of paper, extending his hand. Dante reached to shake it. "Sit down, please."

Dante sat, looking around the room. It had been some time since he'd been in a squad commander's office. It was the same though. They were all the same. Morris was scrutinizing him.

"Let's cut right to the heart of it, Dante," the commander suggested. "The commissioner wants you here, so you and I got no choice. They want to pussyfoot around this dead hooker. Fine. A little politics comes with the job. You get my support, and in exchange, you keep me informed of *everything*. I don't know how you guys worked over in narcotics, but here, I won't tolerate being kept in the dark."

Dante returned his gaze steadily as he spoke. The eyes

belied his otherwise youthful appearance. They were eyes that had seen more in five years than most of his peers would see in thirty. When Morris paused, Dante simply nodded.

"Don't be surprised if some of the guys look a little sideways at you around here. Some of them can read, and all of them watch TV. You're quite the celebrity. That might make them a little nervous." Turning, he hollered out into the squad. "Losada!"

The pretty detective appeared at his door. "You screamed?"

"This is Dante. Point him toward the men's locker room. Get him a cup of coffee. Then I want both of you back here in ten minutes."

Dante followed Rosa Losada around the big island of desks and into an adjoining hall. She indicated the locker room door.

"Coffee's around the corner in the storeroom," she said coolly, proceeding. "Cream or sugar?"

"Black," Dante replied. He pushed his way into the men's inner sanctum.

The lockers and cots, like everything else in city government, were beat-up and green. Dante approached a unit sans padlock and opened it. Besides being just plain filthy, the locker still contained the last tenant's wildlife collection. Mostly beaver. None from *National Geographic*. He peeled them from the inside of the door, dropped them into the wastebasket, and made a mental note to buy a lock and a can of Lysol.

After a quick scan around to get the lay of the place, Dante joined Rosa in the storeroom and accepted the offered coffee.

"You have another name besides Losada?" he asked.

"Detective," she returned coolly.

"Cute." He smiled. "Who picked it, your mother or your father?"

She winced at the mention of her parents.

"C'mon," he pressed. "Just an innocent, friendly question. I'm Joe." He held out his hand.

Cornered, she stared at him defiantly. "The name is Rosa." With unexpected strength, she caught his offered hand, squeezed the knuckles hard, and shook. "Morris is expecting us."

Larry Morris picked up on the chill in the air between them. He smiled to himself. Rosa Losada had no idea that the guy the whole squad had been talking about for a month was about to become her partner. Maybe Gus was right. She needed loosening up. If Joe Dante couldn't do it, she was probably a lost cause. He cleared his throat.

"Losada . . . you've no doubt caught the advance press on Dante here. I'm afraid it's been a little critical. From now on, you're going to have to do your best to forget it."

Dante and the lady detective looked at each other.

"I have no feelings one way or another," Rosa replied.

"Good." Morris flashed a cryptic little smile. "Dante is a sixteen-year veteran. Eleven with a Gold Shield. Before his work in Narcotics, he spent six years on the precinct level as a detective. You've heard that this guy is an oddball. A renegade. What I'm saying here and now is *fuck* the candy asses in the media."

Dante squirmed uncomfortably. Rosa simply stared, increasingly confused.

"Why are you telling me this?" she asked.

Morris shrugged. "Because we have a problem right now that is going to demand the kinds of skills he's developed. The commissioner has assigned him to the Tenth and wants you to work with him."

"I beg your pardon?" Rosa asked incredulously.

"I think you heard me. We have a sticky situation with

this murdered prostitute. The only material witness is some artsy fart who unfortunatley is *the* Paul Garriston's son-in-law. You know if you read the papers that Mr. Garriston lost his wife recently after a tragic illness. The mayor is very anxious that we keep his name out of this. I believe you are familiar with a Willie Davenport, right, Dante?"

The detective's nostrils flared. "Real scum bag," he grumbled. "He beat two raps we fed to the D.A. An animal."

"I beg your pardon, sir," Rosa broke in. "But I'm not sure I understand."

"I'm getting to it." Morris smiled indulgently. "We have the street pretty much blanketed on this thing. So far, nothing much has turned up. We need another angle, and you two are going to supply it. We want you under, working it from their side. Gus Lieberman says you're imaginative, Dante. Give it some thought. However you've got to do it. I'll trust you to come up with something. We need to know what the hell is going on out there to make all the usual mouthpieces so suddenly uninformative. Nobody knows nothing. We need something. Fast."

After spending a month in limbo, Dante's hair had grown to a point where he could just barely comb it. He'd spent some time at the beach. He looked tanned and fit. Stretching his long muscles much as a cat might, he eased back in his chair.

"I'm in the dark, Sergeant. Can you fill me in a little about the murder?"

Morris nodded. "Three nights ago a streetwalker was killed and shoved out of a car on Twenty-seventh Street. The particulars are nasty. Broken neck. Lacerated breasts. A semen-filled rubber stuffed in her mouth. Real sick shit. The girl worked for a small-time pimp named Slick Sloan. Garriston's son-in-law is a trendy sculptor named Brennan. He just happened to be looking out his windows with a pair of binoculars when this all happened. He ran downstairs, found the girl dead, and called us. Apparently, it was too dark in the loading bay where it happened for him to get a good look at the car. Other than noticing that it was small and dark, he can't make it."

"And you think it was Willie D.?"

"Best guess." Morris shrugged. "He runs the show over there, and every couple months, some chiseler tries to move in. We've never been able to make anything stick, but the man's ruthless in his dealings with interlopers."

"You've talked to this Sloan?"

"To no end. To hear it from him, he doesn't even know where the Hudson River is."

"Can we see the body?"

"Sure. She's over at the morgue. No positive I.D. yet. Sloan doesn't know her name either."

Dante's brow had become furrowed in thought. "Is this guy Brennan strictly off-limits?"

"He's a material witness to a homicide." Morris shrugged.

"It'd be nice if we could get him to at least make the model of the car," Dante said.

"Good luck. Just go easy, huh? We've even got Stuart Sprague on our asses."

"Birds of a feather," Dante grunted. "This thing's starting to read like *Who's Who*."

Throughout this conversation, Rosa Losada sat looking lost. They couldn't do this to her. From all she'd heard, this guy Dante was a maniac.

"I don't understand how I'm supposed to be of any help to Dante," she said finally. "Like you say, he's an expert at this sort of thing, and . . ."

"It came from higher up." Morris shook his head, cutting her off. "Maybe they've got something in mind for you and they want you to get some of this sort of experience."

"But I don't necessarily . . ."

"Go have lunch," he said, ending it. "Take a run over to the morgue. I want you two started on this thing right away."

Harry Ransome had set up a lunch with the police commissioner. Stuart Sprague met them at the Four Seasons early Monday afternoon. Even during a crowded lunch hour, Sprague and his guests never failed to be provided with the best table in the house. The maître d' was accustomed to seeing the most influential men and women in the city surrounding the powerful financier. Today was certainly no different from a host of others preceding it.

His guests were already seated and drinking when Sprague entered and hurried across to them.

"Forgive me for being late." He smiled pleasantly. "Chivas," he told the waiter.

Ransome and the commissioner half rose to shake his hand. They made small talk for a few minutes while surveying the menu.

"How's that beautiful wife of yours, Fred?" Sprague asked the commissioner.

"Good, Stuart. Penny?"

"Tan." Sprague smiled cryptically. "You have to come out one weekend before the summer's over." It was like saying they had to have drinks sometime soon.

"That would be nice." Frederick Burnham nodded. "Played any golf lately?"

"Not since Palm Springs last month. Tennis though, right, Harry? Beat the socks off the D.A. here yesterday."

"Bullshit." Ransome grinned. "It's his court. I let him win so he'll invite me back next week."

They ordered food and a bottle of excellent Bordeaux. Sprague believed in exerting influence as civilly as possible.

"I talked to Paul Garriston this morning," he mentioned. "He's still not up to par, I'm afraid."

"That's a tough one to take," the commissioner said sympathetically. "She was a wonderful woman."

"Too bad her daughter didn't have half her sense." Sprague nodded. "Imagine her marrying someone like this Brennan."

'He was no one before she got ahold of him," Ransome said. "By all accounts, she made him what he is today. That's gratitude for you."

"Paul shouldn't have to suffer from his little girl's poor judgment," Sprague said solemnly. "I know that any more attention right now would just about kill him."

"You don't have to worry about it," Burnham assured him. "We're keeping the son-in-law out of it. If we break this one, it won't be because of anything *he* saw."

Sprague eyed him steadily. "You don't know what a relief it will be to Paul to hear that, Fred. All of us appreciate your discretion. You know we think you're doing a wonderful job down there. By the way, how is the PAL doing toward reaching their goal this year?"

"Now that you mention it . . ." the commissioner replied.

SIX

Rosa Losada was predisposed to resent her forced involvement with this ex-narc. She felt like cannon fodder. From what she'd read and heard, this guy was the antithesis of everything a person charged with enforcing the social contract should be. Rosa was big on the social contract. Live and let live. In that the law was enacted to define the limits of acceptable behavior, it upheld the contract. Authorizing people to work outside the law in order to enforce it bothered her. The license granted was just too great. Joe Dante, five years in possession of such license, scared the hell out of her.

Granted, he had done nothing so far to justify her fear. Looking at him there, across the table from her at the Cantina on Twenty-third and Ninth, he didn't exactly look like the killing machine who had recently dispatched four bikers in a pitched gun battle. In his khaki chinos, topsiders, and polo shirt, he looked more like a tennis pro. Long, lithe muscles rippled under a dark tan. He had a good body. Maybe even a great body. And though he was admittedly good-looking, he didn't seem particularly vain. He didn't wear a wedding ring. But then again, he was an Italian male. She wondered.

"Are you married?" she asked casually.

"No." He shook his head. "Why?"

"Just wondering. Divorced?"

"Nope. Never been. Not even close. You?"

"Neither . . . married or divorced."

"How old are you. . . . that is, if you don't mind my asking."

"Twenty-seven."

"You've got your whole life ahead of you," he mused distractedly, attention caught momentarily by a passing redhead. "What made you want to be a cop?"

Her eyes clouded a moment. His attention returned in time to see something close off.

"What makes anyone?" She shrugged. "It was something I wanted to do."

"My dad was a cop," he offered. "Thirty-five years. Never made sergeant."

"Why not?" she asked curiously.

"He wouldn't take. It pissed everyone else off. They thought they couldn't trust him. After a few years they took him off the street and put him behind a desk. He sat there for twenty-five years. Nobody trusted an honest cop back then."

"You sound bitter."

"Maybe." He shrugged. "I suppose I am. You see, I remember how it made me feel as a kid. At picnics and parties, they all treated him like an outsider. Their kids heard them talk. They treated *me* like an outsider. I saw how much it hurt him. For the longest time, I couldn't understand why it made any difference; why he couldn't just be like the rest of them. They were cops after all. I didn't understand what integrity was then."

"He's retired now?"

"Yeah. Two years ago. About ten years ago, the Knapp Commission scared the shit out of everyone. Taking dough under the table, what was left of it, went out of vogue. All of a sudden my pop was a paragon of virtue. They gave him his nightstick and his beat back. I'll never forget the day he went back out on the street again. I was a detective over at the Sixth then. You never saw a happier face in your life."

"As a cop, he must have known how dangerous it was when you went undercover."

"It scared the crap out of him. More than mom, maybe. We didn't tell her much. But he knew, sure. I think he half expected me dead at any time."

"So why did you do it?"

"Because I hate the maggots who think they can laugh at the law and get rich breaking it."

"And that's it?" she asked.

"You gotta understand something," he said seriously, leaning toward her across the table. "In the end, when I finally stopped resenting my dad for being an oddball, I developed a deep respect for what he stood for his whole life. It takes me a while to get around to understanding things sometimes. When I finally do, they stick."

Having lunch with the cowboy made her doubt her instincts. For a guy who had just spent five years in isolation, he was surprisingly open to talking about it. When she compared him to a slob like Pat Meehan, she wondered if maybe this wasn't going to be so bad.

Most guys in the squad insisted on driving, like it was a male prerogative. Dante hadn't batted an eye when she grabbed the keys off the board and climbed behind the wheel. As she drove them across town from the restaurant to the Medical Examiner, he seemed content to ride shotgun and ogle skirts on the sidewalk.

The city morgue was situated in the bowels of the M.E.'s office on 30th and First Avenue. Neither of them relished the idea of their visit. The building was depressing. Morose expanses of dull grey brick. Dingy, institutional green interiors. The morgue was something else again.

They located Rocky Conklin. He was just finishing up with an elderly traffic fatality. Pedestrian. She didn't look too good. As the pale, stooped examiner peeled off his rubber gloves, he was leaning toward a hanging microphone that served to document these proceedings.

"Bases empty and two out in the bottom of the ninth, sports fans. Strike three! We'll be back with the happy recap after a break." He reached to switch off the machine.

"Joey Dante. Hot damn! Long time no see. Hey. Real nice job you did on that load of gorillas they hauled in here. You always were a great shot."

"You never give up, do you, Doc?" Dante grinned and shook his hand. "Be nice to Rosa Losada, will you?"

"Charmed." Conklin smiled ghoulishly. "What can I do for you folks?"

"We're here to see a Jane Doe from the Tenth. Murder victim three nights ago."

"Sure. The professional pincushion. Got her in drawer seven. Help yourself. Don't take anything."

Dante rolled his eyes at Rosa and noticed that encountering the elderly cadaver on the slab had turned her a little green. Conklin and his brand of humor weren't helping matters any. Taking her by the elbow, he guided her out into the refrigerated hallway. The smell of formaldehyde seared their nostrils. Locating number seven, he gripped the handle.

"Got your cookies under control?" he asked.

"I'll be okay."

With a tug, he pulled the stainless steel drawer out into the middle of the passage.

The woman's youth shocked them. She couldn't have been any more than eighteen, tops. The hair, bleached a platinum blond, had dark brown roots. Dante pulled the sheet back from her torso. Rosa, no fan of this aspect of the job, held her mouth.

The breasts were deeply lacerated and bruised. A neat incision had been made from right to left across her shoulder and then down the middle of her chest to the pubis. Dante turned her arm inside up and saw what Conklin meant about pincushion.

As he stood there staring at her, something struck him. Whoever had taken her out genuinely enjoyed his work. The killing had been done without method. There was no weapon employed. The job had been done with bare hands and brute strength. He found that odd. A professional wouldn't take that sort of chance. He might off her and even stuff the rubber in her mouth as a sort of cruel joke, but without at least a garrote or knife?

"Seen enough?" he asked Rosa.

Unable to speak, she managed a faint nod and moved away quickly. Dante was left to shut the drawer.

Back in the car, she just sat there for a full five minutes without starting it. Gradually, a weak color returned to her face.

"They're wrong," Dante said quietly.

"What?"

"About that in there. That's no reprisal killing. A nut did that. A real sick nut."

"How can you be so sure?" she asked.

"I just am." He shook his head. "I can feel certain things, and this one's ringing all the bells. The son of a bitch didn't even use a weapon."

"Yes? I guess I don't understand."

He explained.

SEVEN

“Joey D.!” Sammy Scruggs’s deep bass boomed over the line when he picked up the phone. “What are you doing for dinner, dude?”

“Reheating leftovers,” Dante answered. “You got any better ideas?”

“Yeah. I bring over a six-pack, eat half your leftovers, and we watch the Mets game on your TV.”

“Tell you what,” Dante replied. “Stop by Ray’s on the way and pick up a pizza. No fucking anchovies.”

Sammy mumbled something about then he’d be buying the whole dinner. Dante reminded him that it was his television.

Ever since his days as a rookie in the Sixth Precinct, Joe Dante had lived on Perry Street in the Village. At the time, it had been both cheap and two blocks from work. As time passed, the Village changed. The garden apartment he’d initially rented for $56 was controlled. In sixteen years, his rent soared to an incredible $130. Something comparable, uncontrolled, went for around $1,800. Even if he wanted to, he'd never be able to afford to move on what he made as a cop. Not and live in Manhattan. The large roomy one-bedroom with high ceilings and a walled patio remained everything he needed. Sooner or later it was bound to go co-op. When it did, he would bite the bullet and buy it. He'd be crazy not to. On the open market it would go at $200,000 easy. He'd get it for half of that.

Copter the cat wandered out onto the patio, rubbed up against his leg, and yeowled for his dinner. Dante bent to scratch his ears. Copter continued to yeowl.

"Peristent little fucker, aren't we? C'mon." He scooped the cat up and carried him into the kitchen. "I needed a beer anyway."

Copter had been around the place almost as long as his boss.

He was getting a little long in the tooth. His kidneys weren't what they used to be. Joe fed him special food he got from the vet. Copter didn't like it much. After a couple more pitiful cries from the old guy, Dante relented. Opening a can of 9-Lives, he mixed it in with the prescription food.

"You're a junk food junkie," he growled. "Go ahead. Kill yourself."

Copter dove into the concoction like a fiend.

Carrying his beer back onto the patio, Dante enjoyed the comparative cool of the evening and waited for Sammy to arrive. A half-dozen separate notions roared around in his head like runaway trains in a freight yard. Too much had happened in one day. He'd been assigned to a squad, and the next thing he knew, he was working undercover again. Not the same kind of cover as before, but the ground was too familiar. He'd been saddled with a greenhorn lady detective. Nice enough. But green and female. He didn't need the aggravation. Then there was the murder and the angle they were working it from. It stunk. Finally, there was this soft-shoeing it around a pirate like Paul Garriston. Political considerations guiding the direction of a homicide investigation. That stunk, too. This Brennan guy had to be some sort of pantywaist to hide behind the skirts of some fat cat's dead wife.

"Couldn't make the car my ass." He snorted to himself.

If he had the guy for half an hour, he'd sure have a better idea of what it was than "little and dark."

If pressed, he probably couldn't put his finger on why he didn't want to like the nudie sculptor, but he didn't. Maybe it was a simple matter of origins and station. The guy was rich and got his face in magazines all the time. Maybe that was it. The attention the guy attracted for making that shitty, stylized crap. Joe Dante may have been raised in Brooklyn, but sixteen years had taken him a long way from there now. Even *he* knew the guy's stuff was junk.

What the hell was the man living on the corner of Twenty-seventh and Eleventh Avenue for anyway? He couldn't think of a cruddier spot. He'd soon find out. One of the first things on his list was a visit to this junk peddler.

Sammy arrived in the middle of the second inning. The Mets were already down one nothing and the pizza was lukewarm.

"What the fuck? You came by way of Siberia?"

"I had to make a phone call," Sammy shot back. "What's the matter? Your oven broken or your legs?"

Grumbling, Dante scooped up the whole box and carried it into the kitchen. He was just sliding it into the stove when his ex-partner let out a whoop from the other room.

"What?" he yelled. "What is it?"

"Keith Hernandez just hit one out with two on," Sammy hollered. "You missed it."

It was in the middle of the seventh, with the Mets up by five, that Sammy finally got fed up with his friend's pouting silence and asked him what the problem was.

"Everything." Dante sighed. "They stuck me with a broad, Sammy. They stuck me with a broad and want me to go undercover on a homicide investigation."

"No shit." Scruggs whistled. "Who is she?"

"Woman named Losada. Rosa."

"The one whose parents were murdered?"

"What?"

"Six or seven years ago. Double homicide on East Ninety-third. The woman lingered. They beat her husband to death in front of her and then raped her. Real nasty shit. The only daughter was going to college somewhere up North. She became a cop. Must be the same one."

"Jesus," Dante breathed. "I asked her whether her mother or father named her 'Detective' today."

"You didn't know."

"I should have. I remember it now. I'm stupid."

"What's the homicide that's got them putting people undercover?"

Dante told him about the murder and the operating theory that shaped the direction they were taking.

"That's just the thing, though," he finished. "Willie Davenport is a low-life slime, but this isn't his work. A wacko did this. Go look at that stiff. You'd *know*."

"No thanks." Sammy shook his head. "I believe you. You got the best nose in the department, Joey. You say so, it's so."

"They want me to get inside of Times Square. Set something up where I can get an ear down and see what I hear. Best I've been able to come up with is the basic whiff dealer up from Florida."

Sammy considered it. "You know, maybe we can work this to advantage. With a hand from the Condor, you could get in easy. It'd cut through a lot of this bullshit. Let me think about it. When do you have to set up?"

"Yesterday. It's one of those."

"Let's talk again tomorrow night. I'll sleep on it."

The idea of working something with Sammy again, with or without sanction, gave Dante a badly needed boost. Elevated out of the doldrums, he popped a fresh beer and relaxed to watch the end of the game.

Brian Brennan surveyed the two new faces in the security monitor. Two more detectives. The lid had come off Pandora's box the night he called in that corpse. So far the cops had been reasonable but persistent. Here were more. Some guy named Dante.

The second detective was a woman. Tall, aristocratic bearing. She was introduced as Rosa Losada. Spanish name. But she didn't look Puerto Rican. More a pure Mediterranean. Maybe she *was* Spanish.

Dante seemed somehow different from the others. Shirtsleeves and Levi's instead of an off-the-rack suit. Harder around the edges. Eyes old before their time in an otherwise boyish face. Tall. Athletic. These were the kinds of things Brennan had trained himself to notice. A long time ago; before Lisa. This one had a look of dangerous competence about him.

The woman stood in almost bewildering contrast. Neat and controlled. The very image of thoroughness and order. Maybe a little too tightly wound. It was hard to get a read on her. She was definitely following the tennis pro's lead. Pretty though. She had the goods, even though she went to a lot of trouble to disguise them. No makeup. Hair done back in a simple tie.

"You need I.D.?" Dante asked after introducing them.

The voice belied the looks. Brooklyn with the edge taken off. Brennan was surprised. He didn't look Brooklyn. Topsiders. No gold neck-chains. It was all wrong.

"Not necessary." He shook his head. "Coffee?"

Dante gave Brennan a handshake strong enough to make most men wince. Brennan returned the pressure evenly, ounce for ounce. Dante accepted the offered coffee.

"The studio is probably best," Brennan offered. "It was where I was when I saw . . . it." He led the way.

Brennan's workspace was a cavernous affair. Not counting the living area, it encompassed roughly five thousand square feet. A stranger unfamiliar with his craft would invariably be taken aback by the immensity of the scale. All around the place stood industrial metal- and woodworking tools. Lathes, grinders, planers, power saws. A large kiln stood in one corner. Brennan led them past this and into the drawing and modeling studio. Here, the atmosphere was brighter. Evidence of the sheer productivity of the man abounded.

Crap or not, Dante found himself thinking, Brennan cranked. His eyes were traveling around the room. For some reason, he hadn't expected him to be able to draw so well. There were drawings everywhere. Women, men, animals. Some of them amazingly vivid. Surprisingly, he had yet to see a single one of the works America had come to associate with Brian Brennan. The full-breasted, long-limbed fantasy nudes, generally in bronze but reproduced in other materials now for the mass market. This was the man's house, and there weren't any. Instead, in the middle of the studio stood a life-sized clay rendering of three men in work clothes and hard hats, each reaching to grab a huge hoist hook.

His eyes caught a group of sketches. Hookers. So he

hadn't been watching a blow job in-progress just for the sheer voyeuristic hell of it. Not necessarily anyway. He drew the damn stuff.

"We have to get a make on that car," he said, turning away from the drawings and looking hard into the artist's eyes. "What you've given us so far just isn't good enough."

Brennan seemed unprepared for the brusqueness of the approach. "I'm . . . uh, sorry. Look at the loading area. They were back inside there. It was dark."

"The guy drove out," Dante insisted. "Even if you didn't look straight at it, you must have seen the car out of the corner of your eye. I'm a guy who believes that impressions, right off the top of your head, are the most reliable. High up on its wheels or low-slung?"

"Huh?"

"You heard me."

"Oh, uh . . ."

"Just say it. Impressions."

"Low-slung, I guess."

"Good. Squarish or streamlined?"

"Streamlined."

"Wedge-shaped or more symmetrical front to back."

"The latter. Symmetrical."

"Lot of chrome?"

"Some. Not a lot. There was a dent."

"What?"

"A dent. I remember it now because it was in the passenger door and, even in the low light, I could see how the light hit it differently when it opened. And the gleam of the chrome stopped there, like it might have been broken off."

Dante was beside himself. "You just remembered this?"

"Yeah, I guess so. It wasn't until I actually tried to visualize what I saw again, just now. There was definitely a dent in the passenger door."

"Rosa." Dante turned to motion. "Give me that book."

They'd brought along a book of late-model car makes. Slowly, he began to go through it with Brennan. It took over an hour. Rosa took a note every time they came across something that seemed to fit what had been described. In the end, they had it narrowed down to the Chrysler LeBaron, one of several BMW models, and a new baby Mercedes. Dark in color. With a dent in the door. In other words, they'd narrowed it down to one of a possible couple thousand. The only thing that set theirs apart from the rest was a dented passenger door.

EIGHT

Something came up and Sam Scruggs couldn't make it by Dante's place Tuesday night. He called to suggest meeting for an early breakfast. Joe mentioned a diner on Eleventh in the mid-Forties.

Sammy was late. Dante had just finished his second cup of coffee and was considering food when his buddy pushed through the front door.

"Sleeping Beauty. Come. Sit. Order some of the wonderful cuisine. I'm buying."

Sammy looked at Dante suspiciously. "I dig it. You've lured me here to poison me, right?"

"If you're worried, don't drink the coffee."

Sammy grinned and waved to the waitress. "I've got an idea, Joey."

"Don't keep me in suspense."

"It's simple, really. Downtown thinks this homicide has something to do with the turf wars. You don't. Prove it."

"Huh?"

"Prove it. Your idea's good. Flashy broker up from Florida with the solid Colombian connections. Spread some freebies around and talk quantity. The Condor can help you get inside."

"Aren't you taking an awful risk?" Dante asked suspiciously. "What's in it for you?"

"I want Willie D."

"And you want me to help you set him up."

"That's right. Once and for all. So it will stick. I'm willing to risk the cover to get him, Joey. I don't give a fuck about the cover anymore."

"What are you saying, buddy?"

Sammy sat back and stared out the window a moment, idly watching a cab driver remove his meter from the dash of his car and lock it in the trunk.

"I don't know." He sighed, shaking his head. "I been thinking that five years is a long time. I'm forty next month. Too old for this shit. Two more years and I got my twenty in. I've been wondering what reporting-in every day might feel like."

"It's not all that wonderful," Dante told him.

"You've only been doing it three days. It takes time to get used to."

"Give me an idea of how it runs," Dante pressed.

"All right." Sammy started to grin. "Everybody knows that the Condor is supposed to have the pad down in Colombia. You're the partner of one of his main men. A gringo from . . . Miami, let's say. You're in New York to act as the middleman in a big deal. You're writing orders. There's a shipment of excellent shit on its way north from the Condor's lab. I get some of the blast we stashed from the Morales bust and have a dude I know wash it a couple of times. Clean it up so it sparkles. You remember how good that shit was to begin with. You come on the scene with the Condor's introduction and start passing around free samples."

"And this way I'm right on top of Davenport."

"You got it. Willie's always paranoid about competition. That'll lure him in. Once he sees your product, he'll change his tune. He's got high-end clientele who get tired of snorting that crud he sells."

Dante nodded. "And if there's anything to hear, I'll hear it."

Wednesday afternoon, Dante took Rosa into Larry Morris's office. Leaving out any mention of his extracurricular plans involving Sammy and a quantity of illegally withheld gusto dust, he explained their need for a properly flashy automobile.

"If we cruise in something city-issue, the players on Times Square are gonna laugh us out of midtown," he said. "We need something that a dope dealer would drive. Preferably with out-of-state plates. Florida would be perfect."

To his surprise, Morris offered little argument. With a shrug he told them he would get the request downtown right away.

That night late, Dante got his '84 Corvette out of the parking garage and took a spin over to and up Eleventh Avenue. It wasn't a place he'd ever spent much time around, and he wanted to get the feel of it. With the detachable roof stored in the trunk and the heavy, humid air making him sweat, he rolled slowly in and out of the side streets.

If this really was a psycho and the taste of blood had triggered something that might make him want to do it again, Dante wondered whether he might return here. There were whores all over town. Twelfth Street over in the East Village. Down by the Brooklyn Bridge. The blocks around Twenty-seventh and Broadway. A couple of things occurred to him as he surveyed this wasteland.

For one, homicidal maniacs were a funny bunch. The literature he read suggested territoriality was a significant consideration in analyzing their behavior patterns. Most of them were like homing pigeons. Back to the scene of their kicks. If it was sexual, and again many were, then the guy got his rocks off. That was important. Whatever the conditions were, they'd been right.

Secondly, this place *was* a wasteland. Unlike the other locations where you found prostitution in town, this one was littered with pockets of isolation. Loading bays like the one the killer found. Driveways. Empty lots. Stretches of desolate street. There was virtually no residential occupancy over here. And the area was vast. Twenty blocks, almost a mile, long. Two long blocks wide. Three hundred acres of run-down, rubble-strewn real estate. If a man wanted to get his kicks murdering girls, there had to be a hundred perfect places to do it.

As he pulled around the corner of Twenty-fifth onto Twelfth, he was surprised to see Brian Brennan briskly crossing the West Side Highway on foot. The guy was dressed in gym shorts, running shoes, and a T-shirt. It was two o'clock in the morning.

"Hey!" He hailed him, catching up and pulling alongside.

Brennan looked up, not recognizing the car. The detective from the other day, Dante, was peering up at him.

The sculptor was covered with rivulets of sweat, the shirt plastered to his torso. "Nice night for a run," Dante commented.

"No cars." Brennan nodded, mopping his brow. "I don't need the carbon monoxide."

"You always do this?" Dante asked.

"Usually around eleven-thirty or twelve. I worked late. You too, huh?"

"Sort of." Dante shrugged. "Just doing some thinking."

"Nice car."

"Hop in and I'll give you a ride home."

Brennan walked around to the other side, opened the door, and got in.

"How far do you run?" Dante asked.

"Down to the World Trade Center and back. It's about five miles."

"Jesus. In this heat?"

"You get used to it."

Dante wrinkled his nose. "How about the smell of the river. Do you get used to that, too?"

"It's just in the summer. You look past it. There are other advantages to counter it."

"Like what?"

"The quiet. You get in a rhythm, start the sweat flowing. It really clears your head."

Pulling up in front of Brennan's building, the detective surveyed the forbidding exterior and shook his head.

"Tell me something," he said. "Why does a guy with your dough live in a dump like this?"

Brennan smiled. "It's a longer story than you probably have time for."

"Try me."

"I've got a couple of cold ones in the fridge. You look like you could use one."

Dante was working the four-to-midnight shift the next day. he looked at his watch and shrugged. "Why not?"

He pulled the roof out of the trunk. Brennan gave him a hand, snapping it in place.

"You married, Dante?" the artist asked. They were riding up in the elevator, a gigantic industrial job covered with graffiti.

"No."

"My father-in-law is the CEO of a lending bank. You

know, mergers, Third-World governments . . . that sort of thing. If you can't relate to him on his level, it's like you don't really exist. He always treated his daughter like a commodity. When she married me, he felt like he'd gotten well below market value for her. He's never let it lay. And now I'm in the process of divorcing her."

"So what's that got to do with this?"

"This"—he smiled—"also doesn't exist. Not in Paul Garriston's or my wife Lisa's world. Moving down here was like moving to Mars."

"Kind of extreme, isn't it? I mean, Christ, you've got just as much right to be here as they do."

Brennan snorted derisively. "You've got no idea, do you?"

"Of what?"

"The kind of man Paul Garriston is. How miserable he can make your life. For instance, I've only just gotten representation with a new gallery. The last one dropped me like a hot spud. All it took was a phone call. Paul Garriston spends big money there."

Dante was beginning to get the picture.

"It's funny," he said. He followed Brennan into the loft and sat while the sculptor went for the beers. When Brennan returned Dante said, "You read magazines and a guy like you is famous. It looks like you and Garriston travel in the same lane. No, huh?"

"I was never anything more than a court jester in that world," Brennan returned. He handed Dante a Heineken. "It didn't dawn on me until after you left the other day. You're the undercover cop who was in that shoot-out on the Lower East Side."

"That's right." Dante nodded warily, sipping.

"I can't imagine. Five years?"

Dante smiled. "Yeah. I guess *this* is like moving into

another world for me. Same as you. Different world, same city."

"Then you know what I mean. I'm over here just feeling my way around, trying to get a handle on what it means to start all over again. How are you making out so far?"

The detective shrugged. "About the same as you, I guess. It takes time. Is that the new Brennan?" he asked, nodding at the statue of the three workmen visible through the studio door.

"Might be," the other man said. "Like I was saying. I'm feeling my way around. But yeah, this feels good. They're steelworkers. A commission for a museum in Pittsburgh. Two or three years ago, I never would have chanced it. It runs contrary to the Brennan style."

"You mean the bronze *Playboy* bunnies?"

"Don't start. I already get enough from the critics. Tell me; you've had your Waterloo. Where do *you* go from here?"

"The direction is simple enough." Dante shrugged. "The problem is getting there. In this line of work, reasons for trying to become human again are few and far between."

They ended up having several more than one beer. When Dante left, he had a different feeling for the sculptor and who he was. Starting the Corvette, he reflected on this odd encounter. The temptation, it seemed, was to draw everything in black and white. Nothing ever was. Eager to avoid getting hauled in on a DWI rap, he took it slow on the way home.

As the week wore on, the implications of what he had done finally penetrated Rick's overriding agitation. She hadn't submitted to the promise of money. That is what had surprised him the most. The others always had.

The fact that he killed her upset him at first. But it concerned him little that she was dead. Rick was a planner. He attended to details. When something went awry, it upset him. The death of a whore was no great loss. But she hadn't responded predictably . . . or at least as *he'd* predicted she would. For a planner, nothing was worse than an unforeseen contingency.

By Wednesday, his anger at his own shortsightedness subsided. In its place, the memory of the pleasure he experienced intensified. The way he filled the rubber in great spasms of excitement. No woman had ever fought against him like that. The thrill of the thought made him salivate. She'd been like a terrified rabbit in the clutches of a hound on the hunt.

And she'd looked so much like the girl. In his mind, at the moment he came against her, she *was* the girl. In his mind's eye, the silenced attempts to scream and the look of terror were twisting not the surrogate's, but the girl's own face. He had seen her there like that, under him, fighting him. Just the thought of her terror of the power of his body and of his love made him hard.

By Friday night he could contain himself no longer. He had to return to that place. To see if this was a fluke thing or something sustainable. A new level of relationship with the girl. The muscles of his neck and shoulders quivered at the thought of gripping her, pulling her heaving breasts hard against his chest.

He waited until Joan Rivers finished hosting *The Tonight Show*. Then he got the BMW from the garage, and drove to the brownstone on Twenty-second Street. His mind's eye was now crammed with swirling images of the girl. He couldn't wait to feel the closeness of the black leather around him, to get the smell of it in his nostrils. He knew that if he saw her, he would take her then. No waiting time to let the images mesh. The fever of the image was upon him. A surrogate vessel was out there, awaiting him. He could feel her.

NINE

Joe Dante's phone rang at five o'clock on Saturday morning. Beside him, the dark-haired casting agent he'd brought home from a party at his upstairs neighbor's stirred and pulled the sheet over her head. Reaching, he dragged the receiver across the pillow to his ear.

"You better have good fucking reason to call a man at this hour," he growled.

"Dante?" It was Morris.

"God." He groaned. "What?"

"Get your ass out of bed and over to Thirty-sixth between Tenth and Eleventh. It's the empty lot next to the lumber company. Our friend has left his calling card again."

"You want Rosa?"

"Not necessary. Inspector Lieberman only suggested I call you. He thinks you've got some sort of sixth sense or something."

"What are friends for?" Dante grumbled. "Give me fifteen."

The brunette had more or less come around by then.

"What's the matter?" she asked sleepily.

"Duty calls." He yawned, throwing back the sheet and swinging his feet over the side of the bed. Reaching out, he ran a hand over her exposed hip and fanny. It was a nice setup. Not spectacular but nice. He could make out the tan line, even in the gloom. French-cut, high up on the hip and slashing diagonally down across the cheek. "Stay as long as you want, but don't let the cat out the front door, okay?"

He stumbled into the bathroom and turned on the shower. Cold.

Patrol force had the place sealed off when he arrived. Larry Morris and two other detectives from the squad were busy running the Forensics boys through their paces. Two meat-wagon jockeys leaned against a gurney and smoked cigarettes. The sergeant turned from the gathering and nodded to Dante as he approached.

"She's over here." He pointed. "Even nastier than last time. Whoever it is, he enjoys his work."

Together, they approached the corpse. Lying facedown, head twisted at a funny angle, she appeared to be much the same age as the previous victim. Same hair color.

Dante kept his mouth shut, kneeling to look at her. This was too much of a coincidence. Same hair color, age and general body type. Same exact modus. Gently, he reached to turn her over.

The cheeks and eyes were heavily made up. Not as naturally pretty as the last girl. Even a thick foundation couldn't hide the acne scars. There was the prophylactic stuffed between her lips. The torso was something else again. Not only were there laceractions in her breasts, but this time they were deeper and more extensive.

Like it had taken the guy more effort to get off, he

thought. Taking a deep breath, he rolled her back onto her face and pushed himself to his feet.

"Jesus Christ," he said softly, shaking his head. "Do you know whose she was?"

"Some stoned-out punk who thinks he's a white soul brother or some such shit. Calls himself Danny. That's it. Danny. We've got him across the street."

"What's he got?"

"This guy? About a quarter of the brain cells he was born with. All he knows is that the car was little and black. No make. No plate number. He's tanked to the tits. Eyeballs bulging out of his head like something's kicking them from the inside. God knows there's probably room."

Dante nodded. "I've got a funny feeling about this, Sergeant."

Morris eyed him curiously. "Out with it."

"I think we're barking up the wrong tree. At first I was willing to keep my mouth shut and consider that maybe it *was* a rubout. Made to look like an amateur job. But not now. We've got a sicko on our hands. He's killed twice now, this one nastier than the last. I've got a bad feeling that he's just starting to get warmed up."

The older man stood a moment considering this. He shook his head. "We don't need this," he said. "But I suppose you could be right. I liked the power-struggle angle until I met her doped-up pimp. He's too pathetic to be part of a muscle game. Suddenly, none of it makes sense."

"If our man's a psycho, it won't make sense," Dante said.

Together, they walked a distance from the corpse.

"I want to kill this pimp-war angle," Dante said. "You've got other people who can keep an eye on it. There's something I can feel in my bones about this thing. Let Rosa and me work the psycho angle. If this is a nut, he likes it over here. He feels safe in what he's doing. Maybe he'll get careless."

"I just got you a fuckin' three hundred ZX Turbo with Florida plates," Morris complained, shaking his head.

Dante grinned. "We'll take it. Surveillance we can do in one of the precinct junkers, but the only way we're gonna find this guy is to talk to a lot of whores. He has a type. Blond, tall . . . I'm going to have a lot better luck getting them to talk if I'm behind the wheel of something flashy with out-of-state plates."

"Waste not, want not." Morris grunted. "What the hell."

"It couldn't hurt," Dante said.

"Okay, hotshot. The commissioner thinks you can catch the killer. You do it, and I'm not gonna complain how. Within reason."

"Always," Dante replied solemnly.

Changing strategy meant leaving Sammy holding a ten-ounce bag of sparkling clean coke. Even if he wasn't going to be hopping mad, Dante owed him something for his trouble. As it was, he was going to have to do some quick mental scrambling to appease his ex-partner.

Copter greeted him at the front door, rubbing against his leg and yeowling. The door to his room stood ajar, and there on the bed, the same sheet-covered body lay sleeping. It was just before nine o'clock.

Smiling to himself, Dante slid past, grabbing the phone and carrying it out onto the patio where he wouldn't disturb his guest. Sammy was irritated that he'd call at such an ungodly hour.

"Change of plans, amigo," he told him. "My boy hit again last night, and this time there wasn't any question. Morris is giving me the green light to work the nut angle."

"Goddammit, Joey. What the fuck am I supposed to do with ten ounces of pure flake?"

"I don't know. Snort it, I guess. Listen. There's still Plan B."

"I don't think I want to hear this."

"You want Willie, right?"

"Yeah," Sammy answered cautiously.

"And I owe you that much for helping set this up. So we handle it a little differently, that's all. I've got an idea. If dinner's still on at your place, we can talk about it then."

Sammy carried on awhile, griping to a point where he figured Dante got enough of an earful for throwing a monkey wrench into the works. Dante listened patiently, knowing the big guy was within his rights. Finally able to get off, he hung up and dialed Brooklyn. Ron Gugliano, an old friend from the neighborhood who worked on the docks, was in no better mood about the early hour. Joe let him vent his wrath before outlining his particular problem and making his request. Gugliano told him he'd have to check around and would get back to him. Dante recradled the receiver a final time, thinking about a certain tan line in the other room and wondering whether the casting agent was a morning person.

It was late afternoon before Dante found himself alone again. The idea that he didn't have to go back into the cesspool and play another phony role had come as a great relief. He was relaxed. He'd even bought the lady lunch. Evelyn.

His place needed cleaning in a bad way. Scanning the squalor, he elected to leave it for the following day. He grabbed a Rolling Rock long neck from the ice box and waded through the crap to the patio. Copter, catching him with his guard down, raced into his lap and rolled over onto his back.

"Hiyo, buddy boy," he mumbled, scratching the cat's head. Copter purred, pushing into the pleasure-producing fingers.

The beer felt good in his throat. It was still awful damn hot. Seemed like it had been since the first of June. With August just beginning, there was no sign of relief in sight.

His mind wandered to Rosa. He didn't feel bad about leaving her out of his present plans. To include such an unknown and untried quantity would be foolish. But regardless, there had been developments. The nature of their investigation was changing. He at least owed her an update on that front.

An image of the gung-ho police girl sprang to mind. It wasn't that he didn't like her. That wasn't really it. But the drab crap she wore seemed to match her outlook on life. Somber. Tight-assed. She seemed incapable of loosening up. If she ever smiled, she might even have a pretty face. Jesus, he missed having Sammy around.

After gently dislodging Copter from his lap, Dante ambled inside to retrieve the telephone. He looked up his new partner's number, then dialed her apartment in Park Slope. When Rosa answered, he asked if he could scoot by for a few minutes on his way out that evening. There were a couple of things he wanted to tell her about the case. She kept her response cool, asking in turn why it couldn't wait until Monday morning. Dante wasn't sure. In his guts, he was desperate to break the ice and get their relationship on a more relaxed footing. He didn't say so, explaining instead that the couple of extra hours would give her a chance to mull the whole thing over.

"All right," she sighed. "I've got something at seven-thirty. If you make it before that, we can talk for a few minutes."

At six-thirty, Dante climbed out of a cool shower and dressed. White cotton dress shirt, sleeves rolled a couple turns back from the wrist. Khaki pants.

Traffic was light. The Corvette purred down the West Side Highway, around the bottom of the island, and up the FDR to the Brooklyn Bridge. The sky had closed in since afternoon and now took on a threatening, charcoal-gray cast. Thunder bumpers. The air smelled of rain. Lots of it. It was funny how you could tell how much rain was going to fall, and how hard, by the way the air smelled.

Rosa's building in Park Slope wasn't difficult to locate. A nice, big, clean, white place with polished brass awning poles and a doorman. Park Slope was like that. You seemed to get a lot for your rent dollar this side of the East River. Still, even with apartments being roomier and less expensive, Dante couldn't have faced taking the train into the city every day. Not from Brooklyn. He'd made that break.

After riding the elevator to the sixth floor and locating apartment C, he was greeted at the door by a pert, diminutive woman. Blond with green eyes. Cute. Like one of the girls who was always in demand back in high school.

"Hi! You must be Joe. I'm Cindy." Of course.

Dante smiled and shook her hand.

"Rosa will be down in a minute. Getting dressed for her date is taking her longer than she thought it would."

Dante registered the "date" data. The ice queen had a social life. Well, well.

"Can I get you something to drink?" Cindy asked.

"That's okay," he said.

"It's not any bother," she insisted. "I'm having a vodka and tonic. My date called and said he'd be an hour late." She raised her glass and tinkled the cubes.

"What the hell." He shrugged. "You got a beer?"

She was off to the kitchen, pointing the way to the front room and telling him to make himself comfortable.

The place was good-sized. A duplex. He could have fit his entire apartment into the downstairs alone. And there was a good view of the lower Manhattan skyline and the river. They'd done it up real homey, with art prints framed on the walls and comfortable contemporary furniture.

Cindy returned with a cold Amstel Light.

"Sorry. All we have is this low-cal stuff."

"No sweat," he said, sipping it. He was being polite. Imported or not, the stuff was crap. "This is a real nice place. Who collects the prints?"

"We both do. We've roomed together since sophomore year in college."

Really?" he said. "Where'd you go?"

"Bennington."

Holy smoke, he thought. Sammy said something about her going to college up North. Bennington was rich-girl land. Either that or *real*-smart-girl land. So Rosa Losada had gone to Bennington.

"Is that Joe, Cindy?" A voice came from upstairs. "I'll be down in a minute."

Dante relaxed into a chair opposite Cindy. "So, what do you do?" he asked.

"I'm a forecast analyst for a small investment brokerage."

"No kidding. What was your major?"

"Economics," she replied. "Rosa, too. She was second in our class."

More interesting information. Her parents had been brutally murdered, and five years after joining the force, she was carrying a Gold Shield. He smiled to himself. His partner was proving to be a complex personality with some interesting twists.

And as he reflected, the subject of his rumination appeared beneath the foyer arch. Loose-fitting silk tunic type of thing, belted at the waist. Short. Black patterned tights that ended like pedal pushers, midcalf. Black spiked heels that must have been four inches high. The ordinarily severe ponytail had been liberated and teased into a mass of thick, cascading ringlets. She'd completely done over her face, which now resembled something off a fashion runway in Milan. Dante's jaw dropped.

"Trying to catch flies?" she asked, eyebrows arched.

"Great outfit," Cindy said. "Dynamite. Charlie's going to love it."

Charlie. Dante filed it, confused by the little pang of jealousy the mention of another man in this context raised. It was hard to believe that the woman standing before him was his partner.

"So what's so important that it drags you out to Brooklyn on a Saturday night?" Rosa asked Joe.

Dante snapped out of his daze. "There was another murder last night."

At the mention of murder, Cindy stood and excused herself, leaving the two of them alone.

"And . . . ?" Rosa asked.

"Morris got me out of bed to come take a look. Blonde. Same exact M.O. down to the rubber in her mouth."

"That helps confirm your theory," she said.

He nodded. "I've convinced Morris to let us pursue the psycho angle. You're my partner. I thought you should know."

Rosa appeared to soften slightly. "You could have saved yourself a trip and told me on the phone."

He shook his head. "I've been thinking about how it feels like we've gotten off on the wrong foot with each other. You didn't ask for me, and I didn't ask for you. But that's the way it is. I wanted to come out here to see if maybe we couldn't agree to give this thing a go."

She swallowed hard and smiled. It was difficult for him to read the look in her eye.

"I don't find it an easy thing to trust people right off," she told him. "I appreciate your putting it like this. Most people would let things ride until they sorted themselves out . . . one way or the other."

"We don't have that luxury," he said seriously. "People are dying." Finishing his beer, he set it on the table in front of him and rose to go.

"Okay . . . Joe." She stood with him and extended her hand.

He gripped it. "Rosa." He turned to leave the room, but at the foyer arch he paused and turned back. "And I like your hair like that. You ought to think about exporting it to Manhattan."

TEN

Dante climbed behind the wheel of the late-model Corvette, started it, and pulled away from the curb. The car was his pride and joy, the culmination of a series of horse trades. Two years ago he and Sammy found themselves on loan to the San Francisco department to help them make a big bust. They were out there for three months. During their tenure, the city held an auction of confiscated vehicles and Dante got a great deal on a '56 Porsche Speedster. Two weeks later, he traded it to a collector in Los Angeles for a '57 Thunderbird and $3,000 in cash. He drove the T-bird back to New York and unloaded it for $13,000. That, together with the cash from the Porsche and every last cent in his savings account, went into buying the 'Vette. It was a little ostentatious, but the way Dante saw it, he worked hard, didn't have a family to support, and why the hell not? He figured he could handle the karmic implications, such as they were.

As he recrossed the Brooklyn Bridge, it started to rain as though the floodgates of the Grand Coulee Dam had been opened overhead. Slowly, he threaded his way through the sluggish traffic to the FDR Drive and moved northward as the rain began to let up. Summer rains in New York were like cloudbursts in the tropics. Half a mile from where water was coming down in buckets, he drove abruptly into calm, dry weather. Just beyond Hell Gate and the mouth of Spuyten Duyvil, the FDR branched off across the Willis Avenue Bridge to the Major Deegan Expressway. Across from Yankee Stadium at 155th Street, Dante recrossed the water and turned south on Adam Clayton Powell Boulevard. Saturday night in Harlem, especially in the summer, was a very happening scene.

Thousands of people were out on the street. Girls played double dutch. Kids shot basketballs through the bottom rungs of fire escape ladders. Apartment dwellers hung out their windows, conversing with friends on the pavement. Every couple of blocks, a U-Haul or Ryder van with southern plates stood parked, jammed full of watermelons. As Dante eased the Corvette to the curb at One Twenty-seventh Street, half-a-dozen players leaned on the fender of a Caddy Eldorado just ahead, sipping Schlitz Bull talls and jiving up a storm.

A couple of kids playing stoopball stopped to get a closer look at the ride. As Dante popped his door and climbed out, the kids were gingerly tracing their fingers along the fiberglass quarterpanels.

"It's one of them new ones, ain't it?" a kid asked.

"Yep."

"Is it for real that it'll blow the doors off a Ferrari?"

"That's right. And a Nine Eleven Porsche."

"Strictly bad," the kid said. Stooping, he peered inside. Dante reached into his wallet and handed the kid a five.

"Anybody starts fucking with it, you go to that building there and ring number Twelve. Right?"

The kid stared at the five-dollar bill and then back at the man who'd given it to him. "You got it, mister. Ain't nobody gonna fuck with this car."

Dante strolled to the front door of the Condor's building. The lobby was not elegant, but that changed when he stepped out of the elevator onto Sammy's floor. The carpeting in the hall was a deep red wool pile; the walls were papered in a black-and-gold club print. The only two lighting fixtures were crystal chandeliers. The whole setup leaned a little toward Parisian bordello, but it was clear that no expense had been spared. There was only one door.

When he knocked, a voice rumbled something incoherent from inside, the peephole darkened for an instant, and then a series of dead bolts clicked.

"Joey D.," Sammy said, smiling. He swung the door wide and stood aside.

Dante had been here many times before. The place was immense, covering the entire floor of the building. It was also the most garishly furnished place he had ever seen. There were mirrors and gilt everywhere. Giant-screen television, mammoth stereo, a wall of records, fluff-covered furniture, and a white shag rug that everything stood knee-deep in. The Condor's official nest. Unofficially, Sammy hated it and spent every spare moment he could squeeze out in his crib down in Atlantic Highlands on the Jersey shore.

At about the same time as Dante and Sammy were beginning to work Undercover Narcotics, the unit busted a big-time wholesaler who was in the middle of having the place renovated with illicitly obtained funds. They confiscated it just as the furniture was arriving and sent the poor guy up to Ossining to do a cool twenty. The finishing touches cost the city a little money out of pocket, but the results seemed to be worth it. The Condor had a nest. The way he and Dante worked, Sammy remained clean by feeding the Blade his contacts and letting Joe do the dirty work.

Sammy got Dante a beer and sprawled back on the sofa adjacent to him.

"Before I go to the expense of feeding you and watching you guzzle more of my beer, you'd best spit out your bright idea, little brother . . . and it better be good."

Dante shook his head. "Have I ever left you high and dry before?" he asked. "Have faith."

"Faith is for little old ladies and priests, Joey. Gimme something I can touch."

"What's for dinner?"

"Jambalaya, crab boil, and fried okra . . . if you live that long. But first you gotta tell me what I'm supposed to do with three hundred grams of Bolivian flake."

"It might come in handy in your new line of work."

"I'm listening."

"Willie Davenport's a scum ball, right? There's nothing you'd like more than to mount him in your insect collection."

"Next to the cockroaches," Sammy said, grinning.

"On the other hand, I need an inside track down in Willie's territory. A way to keep an eye on the streets. I was driving around there the other night, but something about his operation didn't hit me until I saw that second dead woman this morning."

He paused to sip his beer and look Sammy straight in the eye.

"He's got a girl in his stable who looks just like the two victims . . . only prettier. Same build. Same hair. It didn't add up until this morning when I realized my man has a type."

"*What* didn't add up?" Sammy asked in confusion. "Make some sense, Joey. You're talking gibberish."

"Think about it, Sammy," Dante urged. "The best way for me to nail my man is to actually *be* there. On the street. Dangling the bait."

"I get it. You want to be a *pimp*." Sammy grunted.

"Uh-uh." Dante shook his head. "I want *you* to."

Sammy was in midswallow when Dante hit him with it. The beer he was ingesting suddenly erupted as he choked, half of it exiting through his nose. Dante was on his feet, handing him a napkin and pounding him on the back. It was some minutes before he had wiped his nose, dried his eyes, and could speak.

"The hell, you say?" he croaked. "Don't do that to me, Joey."

Dante shook his head, focusing in earnest. "Listen to me, Sammy. We tried for five years to get that puke, and he slid on everything we ever tried to pin on him. Loopholes. I started thinking about it, and it got me to wondering if maybe our approach wasn't wrong."

"We did our work, Joey. What else *could* we do?"

"We were angels, Sammy. A couple of *Patrol Guide* boy scouts. Meanwhile, we watch a guy get away who we *know* runs one of the biggst dope operations in the city. Times Square, clubs, discos. And to show everybody just what a stud he is, he runs a string of whores by getting good-looking women strung out on his product."

"Are you saying what I think you're saying?" Sammy asked.

"Only if what you think I'm saying is that it's time to go for the man's balls. We remove Willie, turn the girl, insert you in his place, and I have my bait."

With a self-satisfied grin, Dante sat back and eyed his ex-partner.

"I don't see what I get out of this other than a felony rap," Sammy retorted.

Dante shook his head. "If we do it right, there ain't going to be anyone around to prosecute. I made a call to a dude I know from the old neighborhood. Works on the docks. I've got a plan. Meanwhile, you'll be in a position to service Willie's accounts. Build up cases against a couple dozen guys you're dying to get the goods on. Are you sneezing at that?"

Sammy stood, shaking his head. "Why do I listen to you, Joey. You want another beer?"

ELEVEN

There was something in the papers this time. Not very much. They were playing it down. A prostitute had been found dead on Thirty-sixth Street. No mention of murder. Just that she'd been discovered in the early hours of Saturday morning. There was no naming the woman pending notification of next of kin.

Who could care? She was just a whore. Only a vague shadow of the girl. Still the surrogate but now less a factor in the fantasy he worked to create. Now it was just him and the girl; the whore was simply an instrument. Rick had difficulty suppressing the excitement of his new discovery. An avenue direct to communion with the girl. The memory of the whore's wide, terror-filled eyes flooded him with the intensity of his hunger. Of the subsequent satisfaction. Never in his life had he ejaculated with such ferocity. Now he craved the way it made him feel. He was sure it was exactly how it would feel with the girl. The time of their communion could not be far off. Not when he was peaking in the fevered intensity of his love for her.

The destiny his love would follow had been confirmed now. He had, through the sheer strength of it, willed the path opening before him. The power burned in him. There could be no escaping him now that he had discovered how to feed his hunger for her. He was master. His control was absolute.

On Saturday he got up late, showered, and carried a Bloody Mary onto his shaded terrace. She was sunbathing on the terrace below him. Young, lithe, blond, gorgeous. Lying facedown on a chaise, the tie of her bikini undone, she was unaware of him there above her.

"Oh God, baby," he thought. "You are beautiful." The presence of her there stirred the embers of his fire. Memory of the power came flooding back. Its intensity dizzied him. He knew he would go back. This time he might not be able to wait a week. She was out there, and he had to have her again. Soon. God, how the fire burned now. He would find her again and carry her to it.

When Dante arrived home late from the uptown brainstorming session, there was a message from his new friend Evelyn on the machine.

"Hi, Joe. I'm meeting some friends for brunch tomorrow up on Columbus Avenue. Thought you might like to join us. Give me a call."

There was also a call from his mother wondering when they were going to see him for dinner again.

He opened the door to his patio and pulled up a chair under the night sky. Copter hopped into his lap and purred. It was after two, and he still wasn't quite ready for bed. To his surprise, reaction to his plan had been more positive than he had hoped. He'd known how badly Sammy wanted Willie, counted on it. Five definite contract murders they couldn't prove in court. Half-a-dozen hospitalized prostitutes. Heroin and cocaine by the suitcase. Extortion. It was an offense to them both that Davenport continued to function in the face of all the heat they'd applied.

His thoughts turned to his new partner. Of necessity, she had to be left out in the cold on this one. You didn't implicate yourself in a felony along with someone you didn't know and weren't sure you could trust all the way down the line. Partner or no partner. Still, he'd seen something different in her tonight. The Rosa Losada he met in Park Slope was different from the one he'd met in Larry Morris's office. He thought he might have even caught the hint of appreciation at his going out there just to share the latest movement in the case. And she'd looked great.

Who was Charlie?

Dante wondered if being the Blade for five years had permanently twisted his perception of women and relationships. The available pool in that realm did little to enhance his perception of the fairer sex. Barflies. Lounge lizards. Whiff hounds. Posing as a freelance cocaine broker brought them around like flies to old meat. Hoovers, Sammy called them, a description of their lust for the gusto dust. They would think little or nothing of performing a circus act on a dude's organ for a couple of lines. And even though plenty of them were damn good-looking, the force motivating them could hardly be perceived as heartwarming. The Blade had ridden the wave. Sometimes because it was his job, and sometimes because he thought he wanted it. After a while, he wasn't sure he knew where the line was and wasn't sure he cared.

Now when he met a woman like Rosa Losada, clear-headed, straight, he was all the more confused.

"What the hell am I thinking about?" he asked his cat and only real confidant. "The broad is my fucking partner."

Before turning in, he decided to give Evelyn a call first thing in the morning and accept her invitation.

Rick felt that he was drifting now. In the heat of a Sunday morning, he rested in the shade above her, pretending to read. She was with friends. They had arrived earlier, laughing and smearing suntan oil on each other. Now they lay all three in a row. Young, supple bodies. Dark, golden brown. He was in danger of losing his grounding. Of having the ache tear his heart out. The fire he felt was indescribable. Masturbation helped some. But always, a few hours later, the ache returned, intensity undiminished. The ache transported him to a weightless dimension where he could feel nothing of himself except the fire. He would have her. He must. She was so near.

Monday evening he drove to the custom-processing shop before continuing on to the Chelsea townhouse. The little camera had done a good job. He picked five of the thirty-six to be enlarged. Now he had thirty five-by-seven-inch photographs of the girl's unsuspecting face. Smiles that tore his heart to behold. The crystal-blue eyes. The perfect bone structure. The unblemished skin framed in a halo of white-blond hair. She *was* perfection.

Once in the seclusion of his lair, he undressed and stared once again at his body. The time he spent at the club was paying off. Improved tone and hardness in his muscles was noticeable. She would appreciate that. He was sure.

Sitting cross-legged on the divan in the entertainment room, he studied each gatefold on his walls and matched faces. Then, one by one, he lovingly cut the faces free of the surrounding photographic paper. When he finished, he carried them to the bar and rummaged through a drawer for rubber cement. Then, one at a time, he fastened the faces onto his gallery of pinups. Each imposter's face was covered with the rightful one. He worked with painstaking care to get the angles of the faces just right.

Out there, these imposters strutted in their brazen, prideful bodies, declaring in these pictures their willingness to sacrifice themselves as surrogates at the altar of his love. Them and others like them. Until he could reveal himself to her and she could be his, he would use these. It was no matter that as mere empty shells, they could not withstand the heat of his love. Not as she would one day be able to. When she would forsake the apple for the power of the serpent and they would remake creation.

As much as Brian Brennan loathed these evenings, Lisa Garriston loved them. This one was at the Museum of Modern Art. A cocktails and buffet affair for the sponsors and patrons who shoveled in the really big donations. The museum always arranged that just the right number of presentable luminaries were provided for elbow rubbing. Brennan had long been considered one of these. Tame. Not too outrageous. Married to one of their own. To relieve some of the tension of having to see Lisa, Brian invited Charlie Fung and a date as his guests. Charlie's dates were always bizarre. Any female over the age of nineteen was of no interest to him. He had to be creative considering the limited pool he fished in.

Affixing his white bow tie to the starched butterfly collar of his tux shirt, Brennan eyed himself in the mirror. The best years of her life, she'd said. She had been beautiful then and still was, in that underfed, overcoiffed rich-woman's way. He, on the other hand, showed the tread wear of a long road between then and now. He looked worse before he started running six months ago. But the loose skin under the eyes was still there. The deep lines furrowing his forehead. Now that he no longer drank to escape, he had cut way down on his intake. Most of the puffiness in his skin was gone. But it was still a drinker's face. His years with Lisa were written on it. God, he wasn't looking forward to this thing at all.

At seven-thirty, he collected Charlie and his date from the old building in SoHo. True to form, the girl Fung had hanging on his arm was a towering, statuesque brunette, just out of pigtails.

"Brennan," he called out, pushing the girl ahead of him. "Meet Bambi Budowski."

She was built like a young Sophia Loren. Brennan couldn't figure out where Charlie found them.

"Bambi?" he asked, extending a hand.

"You're Brian Brennan?" she bubbled. "Wow! My acting teacher has one of those statues of yours. He'll flip when I tell him I actually met you. Jeez."

Brennan gritted his teeth. Charlie looked over at him.

"Why are you doing this, buddy?"

"My attorney tells me I've got to be nice."

"What the hell for? You've got dough. She's got dough. There ought to be plenty to go around."

Brian smiled wanly. "That isn't how it works. If Lisa decides to be vindictive, she could tie my assets up for years. Litigating. Moving and countermoving. Don't forget, we haven't even started to talk divorce yet. The way I see it, I do a little glad-handing now to save myself a lot of grief later."

"And you're actually naive enough to hope it might make a difference?"

"Maybe." He shrugged. "I'm not sure I hope much at all. Or even care for that matter. But you can't let eight-and-a-half million bucks in community property go without at least giving it a shot."

Bambi was listening with a confused look on her face.

"I don't see why you're worried," she offered vacantly. "You're already a star and that's all that really matters."

When they climbed out of the cab at the museum on Fifty-third Street, Brennan muttered "Peachy," in Fung's ear.

Charlie grinned. "I still say it beats the Ice Queen. If I know you, you're going to have a miserable time, get wasted, and I, your shallow and insincere friend, am going to have to carry you out of there."

Brennan eyed Bambi, considering the alternative, and shrugged.

"What the fuck." He smiled. "The fortunes of war."

Ever since he left her, Lisa had thrown herself into the production of these gala affairs. Everyone in this rarefied little world knew that Brennan had flown the coop, leaving her in her own cushioned version of the lurch. Without an actual live one to put on proud display, her vigorous support of artistic institutions was seen as affirmation of her deep and passionate love for the beautiful things even boorish and insensitive people could produce. She'd thrown herself into this event like an Aztec virgin leaping from a high promontory into a raging river.

When Brian entered the museum, a dozen pairs of eyes singled him out with looks of disapproval and accusation. He doubted if this was her therapist's idea of neutral territory. Lisa always knew how to play a crowd. Picking his way through the throng to the bar, he ordered a bourbon on ice. Agreeing to come here was beginning to feel like it might have been a mistake. The feeling put him in one of those dangerous moods. In a lighter moment, he'd once termed it social claustrophobia. That feeling of being trapped in a crowded environment both alien and hostile to him. It was remarkable to him that just a year ago, these same people would have been fawning over him. Loyalties. He knew which side the buck was buttered on.

"Brian! I had no idea you were here yet." Lisa approached as if she'd stumbled on him by accident. Fat chance.

"Nice turnout," he commented, eyeing the room. "Get you a drink?"

"Not while I'm working." She shook her head, smiling an icy smile. "I hope you'll be doing that in moderation."

He rattled the cubes in his glass, grinning. "Could I heel, roll over, do a few other tricks for you?"

"I was hoping you wouldn't be like this." She frowned. "We have to talk, Brian."

"About what, Lisa?"

"About this irresponsible behavior of yours. I understand how a man your age needs to break loose and blow off a little steam. But don't you think you've taken it far enough?"

"Is that what I'm doing?" he asked. "Blowing off steam? Sowing oats? You don't get it, do you?"

"I don't think there's anything to get. My therapist says that I have to try to be understanding. To keep the lines of communication open."

"No shit? That's great. Is the line open now?"

"Of course it is."

"Then try to understand this. I'm getting a divorce. *Comprende?* I don't want to be married to you anymore." He gulped his drink, finishing it. Setting it on the bar, he ordered another. "When is it going to finally sink in with you?"

"Brian, please. People are watching."

"Fuck them!" he spat. "They're your fucking friends. And a pack of back-stabbing hypocrites at that."

Brennan noticed his father-in-law approaching the bar with a frown on his face. He was a big man with a shock of white hair and an impeccable tan. In his wake, the Manhattan District Attorney Harry Ransome and tycoon billionaire Stuart Sprague hurried to back him up. They looked like a matched pair. Spragaue a little heavier-set, but both square-jawed, tanned, and fit.

"I thought we were rid of you." Garriston snarled at Brennan. "Now here you are making an ass of yourself in my daughter's company."

"We're just communicating, Paul. It was her therapist's idea." Brian gulped more whiskey, the glow if it starting to move outward from his stomach and along his limbs.

"I won't have you ruining all the hard work she put in to create a nice evening for these people," Garriston insisted.

"Every evening's a nice evening for these people." Brennan snickered. "You just can't stand the idea of a Garriston looking pathetic in public. Tough tittie, Pablo. Even *you* can't control matters of fact."

Stuart Sprague stepped up next to Garriston. "I think the man asked you to leave, Brennan."

"Really? Is that what he was doing? You fat cats have real trouble getting to the point, don't you?"

"Now *I'm* insisting," Sprague shot back.

"Calm your bomb, Stuart," Garriston cautioned.

"Like hell." Sprague shook his head. "Who the hell does art boy here think he'd be if we didn't buy his lousy crap?"

Brennan smiled at him. "Oh, I know who I'd be, Stuart. I'd be a damn sight less confused than I am right now. But there's one thing I'm not confused at all about. And that's whether a fat-ass fuck like you could throw me out of here, even if he wanted to."

The effect of the statement was like pushing a button. Sprague gave no indication that he was coming after him. He simply launched himself, bringing his fist up from down low. The impact caught Brennan square in the solar plexus, doubling him up. Pulling back half a step, Sprague set up the surprised face with a quick jab and then clubbed him to the floor with a hard right cross. Brennan's face turned blue; his knees buckled just before he hit the ground. Lisa screamed and leaped in front of the enraged financier.

Brennan moaned, writhing on the ground and fighting for air.

"Someone call the police," he finally gasped.

"For what?" Sprague snarled. "You got drunk, tripped, and hit your head on the bar. Isn't that the way you folks saw it?" He turned to the knot of onlookers.

"I'll bet they'll swear to it," Harry Ransome said, giving them all hard looks. "I'd go and take care of that ear, Brennan. The bar seems to have taken a nasty chunk out of it."

The D.A., Sprague, and Garriston looked on impassively as the sculptor struggled to his feet, blood from the ear trickling down his neck and into the collar of the formal shirt.

Brennan looked at Lisa and shook his head. "You're out of your fucking mind, thinking I'd want to live in your world."

TWELVE

Rosa Losada sat at the large island of desks in the middle of the cramped squad room. She and Dante were working an eight-to-four and Joe had just gone out for coffee and doughnuts. Larry Morris agreed that the psychopath angle was important enough for them to pursue, authorizing any surveillance overtime they might reasonably incur following it. Pat Meehan and his partner, Tommy Naglack, would remain working the Times Square theory. It was Downtown's opinion that this was still the best direction of inquiry. Morris confided that at this point, he thought they were allowing themselves the luxury of wishful thinking.

"Hey, Rosa." A voice came from the door. Meehan and Naglack were returning from following up on a convenience-store robbery from the previous night. "Bum luck you drawing the narc. Has he tried to teach you anything about *undercover* work yet?" The lewd grin matched the implication.

Meehan had been the first and the most persistent of the Tenth squad lotharios harassing her when she'd first come aboard. Married with three kids and an overweight wife stashed in Yonkers, he was a bulbous-nosed slob who smelled of old cigars.

"When was the last time you looked at yourself in a mirror, Pat?" she returned evenly. "It's a pretty disgusting sight."

Meehan sputtered and spun on his heels. Stomping into the locker room, he kicked the metal trash basket.

"Cool it, Pat," Naglack cautioned him. "Morris is due back any second."

"Fuck her!" Meehan snarled, loud enough to be heard in the other room. "I'd offer to let her blow me, but I don't have that big a grudge against my dick."

"That does it," Rosa shouted, leaping up so fast her chair fell over. Throwing her pen onto the desk, she stormed after her antagonist. "You're a bastard, Meehan," she snarled, confronting him. "I've taken just about all I'm going to take from you."

"Suck mine, bitch." He laughed. "What the fuck are you going to do about it?"

"She's not going to have to do anything about it." A voice came from behind them. They turned to find Joe Dante in the doorway, doughnuts and coffee in hand. "You got a foul mouth, Pat."

"This is between me and her," Meehan returned.

Dante shrugged. "Probably so. Too bad running your mouth isn't aerobic, Pat. It'd take a little of that strain off your heart."

Rosa suddenly realized she was standing in the middle of the men's locker room. Turning quickly, she hurried out. Meehan, meanwhile, was reddening at Dante's reference to his weight. Dante just shook his head and carried his doughnuts out into the squad room. He set them on the desk in front of Rosa and pulled up a chair.

"You can't let assholes like that get to you," he said quietly.

"I usually don't." She shook her head. "I don't know what got into me. I have a thicker skin than that."

"We all have our buttons," he said. "He pushed yours."

Rosa picked up the bag of doughnuts and extracted a glazed. She tore off a chunk and dipped it in her coffee. "Nasty habit," she apologized.

"I've seen worse," he assured her. "Lets go for a ride, huh?"

The recently confiscated 300 ZX Turbo, fitted with Florida plates, was parked diagonally in front of the precinct house. Even at 8:30 A.M., the day was starting to feel close and muggy. Across the street, a driver from city traffic was busy hauling off an illegally parked car. The owner was in a snit, screaming right in the man's face. Dante wandered across and held up a hand.

"It's a no-win situation, pal."

"It's a hundred fucking bucks," the florid businessman yelled in return. "I'm getting the cops."

"You just got one." Dante showed him his shield. "And I'm telling you to let the man do his job. If you don't, I'm taking you across the street and letting you cool off there."

At that point, a pair of uniforms in a squad car pulled alongside. The driver ran down his window.

"Problem?"

"No problem," Dante told him. "This gentleman was just getting ready to flag a cab on the corner." He stared hard at the poor guy, knowing inside just how he felt. Getting your car towed was an unbelievable drag. Hitting a tow-truck driver, on the other hand, was worse.

As the little drama broke up, Dante strolled back across

the street. He dug the Nissan's keys from his pocket and dangled them in front of Rosa.

"Ever driven anything like this before?" he asked.

She shook her head. Dante tossed her the keys and opened the passenger door. "The West Side Highway's nice. Especially on up toward the G.W. Bridge."

Moving north on the potholed roadway they were past the Thirty-fourth Street heliport and alongside the cruise line piers before Dante spoke again.

"I liked your apartment. How's living in Park Slope?"

"Cheap," she replied, allowing a quick little smile.

"I had dinner with my ex-partner the other night. He told me about your parents."

She stiffened visibly, knuckles whitening as they gripped the wheel.

"If you don't want to talk about it . . ." he said.

She shook her head. "No. It's okay. You just caught me by surprise."

"Cindy said you both went to Bennington. Is that where you were when it happened?"

She nodded. "My sophomore year. The Seventeenth caught it. A guy named Booker. I try to talk to him every month or so just to make sure he hasn't forgotten."

"I'm sure he hasn't," Dante said. "A thing like that sticks in a guy's craw for years and years. You don't forget a thing like that."

"I was the only one she had. My mother. They raped her and then tore her up so bad inside that nobody could do anything for her. Eventually, infection reached her kidneys and she died of renal failure. I sat there for three days and watched her die."

"What were you, about twenty?"

She swallowed hard as the memory flooded back. "They called me up at school and told me to get down to the city as fast as I could. I had no idea what was going on until a policeman picked me up at the airport and drove me to the hospital. Lenox Hill. Three days later I was an orphan trying to figure out where I was going to get the money to bury them."

"And now you're a cop," he said. "I won't try to tell you that I know how it feels. I don't. But I'm sorry."

Rosa shook her head. "I'm not carrying the anger with me anymore. I keep it stored in a little locked box now. It took five years of visits to my therapist, but I have a handle on it now."

Touching her face with a knuckle, she pushed away a tear. "Shit," she muttered.

Dante pointed at the road ahead. "It starts to smooth out right up here. Give it a little gas."

For the next two nights, Dante used the excuse of familiarizing themselves with the territory to work the no-man's land shared by the Tenth with Midtown South. Times Square was technically the other precinct's territory, but the lines got hazy as the real estate moved west. The whores tended to move freely between the two precincts as the heat pushed them back and forth from one to the other. To get a reasonable feel for what they were up against, the two detectives worked both territories. Unbeknownst to Rosa, Dante had an ulterior motive. He was watching Willie Davenport. Checking out his patterns.

In order to spring his trap, Joe needed tools. Photographs of transactions Willie reportedly made, using his girls as runners. By tracking him through Times Square, Dante could watch his operation and plan the action. By Wednesday, he was ready to take the first steps toward realizing it.

While he and Rosa cruised the area midtown, Sammy

was working the Harlem end, where he'd been shadowing Davenport on and off since Sunday. He'd ascertained what the pimp's rough routine was. What time he left his place every night. Where he ate. Who his girls were.

When Dante, off-duty and working alone, pulled abreast of the Condor Wednesday night, he was leaning on the fender of a sleek Jaguar XJS on Lenox Avenue. All white with leather interior. The Condor in full regalia was a beautiful sight to behold.

Dead in the middle of heavy traffic, Dante reached to turn off the ignition of the Corvette. As the light changed, horns began to blare. He hopped out and while motioning people around him, lifted the hood. After quickly disconnecting the lead from the electronic ignition to the distributor, he dropped the hood and slid back behind the wheel. When he turned the key, the starter motor ground away to no effect. He climbed out and started pushing the vehicle toward the curb.

Right on cue, Sammy was there to help.

"Any sign of him?" Dante asked, trying to steer with one hand and push with his shoulder.

"Not a peep. I been checking around, Joey. The blonde you saw the other night calls herself Cheri. Every one of them broads is money machines. You just don't see stuff looks that good walking Eleventh Avenue."

"What time do you figure he moves on a Wednesday?"

"Don't make much difference what day. The pimpin' might be slow, but there's always Mister Jones. He'll be on the street inside forty-five. Takes 'em all to get something to eat and heads downtown around eleven."

Once they reached the curb, the Condor strode back to his wheels while Dante undertook some fake fiddling under the hood. A couple of kids came by to check out the 'Vette up close. Every once in a while, just for effect, he climbed back behind the wheel and ran down the battery.

When, at nine-fifty, Willie and his girls appeared outside his building and all piled into his white Lincoln stretch, the Corvette made a sudden and miraculous recovery.

"Here we go," Dante said to himself. Ahead of him, the enormous limousine, sprouting more antennas from its trunk lid than the roof of the Cuban Mission, moved away from the curb. It eased left at 118th Street and crawled west, around Morningside Park, to Broadway. There, just south of the Columbia University campus, they paid a visit to a chicken and ribs joint. Dante, suddenly hungry, climbed out of the car.

He'd seen the blonde from a distance on a number of occasions now, and the temptation to catch a glimpse up close was just too great. Inside, the clientele was about 75 percent black, with the rest being made up of the summer school college crowd. Preppy kids from Columbia and Barnard. Dante walked to the takeout window and scanned the menu. Three tables behind, Willie sat with his four women: two black and two white. They were talking loudly, laughing and trying to make a scene. The way they were dressed, it would have been difficult not to. Once Joe ordered, he turned nonchalantly and leaned, arms folded, against the wall to wait.

The target girl was a great-looking number. In hot pants and a skimpy halter top, she slouched smoking cigarettes, legs outstretched alongside Davenport's chair. And what a pair of legs. Standing, she must have been five-nine or ten. Better than half of that was gam. Slender but well-shaped. As a matter of fact, everything was well-shaped. She even had a good face. Dante wondered what Willie had done to turn her . . . and what he had to supply to keep her around. This was half-a-dozen cuts above the usual tunnel blow job fare.

Twenty minutes later, Dante sat in his car, licking his fingers.

* * *

Davenport parked his pimpmobile on Forty-second Street just around the corner from the Port Authority Bus Terminal. From the size of the throng on the sidewalks, it would have been difficult to guess that this was a slow night on Times Square. Just another block over, the legitimate houses were doing a brisk tourist business, while here on the sleazeway, marquees proclaimed such delights as *Ballbusters, Cherry Pickers, Slave Drivers,* and Live Love Acts. Everything that wasn't sexually oriented seemed to have something to do with kung-fu or zombies. In the one block between Eighth Avenue and Broadway, several hundred weasels peddled dope. Scraggly facial fuzz, fishnet T-shirts, jail tattoos, jauntily angled hats. They stood just feet away from knots of nervous-looking rookie cops, brazenly hawking their wares. These were the players on the turf Willie Davenport had consolidated and now worked to control. If a freelancer moved in, it wasn't long before he was nursing a nice gut wound up at Roosevelt–Saint Lukes. If he made it back on to the street, he always had the option of buying from the man. Chronic troublemakers were left stuffed in dumpsters.

"The Man" always showed up around the same time every night to service his franchises. The girls did the legwork, making the exchanges on the sidewalk, while Willie waited in the car, ready to scoot if the heat showed.

Dante had a 35-mm camera equipped with a power zoom lens and motor drive. Slipping to the curb next to a hydrant, he slouched low in the seat and took aim at the activity on the sidewalk around Willie's car. As the girl called Cheri moved to make an exchange with an anxious-looking Hispanic kid, the motor drive whirred, shutter clicking away. He caught the blonde red-handed, with a good angle. Just to make sure, he pulled back into traffic, around the block, and parked to reload. One more time, he slipped in next to the hydrant and muttered, "Say cheese."

THIRTEEN

It had been a long night. For some reason Willie didn't understand, the heat gave dudes the itch. It didn't matter what night it was that he got it. By two in the morning, the johns were still crawling the neighborhood, thick as flies. He had his bitches on a short leash. All four stood working just a stone's throw away while he jawed with some of the other players on the corner of Thirty-ninth and Eleventh. Rumors were flying about the whore they'd found dead down on Thirty-sixth. Some people were saying it had been murder. He knew that jive junkie Danny was capable of almost anything, but he wouldn't have offed his meal ticket. The heat was around. That fat slob and his partner from the Tenth even tried to shake *him* down. Willie didn't like being bugged like that on his turf.

Still, the money had been real good that night. Demand on Forty-second was always up in the summer. Kids looking to cop drifted in from Jersey and the boroughs. Catch a kung fu flick and snort a little something. Make the scene. Be bad. Maybe your teenybopper might do you tonight.

At four, with things thinning out, Willie rounded up his charges and herded them back into the ride. When they got back to the pad, nobody was quite ready for bed. Music cranked up, he laid out some lines and watched with pleasure as his bitches horned them up their eager nostrils.

Willie Davenport was a man who had achieved a balanced relationship with his environment. The way he saw it, a man should be able to have whatever he wanted and could get. He should be able to hold it as long as no one else could take it away from him. Simple, straightforward logic. He prided himself on his mixture of brute strength, street savvy, and persuasiveness. He had it together. Nice pad. Nice wheels. Real nice little business. And a nice piece of ass whenever he wanted it.

In fact, Willie was a man at peace with fate. He had gone out there into a world accustomed to breaking a man's will and taken what he wanted. Plenty of others tried to take it away from him. Big dudes. Bad dudes. The way Willie saw it, they just must not have wanted it as much as he did.

It would be difficult for Willie's adversaries to argue with him. You got only one chance to cross Willie Davenport. There was little he could do to stop another man's envy and greed. Except kill him.

Brian Brennan returned from the debacle at the Museum of Modern Art, cracked a fresh bottle of Johnnie Walker, and drank himself into oblivion. When he awoke the next day, it was because the phone next to his head had been ringing for over a minute. Reaching out, he swept his arm across the nightstand, knocking the instrument on to the floor. The ringing stopped.

God, he felt awful. His stomach was bruised. The side of

his face ached. The inside of his head felt like it had been fed into a Cuisinart.

"Brian?" a little voice squawked from the floor. "Goddammit, answer me."

Feeling around, he located the receiver and pulled it to his ear. "Don't bother me," he croaked. "Good-bye."

"Wait!" It was Diana.

"Why?"

"Charlie called this morning. He said you got into a fight with Stuart Sprague at MOMA last night. What the hell's going on? Are you all right?"

"No, I'm not all right. I feel like I jumped in front of an uptown express and then fell into a vat at the Dewar's distillery."

"I'm coming over there," she said.

"No," he moaned. "Please don . . ." She hung up.

When Diana finally got Brennan to answer his door, she found the barely upright, battered ghost of the evening past. His eyes were rheumy crimson pools. The side of his face was swollen like a volleyball. The skin that wasn't blue was gray. Under his eyes, puffy bags bulged pitifully.

"Why do I care?" she asked in exasperation, pushing past him.

"Because I'm a basically nice guy," he mumbled, shuffling slowly toward the sofa and collapsing on it.

"You're an asshole. Don't kid yourself."

"Why have you come here to abuse me?"

"Someone has to. What the hell did you think you were doing last night?"

"He swung at me first."

"You know as well as I do that it didn't have anything to do with Stuart Sprague."

"He was as good as any of them. And he's the only one I thought I could provoke."

"Oh, God." She threw up her hands. "You're impossible."

"After all this time, they still treat me like the delivery boy."

"Whose fucking problem is that? Yours? You can't keep doing this to yourself, Brian. You're going to kill yourself."

"Who cares?" He shrugged. "First I let the bastards stroke me off. Then I spend fifteen years producing shit. Do you have any idea of what selling your soul to the devil feels like?"

"No." She shook her head. "But at this point, I'd *like* somebody to pay me to make shit. Christ, about now I'd do duets with Tony Orlando."

He chuckled, and that made his head hurt worse. "Don't do that to me."

"I'm not kidding. Fuck it, Brian. Shine these people on. There's no percentage in doing anything but telling Lisa to screw herself when she calls. Fuck the money."

"That's easy for you to say," he grumbled.

"It's easy because I'm right," she retorted.

By Wednesday night, Rick could no longer contain the urge to prowl. A little voice was now preventing him from going directly after the satisfaction he now craved. It cautioned him. The rest of the world couldn't understand his love. There would be police. He would have to be careful. To pick his times and places with calculation. But tonight he had to just see the one who would be next. The pictures on the wall made him ache with his love for the girl. And he had seen her sunbathing again. His mind could concentrate on nothing but the image of her body burned in his mind. He had to find a vessel.

A pattern was established for covering the far West Side. First, he would do a quick sweep of Tenth, Eleventh, and Twelfth avenues, looking for police activity. All three of the area precincts along the greater "stroll" regularly harassed the girls with tickets for loitering, trying to keep them moving. After reconnoitering the entire area, he settled down to a methodic sweep of each street. The concentration of hookers seemed to be divided in half over the twenty blocks they generally worked. Initially, he would cruise up to Forty-fifth and across to Eleventh. From there he would wind in and out of the cross streets, moving slowly, looking. Down around Thirty-third, they seemed to thin out until he reached the high Twenties. Then, for the next five blocks or so, there would be more of them. Unless, of course, one or another precinct had the heat on. Then one or another area might be like a ghost town. But never, it seemed, both at once. The cops appeared to be engaged in a constant seesaw battle of pushing the whores back and forth between each other's jurisdictions.

Most of the whores were black, and a majority, white and black, were fat. Fat was repugnant to Rick and black had nothing to do with the girl. Still, every once in a while, one who looked like her would appear. These he sometimes stopped to converse with. The girl he had his first experience with had been one he'd talked to on a number of occasions. They had to stick in his mind. That was the sign. She had been one of many to become an obsession but the first to die under the weight of his love. The second was different. He'd needed no time with her; his love had reached new levels of expression. Now the voice was warning him.

Tonight he needed just to find her. To see who she was working with. Maybe say just a couple of words; to hear the voice.

Brennan spent most of Wednesday trying to pull himself together again. The hangover had lasted all of the day before and well into the evening. Diana had been on the money. When you feel like you've got to punch some poor old fart and then rush home to dump a quart of whiskey down the hatch, you are in trouble. He had to quit dragging his tail and get out of town. Pour some metal. Sweat out some of the frustration. The ocean side of the house needed painting. He'd been putting it off. It was time to get on the stick.

In the afternoon, he called the movers and scheduled them to crate the new piece Friday morning for shipment to Connecticut. Later, he hiked over to Ninth and Twenty-third to buy groceries. He was going to cook himself a decent meal. Swanson's just didn't do it anymore.

By nightfall he was back at the steelworkers, putting on some finishing touches. Blessedly, he hadn't heard from Lisa. Charlie called to offer his sympathies and tell him he hadn't seen any of it. Not a lot of help in a lawsuit against Sprague. Apparently, nobody about to step forward had seen anything. Anybody even leaning in that direction would most likely be in receipt of a gift subscription to the season at the Met. Just a friendly reminder that they were who they were and that he represented the forces of instability.

While his face still hurt to the touch, the swelling was down. The muscles across his stomach and up the back of his neck were stiff and sore. He knew he wouldn't be able to get to sleep unless he attempted to get some of the kinks out. At twelve-thirty, he decided to take a run.

It hadn't cooled off much that night. The hot humid air of the street hit him like a blast furnace as he gained the sidewalk. A couple of regulars loitering on the corner greeted him as he started to stretch out.

"Bry-un." A big, busty black woman named Ellie beckoned. "When you gonna give up doin' that nasty shit to your body and do something nice for it?"

"Woman like you'd be too much for me, Ellie. Especially in my present condition." He threw a leg up atop a fire hydrant and leaned over it.

"Aw, come on. You oughtta see some of the wrecks I get."

"Thanks."

"That's not what I meant. I'm sure you'd be a real pleasure workin' with. I seen the blond, punky-lookin' pussy you got around. Good enough lookin', I guess, but she ain't black."

She wandered over and was leaning against the wall next to him. "Try black, and you'll never go back." She smiled.

"So I've heard." He grinned. Swinging his arms, he gave his back a final loosening up. "Don't take it personally, Ellie," he said, "but I've gotta run."

Taking it slowly at first, he jogged down Eleventh Avenue to where it intersected the highway along the river. Staying to the city side, he began picking up the pace, running south into the meat-packing district. When he reached the area where the leather bars proliferated, he generally crossed over to the river side and continued on down from there. Most of the old piers along this stretch either had been razed or had burned. Several lay stripped clean and fairly intact. Sunbathers from the Village flocked to them during the summer months, and at night, the more adventurous gays used them as an after-hours rendezvous. There wasn't much of a moon this time of the month, and what there was wasn't around at that hour. Deep in the shadows, he could barely make out the movements of silhouettes out over the water. The river itself reeked. It was a heavy, decaying garbage odor. Across it, the lights of Jersey City and Hoboken were reflected in long, sparkling bands of color. When the wind was right, the heavy smell of roasting coffee floated over from the giant Maxwell House plant on the opposite shore.

He loved it. Being out here, moving, sweating, sucking it all in. The entire skyline of the city loomed behind him, massive and hulking but just remote enough to give him that rare feeling of detachment. In a city of millions, he was alone in the open air. Alone with his thoughts. The burning of his breath in his lungs. The pouring sweat. Ahead, the twin towers of the World Trade Center beckoned. Huge, perverse obelisks shimmering in the humid air.

Tonight, he was working the poison out of his system. At first he felt ill, his stomach twisting in knots. It was almost two miles before the urge to vomit completely passed. Making his turn at the towers, he began to get his second wind. He felt good now. Loose. In the groove. He was leaving for the beach Saturday. Each day he would scrape a little more of the side of the house. By the time the month was up, it would be painted. Maybe Diana would come up. That would be good. He hated to admit it, but she seemed to be a grounding influence. And it wasn't that he didn't appreciate her caring. He just resented any woman's being important right now. But what the hell, she was fun, too. When she wasn't reminding him of what a jackass he could be.

As he approached the Eleventh Avenue cutover, the noise of music and laughter floated up behind him. Looking over his shoulder, he caught sight of one of the big Circle Line tour boats churning toward him up-river. Slowing to a walk, chest heaving up and down, he watched. The deck was crowded with men in black tie and women in evening gowns. An orchestra was set up amidships, cranking out lively soft-rock dance tunes. The boats would dock up in the mid-Forties and were used during the daytime hours for sightseeing circuits of Manhattan Island. At night, groups and organizations often rented them for floating buffet parties. From the sound of it, this gang was feeling no pain.

The party came abreast of him and then slowly made its way north. He walked, watching it cut deeper into the gloom until only snippets of gaiety reached him on the breeze. He crossed the highway to the city side and walked slowly toward home.

Opposite his building, he noticed an immense white limousine two short blocks up, on the corner of Twenty-ninth. He had seen it in the neighborhood off and on. What caught his attention tonight was the scantily clad ass of a lanky white whore with her head in the window of a small black car. It was very similar to the one he'd seen the night the woman was killed. When the hooker finally stood erect, the car's engine revved as it swung into a slow U-turn. Brennan couldn't make out the plate from that distance, but in the streetlight, he saw the hubcap-sized dent in the passenger door, the chrome that should have spanned it missing. "Holy shit!" he murmured. And the woman. She was blond, unusually pretty for a street-walker, and bore a striking resemblance to the girl he'd found dead in the loading bay.

FOURTEEN

Joe Dante arrived at work first thing Thursday morning to find a message from Brian Brennan. He'd said it was urgent. Trying the number, he found the sculptor still half-asleep.

"Late night?" he asked, checking his watch. It was half-past eight.

"Always." Brennan yawned. "I saw the car again last night. That is, I'm pretty sure I did."

"You what?"

"I was coming back from my run. There was this big white limo parked up from my place, and one of the girls had her head in the window of the car. It had the dent in the door, just like I thought. And this time I got a good enough look that if you showed me the book again, I'm sure I could pick it out."

Dante couldn't believe it. The limousine had to be Davenport's.

"What did the girl look like?" he asked, trying to curb his excitement.

"That's the spookiest part," Brennan returned. "She could have been the woman I found's sister. Tall, blond, nice body, and real good-looking for this part of town."

"Listen," Dante said. "Are you going to be home for the next couple of hours?"

"All day," Brennan replied.

"I'm coming by with the book. And I have some other pictures I want you to look at." Dante hung up the phone as Rosa walked into the squad room.

"Get ready to roll," he told her. "That was Brian Brennan. He thinks he saw the car again last night . . . and what sounds like a blonde I might be able to finger talking to the driver."

On the way to Brennan's, Dante made a detour past a photo-processing shop. When he tossed the results of the prior night's moonlighting into her lap, Rosa opened the first of two envelopes.

"Where did you get these?" she asked, examining a grainy close-up of Cheri making an exchange on Forty-second Street.

"I couldn't sleep last night," he lied. "I took a drive and ended up tailing that girl for a couple of hours."

"With a camera and telephoto lens?" she asked.

"Zoom," he corrected. "You never know. I'm hoping Brennan might be able to make her from them."

They parked in front of Brennan's industrial building and Dante took the envelopes. Pawing through the work, pausing from time to time and admiring a nice angle, he eventually found what he was looking for. A good, clear shot of Cheri, as close to full-front as he could hope for. Secretly, he was encouraged by a lot of what was there. Nothing that could be called incriminating in a court of law but, outside of one, definitely intimidating.

"Got the car book?" he asked Rosa.

"Right here," she said, gathering it up with her bag and pushing open her door. "Do you realize what it means if Brennan can put your woman and that car together?"

"I don't even want to hope," Dante said.

Brian Brennan received them with almost as much excitement as they felt themselves.

"It was like I was having a déjà vu flash," he said, seating them in his front room. "Something to drink? I've got beer and coffee."

They took coffee. Once they were settled, Dante took the car book from Rosa and opened it on the table.

"Let's try the car first," he said. "These five were what we narrowed it down to before." He opened the book to the paper-clipped pages and showed them to Brennan again.

Brow furrowed, the sculptor studied them silently, giving no indication of what he was thinking.

"Problem." He grunted, shaking his head.

"What's that?" Dante asked.

"The BMW and the Chrysler LeBaron. Couldn't they have made the rip off a little less blatant?"

Dante looked at the two pictures. Both profiles and rear ends looked almost identical in silhouette. The grilles were different, but he could see the man's point. In the dark, it would have been tough to distinguish between them.

"It's definitely one of those two," Brennan said conclusively. "And I'm sure it was black now. The dent was about a foot in diameter and pretty clean, just like a bowl. The chrome is missing right across here." He pointed.

"It's something," Dante said to Rosa. "We've probably cut it down from several thousand to less than one. Might as well have Albany run whatever they can." Reaching into his briefcase again, he extracted an envelope.

"Now," he said, looking hard at Brennan. "Do you ever play hunches?"

"All the time," Brian answered.

"I do, too. I'm playing one now. I've got a photograph of a woman here. I want you to look at it and just tell me what hits you." Opening the envelope, he extracted the picture of Cheri and handed it to him.

"It's her," Brennan said almost immediately. "The one I saw last night."

"Are you sure?"

"Believe me." The sculptor smiled. "You're a detective, I'm a sculptor. I study bodies. I don't even have to look at this face. It's the last thing I usually notice about a woman anyway. I see proportions, phenotypes. This is her. Positive."

Dante looked at Rosa.

"What's it mean?" Brennan asked. "Who is she?"

"Just a prostitute," Dante told him. "But we're working on a theory based on another hunch. If it's correct, you don't know what a help you've just been."

He shrugged. "Any time. By the way, if you come up with something on the car and need me, I'm going to be up in Connecticut for most of the month. I should leave you my number."

It was difficult for them to contain their excitement. In the car, riding back to the precinct, Dante was grinning like a kid on Christmas.

"Dovetails pretty nicely, huh?" he said.

"Take it easy, or you'll sprain your face," Rosa said.

"The man has a type. Hot damn! I was right. The son of a bitch is sniffing her out. He could move any time. I don't want to lose this."

Joe and Sammy sat quietly in a dented '79 Ford Fairmont on the north side of Forty-second Street between

Eighth and Ninth. It was almost midnight and still no sign of Willie. Over toward Times Square, Thursday night was the official start of the nightlife weekend. Business was most likely brisk. Besides, it had rained hard for about half an hour a little earlier, and the pimp had most likely let the girls ride it out inside the car. It's hard for a whore to make money when she looks like a drowned rat. When Willie finally came west, he was going to pass them. He'd taken the same route four nights in a row. Joe and Sammy were relaxed and watching girls.

Directly behind them, beside the bus stop, was the entrance to the Eighth Avenue Independent line subway. With the side and rearview mirrors cocked just right, they could watch people come and go as well as keep an eye on the street behind. Directly across the street stood the side of the Port Authority. Plenty more pedestrian traffic there. And down the way to the west loomed the towers of the Manhattan Plaza, a federally-subsidized theater arts colony. Across the street from them were the Off-Broadway houses of Theater Row. Once the shows let out, there had been a steady trickle of upscale types. Every once in a while a truly hot number would happen by. In such an instance, they paused to admire and compare notes.

"You know, Joey," Sammy said, breaking open a peanut, emptying the meat into the palm of his hand, and flipping the shell onto the floor. "I been thinking about what you've done."

"What's that?"

"Getting out of this rat race. Once this thing blows over and I can make some wholesale busts down here, I'm thinking about throwing in the towel. I only got two years now, you know."

"Think you'll ever be able to get married and settle down like normal people?" Dante asked. "I've wondered about it myself."

"I dunno," Sammy said. "I got a grandma getting old down in North Carolina. She's startin' to have trouble running the farm. I talked to my brother the other night. His old lady won't leave D.C. I'm the only other one she's got. I been thinking lately that it wouldn't be so hard leaving this hellhole."

Dante grinned. "To become a farmer? What the fuck do you know about farming?"

"More than you'd suppose. I was born and raised on that land. It's beautiful, Joey. Like nothing you've ever seen. Three hundred and fifty acres of rich, black bottomland. Bought and paid for seventy-five years ago. If I worked it hard, I could clear a hundred thou a year growing tobacco."

Dante whistled. "That's decent. If you can make that kind of bread, what the hell are you doing here?"

"Same thing you are, little brother. Fighting for truth, justice, and the American way."

"Before we went under, I almost had my master's degree in Criminal Psychology," Dante said. "I've been thinking about the academy again. If I keep doing harebrained shit like this, I'm gonna be out of a job sooner or later."

"I always said you'd be good. You've got the service record. I don't see how they could turn you down. You're the best."

"Maybe." Dante shrugged. "First thing I have to do though is catch this murdering son of a bitch."

"Willie D. at seven o'clock," Sammy said.

Joe reached for the ignition key as Davenport's pimpmobile loomed in his side mirror. "Hate to break up such a happy family," he grunted as the stretch shot by.

They followed them to Eleventh just south of Thirtieth. It appeared that they were going to work the southern half of the territory. The girls got out and stretched their legs while Willie backed the car around the corner and parked it on the side street. There were already a couple of other players running their strings on nearby corners. Two of them loped over, shaking hands, posing bad, and talking loud. Willie eventually went to a breast pocket and brought out a little vial. They all had a snort. Another of the players repaid in kind, passing his own stash around. Willie shooed his drooling girls on their way.

Dante and Sammy continued on down to Twenty-third Street and parked in front of the big U-Haul rental joint. Sammy climbed out and unlocked the trunk.

"Pick whoever's closest to him," he said. "Once he starts for you, lead him about fifty yards if you can. I don't want any of those other fuckers deciding to lend a hand."

"What if he doesn't come at all?"

"He'll come all right. That's his pussy you're fuckin' with. And Joey; I'll take care of him. You just make sure the bitch don't see me." He stepped gently into the trunk, coiled up, and pulled down the lid.

Slipping the battered Ford into drive, Dante pulled slowly onto Eleventh and on uptown. Alone in the front seat now, he felt a little strange, girls waving to him, some flashing tits. As he approached Willie's wheels, he scanned the pavement for his whores. It stood to reason that they'd be busier than a lot of these others. It wasn't until he'd passed the assembly of shucking pimps that he spotted Davenport's stable. He turned into Twenty-eighth Street.

The landscape down here was like something left in the aftermath of a war. Forbidding, monolithic warehouses stood absolutely pitch-black. The streets were all but deserted.

A car trolling directly ahead of him spotted the good-looking white girl and got to her first. Dante cursed under his breath and rolled back around the block, past the building Brian Brennan lived in and back up. Cheri was already finished with her john. She hustled up to Willie, handed him something, and hurried back into the street. Real enterprising. Dante made his move, not wanting to be beaten to the punch a second time. When he slowed and stopped, she leaned to look inside.

This was the second time he'd seen her face-to-face, the other time being in the Broadway rib joint. He hoped to God she wouldn't recognize him. But Cheri saw lots of men. Hundreds of them every night. He was just another face.

"Twenty bucks, buddy. Let's see it."

Dante pulled the green from his shirt pocket, and she popped the door handle.

"Pull around the corner," she directed. "I suck you off. You keep your hands to yourself. Give me the money."

He handed her the twenty. She slipped it into the bodice of her Bo-peep corset and reached for his fly.

"Right here's fine." She nodded, indicating a spot under a broken streetlamp. "Keep it running."

Joe hoped he was far enough away from the corner for Sammy's purposes. He didn't want to risk riling the quarry by pushing his luck. She began to unzip him, and he reflected on the sacrifices a cop is called upon to make in the line of duty.

"You're sure pretty," he told her.

"Yeah, sure."

He reached to touch her hair.

"Hands off, buster," she snarled.

"Come on," he said. "I just want to touch you."

"Nobody touches me." She shook her head. "You want to push it, I take your twenty bucks and split."

Here goes, he thought to himself. Catching hold of her hair, he quickly slid his other hand into the top of her corset. She was already inside his pants. In fury, she dug in her nails and yanked. A searing pain shot through his groin. He yeowled as she grabbed for the door handle.

"You fucking bastard!" she hissed.

Struggling to keep his mind on the job at hand, Dante dived for her. "Oh no, you don't, sweetheart." Catching her shoulder, he jerked her back toward him. Finally she screamed.

In the rearview, he saw Davenport break away from his cronies and sprint pell-mell down the sidewalk. Slipping it into drive, he let the car roll forward, while he wrestled to keep Cheri from disemboweling him.

Willie could run. The pimp covered the ground in a hurry. They'd rolled about thirty yards when he caught them. And then all hell broke loose.

Sammy's leap from the trunk caught Davenport completely by surprise. Before he knew what had happened, a massive, ski-masked monster coldcocked him and stuffed him into the trunk he had just erupted from. Jerking open the passenger door, Sammy grabbed Cheri and pulled her out onto the sidewalk. As he leaped in, Joe gunned it and yanked the wheel around hard, throwing it into a skidding about-face. They raced the wrong way back toward Eleventh Avenue. Two of Willie's other women had seen what went down and charged into the Fairmont's path. Dante took to the sidewalk, swerving to avoid them. One threw a beer bottle, shattering the back window. A pimp was hurriedly jerking out his piece as they rocketed through the red and careened around the corner heading south.

"Oh, Jesus!" Dante groaned. There, in the middle of the street, stood a sweat-soaked, open-mouthed Brian Brennan. Two shots rang out an instant after a neat hole appeared in the windshield. Ducking, Dante floored it. There was no doubt in his mind that Brennan had seen him.

"That was our sculptor," he muttered, gaining the West Side Highway and heading for Brooklyn.

"You're shittin' me," Sammy said.

"I wish I was."

FIFTEEN

Ron Gugliano sat waiting in a Ryder truck off Flatbush Avenue. Inside the locked cargo box sat a piano crate purchased from Baldwin and stocked with canned goods and water. When the dented Ford eased up behind him and killed its lights, he climbed down from the cab and inserted his key into the padlock.

"All set, Ronnie?" Dante asked.

"Have I ever let you down, Joey. Hey, Sammy. Christ!" He noticed the bullet hole in the windshield and the shattered back glass. "What the hell happened?"

"Nothing, thank God. When does the ship sail?"

"Six forty-five. They're loading your container second to last. No problem."

Sammy collected Willie from the trunk and carried him to the crate. He was beginning to come around as they cleaned his left bicep with alcohol and injected him with enough phenobarb to put him out for at least twenty-four hours. Next, they stripped him and took his clothes.

"You ought to like Saudi Arabia this time of year," Sammy said, patting the unconscious man on the back. "I hear it's . . . sandy."

Dante turned to Ron. "Do you know someplace we could get a guy to replace this glass and keep his mouth shut?"

"There's a Polish dude who's good. In Greenpoint. Put it in my garage and take the Rabbit." He dug into his pocket and handed him the keys. "I'll give a call when it's ready."

"Thanks." Dante nodded. "I owe you one."

"You kiddin'? More like three. Get outta here."

Sammy was grumbling about the tight fit as they crossed the Williamsburg Bridge into Manhattan.

"I've gotta go talk to someone," Dante said. "You want to crash at my place?"

"Later," Sammy said. "I'm goin' with you."

When they pulled the Volkswagon to a stop in front of Brennan's building, the big Lincoln and all the action had departed. A lone police cruiser sat idling near the scene of the earlier incident, dome lights flashing. They imagined that an hour earlier, there had been a good many more of them. Kidnappings and the discharging of firearms tended to bring the uniforms out in hordes.

Dante pushed Brennan's buzzer and waited. It was almost a minute before an irritated voice growled over the intercom.

"Who is it?" He didn't have the video monitor on.

"Dante, Brennan. Sorry. We've gotta talk."

The door release hummed. They pushed through and rode the elevator to the sculptor's floor.

Brennan stood waiting for them at the front door, bleary-eyed and tousle-haired. "I figured you'd be back," he said matter-of-factly. "Come on in."

"This is Sam Scruggs," Dante said, indicating one of the biggest humans Brennan had ever seen. They shook hands.

"You mind telling me what that was all about?" Brennan asked. "The son of a bitch almost shot me. Your team had me in the backseat of a squad car for over half an hour. They are still your team, aren't they?"

"What did you tell them?" Sammy asked.

"Just that some maniac tried to run me down and one of the local Superflies got a little trigger-happy."

"But you saw me, plain as day," Dante said.

"I did." Brennan nodded. "And I figured there was some sort of explanation. Is there?"

"Mind if we sit down?" Dante asked.

"Please. A beer? Coffee?"

They both thought a beer sounded good.

"I'll cut right to it," Dante said once he'd gotten settled. "The uniforms talked to you. What do you know about what happened?"

"Only that the big pimp who drives the white Lincoln limo was abducted. I assume you guys were the ones who did it."

"Willie Davenport," Joe nodded. "He controls the street action around Times Square and the west side of Midtown. Or controlled. He's taking a little unscheduled vacation."

"It has something to do with the picture of the girl you showed me. She's one of his, right?"

Dante nodded. "Remember talking about hunches the other day? Well, mine is that a psychopath is responsible for killing the woman you found. There was another just like her last week. The woman in the picture fits a type. Your seeing her talking to the driver of that car only further cinches it. We decided we had to move Willie out of the picture so we can turn the girl. What we did wasn't exactly . . . uh . . . regulation procedure."

Brennan looked from one of them to the other. "And you're asking me to look the other way."

"In a nutshell."

"I don't consider myself a knee-jerk liberal," Brennan said. "But isn't prostitution a victimless crime?"

"Murder isn't," Sammy returned. "We know of at least ten for a fact and can't pin any of them on him. Joey and I have tried three times to put the fucker away, and he's always slipped it in the courts."

"And you gentlemen have arranged a change of air for him?"

"You might say that."

"Like I told you, Dante. I'm off to Connecticut for the rest of the month. If you need to talk to me about that car, you know where I can be reached. Anyone need another beer?"

Charlie Fung called Brian Brennan Friday afternoon. The sculptor was busy packing up whatever he thought he'd need for the month at Pleasure Beach. Whenever Charlie heard that he was making the extended trip to the Sound, it wasn't long after that he'd phone to invite himself up. Brennan didn't mind. There was generally a fifty-fifty chance that Fung's date could complete a sentence. And she was guaranteed to look great in a string bikini.

"Hi, buddy," Charlie chirped over the wire. "You still planning to make the break tomorrow morning?"

"Sure, bring her along," Brennan grunted.

"You don't have to be that way. This one is a little surprise. And dig this: she can draw."

"Let me guess. Forest? Dawn? Sky? Fern?"

"Fuck you. Lunch?"

"Only if you bring it. The movers are coming first thing to haul the new piece up. I'm gonna have my hands full. Should be there by noon though."

Diana called a little later.

"Charlie cancelled on me. He thinks he's in love again."

"Yeah. He's bringing her up to my place. Who is she?"

"I don't know. So far it's hush-hush. From what I could gather, she some budding little artiste who worships the ground he walks on. He said something about how she was going to throw you for a loop."

"Just what I need. So you can come up?"

"For the weekend anyway," she said. "I'm sure his infatuation will be over by then. She'll probably have a birthday or something."

Brennan chuckled. "Why don't you drive up with me? The movers are going to be here at seven-thirty. We ought to be ready to roll by nine-thirty–ten o'clock."

The sleek Jaguar of the Condor sat curbside on Lenox Avenue while the man himself leaned on the front fender and held court. Half-a-dozen players, all of them minor leaguers, stood around him. A sighting of the Condor was a rare enough thing to be an occasion. Everyone knew he had a pad over on Adam Clayton Powell, but it seemed he was scarcely there. Some stories had it that the man owned a huge estate on the North Shore of Long Island. Others had him spending most of his time in a heavily guarded hacienda outside Popayán in Colombia. Sammy started the Colombian rumor himself. He had no idea where the other had come from.

Whenever he showed up on the street, people noticed. Low-key but elegant in his dress, he nevertheless dominated the landscape with his sheer size. By any standard, he was one huge, hulking mother of a man. And in terrific shape. At six-ten, three hundred pounds, there wasn't an ounce of fat on him. If that weren't enough to make him formidable, he was perpetually strapped with a Walther P-5. Everyone who dealt with him knew it. *And* that he was quick as a cobra. You didn't mess with the Condor unless you wanted to be staring through a pair of nickels at the lid of a pine box.

Today the Condor was laying the groundwork for taking over Willie Davenport's Times Square dope operation. He had spotted Jackson Salaam after searching half a day for him. The man would suit his purposes as the middleman in his little squeeze play. Greedy and as slippery as a well-oiled bearing, Jackson was forever looking for new territory and opportunity. With Davenport dominating the Midtown game, he'd had sense enough not to attempt crossing him. Jackson was interested in living to enjoy the fruits of his avarice. He muscled in only on weaker fish. Now that word was out on the disappearance of Willie D., there was little doubt in Sammy's mind that Jackson would be contemplating a move. And Sammy's plan was to have the Condor condone it, for a piece of the action.

"Listen, brothers," the Condor said smoothly. He'd just passed around his vial and bought them all a King Cobra. "Jackson and I have a little business to discuss. Why don't you excuse us for a few minutes?"

A moment later, the Condor was smiling his big, bull-shit street smile into the eyes of a curious and slightly uneasy Jackson Salaam.

"We got us a little problem, friend," the Condor said.

Jackson gulped visibly.

"I'm afraid that the vacuum created by the disappearance of Willie is gonna create problems downtown. I can only assume that whoever did the work is gonna jump in. I got a feeling that *you* are gonna jump in. I got just one interest in all this. Smooth, businesslike distribution of product. I ain't interested in no war."

Jackson was studying him, nervously, his feet making little herky jerky tappings against the pavement.

"So I been thinking, in the interest of peace and brotherhood, that you ought to be the man to run that operation."

This wasn't what Jackson had expected. His eyes widened as he comprehended what had been said to him. "Me? Are you offering me some sort of partnership?"

"Not exactly. I'm offering you an exclusive *distributorship*. Like McDonald's or Anheuser-Busch."

Salaam considered this, quickly realizing that if he wanted the territory, he was going to have to make compromises. If he refused the Condor, the big man would go somewhere else. Once he did, opportunity's door would slam shut in his face.

"What about the man's bitches?" he asked. "I hear they're holed up in that big pad, snortin' up the rest of the man's stash and threatening to shoot anyone who tries to come through the front door."

"They're my problem for now." The Condor smiled. "The big one has eyes like a tiger. I wouldn't mind goin' a couple rounds with that."

"You planning on workin' them?" Salaam asked, surprised.

"Might not be a bad idea. For a while I'm gonna have to look after my interests downtown. Might as well have a little sport while I'm at it. Depending on how things work out, I might see clear to cut a couple of 'em over to you. They gotta be worth an extra two grand a week apiece."

He could see Jackson's mouth watering. There wasn't anything in his stable to compare to what Willie'd had. All he had to do was play the game awhile.

"We'll give it a couple weeks and see how it goes," he continued.

"You goin' up there now?" Salaam asked, nodding at Willie's building.

"That's right." The Condor smiled.

* * *

To gain access to the place, Sammy pressed every button on the intercom board and waited for the inevitable chorus of "Who's there?" As expected, someone who couldn't be bothered simply buzzed him in.

Pushing through, he took the elevator to Willie's floor and approached his front door. It was a nice building, with well-kept common space. And like his own, the hall outside the pimp's place of residence was garishly decorated.

A voice told him to beat it when he rang. Undaunted, he continued to work the button insistently.

"I said go away," the voice repeated.

"It's the Condor, honey. We gotta talk."

The cover to the peephole scraped open. The voice turned back into the room. "It *is* him."

"Bullshit!" A deeper voice, further back.

"No bullshit, Mama," he said loudly. "It's me, and I'm gettin' impatient being made to stand out here in this hallway. I hope you can shoot straight, because in about five seconds, I'm comin' through this door whether you open it or not."

A chain rattled, bolts clicked, and a young white face peered out at him. It was the other one. Pam. Slowly, she opened the door to him. Directly across the room, sitting cross-legged on a leather sofa, sat the big amazon, Lila. She was training a 9-mm Beretta on him.

"Easy, Mama," he said. "I ain't here to break up your party. Just to talk a little business." He stepped into the room. The other two girls, Rhonda and Cheri, sat in other chairs around the room. A good quarter ounce of cocaine lay dumped on the surface of a large, mirrored coffee table. Two shortened soda straws and straight-edged razor blade lay alongside it.

"Enjoyin' your little vacation?" he asked them, smiling. Moving to an empty chair, he sat. "You ladies got anything to drink?"

Lila's automatic had followed him as he moved. "What do you want?" she growled.

"A beer would be fine," he said.

"That's not what I meant. What are you here for?"

"You get me the beer and we'll talk about it, okay?"

Lila nodded at Pam, who scurried off to the kitchen. There wasn't much doubt about the pecking order among them. When she returned with a Colt 45, he eased it to his lips, smacked them appreciatively, and smiled at Lila.

"A man gets thirsty on a day like this."

"You did it, didn't you?" Lila said accusingly.

"Did what, Mama?"

"Took Willie down."

He shook his head. "Not me. The Condor don't take productive members of his society down, honey. There ain't no percentage in it. Willie had his territory stabilized. That's nothing but profitable for a man like me. There ain't no reason I'd want it any other way. But now I've got a problem. You see, whoever *did* do Willie is obviously planning somethin' down there. And the Condor don't like unknown factors fucking with the stability of the structure. Know what I mean?"

"How is any of this *my* problem?" Lila sneered.

"Oh, I don't know, Mama. Sooner or later all this snort you're hornin's gonna run out. Where are you gonna get more? How you gonna buy groceries? You try to waltz downtown and work a little freelance and that structure I been talkin' about's gonna make dog meat outta you. I guess *that's* how it's your problem."

Lila just stared at him.

"The way I see it," he continued, "is that you and me can effect a little alliance. You see, my problem is quick stability. Your problem is supply and protection. For the next month or so, I'm gonna be spendin' a lot of time down there, keeping an eye on things. You girls are gonna have to go back to work sooner or later.'' Smiling, he reached into his pocket and removed an ounce of the cleaned-up Morales stash. Reaching out, he placed it on the coffee table. ''I thought maybe we could work something out.''

They all eyed the drug. Sparkling there in the light, it looked like diamonds next to their paste.

''Who knows?'' He shrugged. ''I got me a big house down in Colombia. A couple of you bitches might like it down there.''

''What's the deal?'' Lila asked.

''You work for me. You keep your eyes and ears open for any trouble. Talk to the other girls. You move outta this dump and into my pad. You work just like you did for Willie. Dude like me has certain . . . needs. You accommodate me when I ask you to. We'll all get along fine.''

The glint in Lila's eye had been replaced by a sparkle. While the Condor had been talking about his needs, he had been looking directly at her. He was a big, strong man. He had power. His drugs were beautiful. She smiled her best submissive smile.

''It sounds like an offer we can't refuse.''

''One other thing.'' He grinned back. ''I get the gun. Ain't no way we're gonna have equal distribution of firepower around here. That's my department.'' Standing, he approached the leather sofa and held out his hand.

Lila handed the Beretta to him, butt first. As he took it, she held on playfully, batting her eyes at him.

''You're a big man, and I'm a big woman,'' she cooed. ''I bet we could make big, bad music together.''

''I bet we could.'' He smiled back, taking the gun. Already he could tell that this little setup was going to involve great sacrifice.

SIXTEEN

He had seen her. Talked to her. Just Wednesday night. But on Friday, she wasn't there. He'd looked everywhere. And she was so much like the girl. Tall, slender, truly beautiful.

She had tauntd him, reaching in to run her fingers across his chest, feeling the gold around his neck. Her eyes had flashed as she licked her lips. If it hadn't been for the little voice, shouting at him, he would have taken her then. And now, with the voice calmer, just wary now, he could not find her. A savage resentment built inside him. She was with someone else. He knew it. The big white Lincoln was nowhere to be seen. That bastard had taken her away from him.

Feeling murderous instead of loving now, he gripped the wheel until his knuckles whitened. Rage consumed him.

There, ahead of him, stood a fat whore. Her bleached hair showed heavy black roots. Huge, pendulous breasts hung sloppily, encased in an absurd leotard. Bright red lips made kissing gestures at him as he rolled past. This grotesque caricature of his desire was mocking him. He hit his brakes, screeching to a halt.

"Hi, honey. You look hot. Looking for someone to cool you off?"

"Get in," he breathed, struggling to keep the snarl from his voice.

"Money, baby."

"I got money," he hissed. Reaching into his open jacket, he showed her a fistful of twenties. "Lots of money."

The fat blonde's eyes lit up. Quickly opening the door, she climbed in. "Listen," she said. "I've got a friend, and . . ."

Rick's eyes hardened. Not only was she mocking him, she was trying to set him up. "You'll do fine." He forced a smile. "Tell me. How much of this money would you like to make?"

"That depends on what you've got in mind."

"I've got a place about five blocks from here. Two hundred, if you'll let me take you there."

A couple hundred dollars was as much as she could expect to make on a good night. An hour off the street with one john and she was already way ahead of the game.

"Up front," she said cautiously. "All of it."

"Fine." He smiled, peeling and counting ten twenties. Pushing the BMW into gear, he set off for Twenty-second Street.

The big whore *ooh*ed when the electric door to his garage came up and they drove in. "Pretty nice setup, mister. I hope we can do this again soon." Reaching over, she caressed his crotch. "Looks like you're one of those that takes a little while to warm up, huh, honey? Don't worry." In one quick move, she slipped the shoulder straps of the leotard and revealed her monstrous breasts. Taking his left hand, she pulled it to her. "There, baby. Now close your eyes." She reached for his belt buckle.

Inside, Rick's rage had built like a torrent, coursing against the floodgates of disgust. As she pulled his hand toward that giant, grotesque parody of a tit, it trembled. The loathing he felt was absolute. And now she was going to touch him, to violate the holiness of his longing with the cheap playacting of commerce. His trembling hand, the weight of her heavy flesh in his palm, suddenly clenched closed. As her mouth came open to scream, he hit her with all his strength.

Joe Dante had gotten to bed early for a change. This Evelyn dame called again that evening, this time to complain that he hadn't phoned. It was true that he'd said he would. But that was in the throes of lust, she having just been most accommodating with brunch and a quickie afterward. But nice tan and all, he wasn't really interested in her. He'd never intended it to go on and hadn't expected her to. He was wrong. She told him she'd thought he was a nice guy and that he could go to hell. He had some reading on personality disorders he wanted to do. With a beer and the book, he crawled into bed at ten.

At four the phone rang. It was Morris again. This was starting to get on his nerves.

"Don't tell me," he said sleepily. "Just tell me where and I'll be there in ten minutes."

This time it was on Forty-fifth between Tenth and Eleventh. In the driveway of a place where commuter buses were washed during the day. There were two units from Midtown North and an unmarked car. Otherwise, the area was quiet. Larry Morris was huddled with his opposite from the other precinct.

"Joe, this is Lieutenant Cobb. Lieutenant, Joe Dante. He's the man we've got on the psycho angle."

"The detective's reputation preceeds him." Cobb nodded. Quickly, he shook hands. "I understand it's been pretty dry so far, Dante."

Joe nodded. "That's right, Lou. We've got a couple of theories we're working on."

"How does this fit in with your theory?" the lieutenant asked, pointing at a blanket-covered mound five feet away. "The sergeant tells me you think he has a type."

"That's right." Dante had moved to the body and knelt. Lifting the blanket, his eyes widened. The face had been beaten almost beyond recognition. The hair was bleached blond, but it was a bad job. And the woman was huge. It didn't make sense. "Jesus," he muttered. "Cause of death?"

"Preliminary examination says multiple contusions. The paramedic thinks the skull is fractured. It looks like the bastard did it with his bare hands."

"I don't get it." Dante shook his head. But there it was. The semen-filled rubber wedged between her lips. A copycat couldn't have known about this. They'd been careful to keep it under wraps.

"I'm inclined to be skeptical of your theories, Detective," Cobb said. "The biggest operator in the area is abducted just yesterday, and now this? I say they're tied together. And I think we have more than one murderer."

"Analysis of the semen will tell us that." Dante shrugged. "Frankly, I don't know what to think, Lou. I'll be interested to find out whose fingerprints they find on that rubber."

"How so?"

"The other two had the victim's prints and glove smudges. This killing looks to me like it was done in a frenzy. It's different." He shook his head. "That's all."

* * *

When Charlie Fung pulled down the long gravel drive to the house and parked, Brennan and Diana were in the old carriage house, which had been converted into a foundry, uncrating *The Steelworkers*.

"It's Charlie," Diana said, returning from peering outside and waving to them.

"I hope he listened to me and brought lunch," Brennan said. "There isn't a thing in the house."

A pair of shadows loomed outside, and then Fung and his date stepped through the open double doors.

"In Pleasure Beach, Connecticut, the word around town is Becks." Charlie was grinning as he pulled a six-pack out of the bag he carried. "I want you to meet Jill Warren Sprague."

Brennan literally jerked around to stare openmouthed. Fung was getting a big kick out of this.

"Warren," the girl next to him corrected him. "Stuart is my *step*father."

"Uh, listen . . ." Brennan started to explain.

"Forget it," she said. "I probably think he's a bigger asshole than you do."

Fung popped the caps of a couple beers with his pocketknife and handed them around. "We met at the party," he said. "I haven't had the opportunity to properly thank you, buddy."

"What happened to your date?" Brennan asked.

"Bambi? She met a Broadway producer."

Brian shook his head, took a swig of his beer, and threw the pry bar he was carrying onto a nearby bench. "I'm starving," he said. "What did you bring to eat?"

In the light of day, the young stepdaughter of Stuart Sprague was something to behold. The lunatic Chinaman sure had the touch. When it came down to it, Brennan had to admit that he'd never seen the man with a woman who wasn't physically exceptional. Their brains were generally another thing. He'd said this one could draw. Brennan wondered what. Butter maybe?

"We stopped by Balducci's and bought the fucking store," Charlie said, dragging bags of groceries out of the car and handing one to each of them. Except Jill. Instead, he carried two as they walked to the house.

The beach cottage Brennan had bought was some Victorian's idea of roughing it on the Sound. Long since, the power company had built a generating plant across the bay, and the support of such eccentricity had become almost as expensive as manufacturing electricity. The place fell into disrepair, and he'd picked it up for a song. Covered in about an acre of white shingle, it was a bit of a beast to maintain. But it was paid for, comfortable, and even weirdly elegant.

The country kitchen was one of those cavernous rooms full of maple cabinets, tile counters, a waxed brick floor, and a huge solid maple prep table in the center. The giant cast iron stove was original, providing wood heat as well as cooking surface.

They carried the groceries into the place, where they proceeded to unload them while the Sprague girl pulled up a chair and sat.

"Pasta salad. Tortellini, I think," Charlie said. "Antipasto. Chilled green bean salad. Steaks for tonight. I knew you wouldn't have gone shopping. Coffee. More beer. Red and white wine. I figured there wouldn't be a drop of alcohol in the place either. Eggs. Butter . . ."

He *had* bought the store. But then again, Brian was famous for inviting people up and having nothing in the larder. Charlie was probably his most frequent guest. He'd learned.

"I figured we'd have some of the salads and maybe make ham sandwiches for lunch. This Virginia ham is dynamite."

Brian and Diana started putting things into the refrigerator while Charlie began slicing bread and meat. Jill still hadn't raised a finger.

"Do you go to school?" Brennan asked her.

She nodded. "Brown. I just finished my sophomore year."

"Charlie tells me you draw."

"I'm a fine arts major."

"What's your discipline?"

"I paint," she said.

"How about grabbing some plates and silver. They're in that cabinet over there."

"I beg your pardon?"

"Plates. We have to eat *off* something." Turning, he started to spread mustard on the bread.

Diana was slicing tomatoes. Looking up, she rolled her eyes at him.

Jill stood, looking vaguely shocked, and crossed to the Hoosier cabinet in the corner. The idea of actually touching plates and utensils appeared to be alien to her. Opening the upper doors, she stood and stared at the china for a moment before slowly counting out four dinner plates and taking them down. Carrying them to the table, she turned to Charlie.

"I think I'll freshen up. Where is our room?"

Brennan looked at the four plates, still without silverware. Then he looked to Charlie.

"Uh . . ." Fung said. "I . . . uh . . ."

"Let me show you," Diana said, leading the way into the dining room beyond. "Bring your bag."

Again Jill turned to Charlie, looking expectantly. Fung pretended not to notice, and after a few pregnant seconds, the girl picked up her own case and lugged it out of the room.

"What the fuck's going on?" Brennan demanded.

"She not used to having to do things for herself." Fung shrugged. "I don't know. Her mother spoils her."

"What are you, soft in the head?"

"Look at her, man. That's inspired creation. And you've got to see her work. It's awesome."

"Bullshit. You're addled. I'm not ready for a weekend of 'The Princess and the Pea.' "

"She grows on you," Charlie argued defensively. "You'll see."

"You're out of your league this time, friend." Brian shook his head. "I thought Diana said *she* worships the ground *you* walk on."

"She does. And she's terrific in the sack."

"Now I know you're addled. There isn't a nineteen-year-old in the Western world who's worth a fuck in bed. What does she paint? Her Cabbage Patch dolls?"

Fung got something caught in his throat and began to choke, coughing uncontrollably. Brennan rushed to his aid, thumping him on the back.

SEVENTEEN

Dante called Rosa on the morning of her Sunday off to tell her he had something urgent to discuss. An hour later, clad simply in a pair of shorts and a T-shirt with St. Thomas emblazoned across the front, she padded barefoot across the foyer to answer her front door. For the past two days the precinct had been rocked by the sudden abduction of the man who seemed their best shot at snaring the murderer, coupled with the butchering of the fat hooker by roughly the same M.O. Dante's theory seemed flawed. Larry Morris was back to operating on his pet premise that the deaths were drug-war related. People were snickering at Rosa's ex-narc partner behind their hands.

Dante smiled at her informal getup as he stepped inside. "Nice legs," he commented, moving past her.

"*Great* legs," she returned. "You mind telling me what the hell's going on?"

Her partner made his way into her front room uninvited and sat.

"Hope I didn't, uh . . . *disturb* anything," he said. There was the hint of prurience in his voice.

"He gets up early to do his paper route," she replied. "I hope you didn't come all the way over here to critique my social life."

Dante found himself smiling. "Something a lot more interesting. Sammy called last night. Something real strange has come up."

"I hang on your every word."

"Seriously. You remember me telling you how many times he and I tried to stick it to Davenport?"

"The Dante Domino Theory," she said. "Get him and the rest fall down the line."

"Right. Friday afternoon Sammy moved on Willie's operation."

"How do you mean?"

"I mean the Condor muscled right in. Took over the man's crib, his string of girls, his business, everything. He figures it'll lead to at least a dozen solid collars over the next five or six weeks. Suppliers, buyers."

"But he's exposing himself," Rosa argued. "It will destroy his cover."

"He's getting out, just like me. This is his last stand. I think he hates it as much as I did."

"What does this mean to us?" she asked. "I assume there's more in it, right?"

Dante eyed her steadily. "I laid the whole Cheri thing out to him. Told him how close I think we're getting. He's willing to let us have access and her complete cooperation."

"What does that mean?"

Dante smiled. "I have a couple of ideas. For one, I want to wire her."

"A civilian?" Rosa asked, incredulous. "They'll never let you."

Dante shook his head. "I wasn't going to ask."

A look that had been only disbelief suddenly became troubled. Rosa paced nervously across the room, her back to him.

"Look," he said. "If you don't want any part of it, you're clean. You don't know anything about it."

"But I *do*."

"We've got a butcher out there, and I don't care what Larry Morris or anyone else thinks. I saw the lab reports last night. Same blood grouping for the semen. Same cause of death. Our boy's just gotten a little kinkier, Rosa. We've linked him to this Cheri by eyewitness account. Brennan's a fucking artist. He makes his living studying women. That's as good as you could ask for."

"Rigging an unauthorized surveillance wire is grounds for being kicked out of the department, Joe."

Dante slammed his palm with his fist.

"What's another couple dead whores to them? I try to talk to the lou over at Midtown South yesterday, he thinks it's some sort of joke. Animals killing each other off and good riddance. He's a fucking asshole!"

Rosa sat heavily in the chair opposite, taking a deep breath and letting it out slowly. "How are you going to get her to cooperate?"

Dante allowed himself a weak smile. "The pictures I took. Sammy's willing to make it look like we're going into the extortion business together. License numbers matched with cute tapes of Daddy copping a quick blow job on his way home to the wife and kids in New Jersey. If she won't cooperate, we threaten to turn the pictures over to the cops."

"Pretty nasty," she said matter-of-factly.

Dante shook his head. "She won't work if we don't scare the shit out of her."

Rosa sat and thought, eyes to the floor. Dante watched

her, determined to wait as long as it took. She was going to talk first.

"Why do you trust me?" she asked at last.

"Because you believe the same thing I do," he said. "There's a nut out there . . . and this is our best shot at nailing him."

"This is crazy." She sighed. "*I'm* crazy. What do you want me to do?"

Dante was grinning from ear to ear now. "I want Sammy to bring her by here this afternoon. You talk to her, show the pictures, and explain how you hope you don't have to give them to the cops. Then you tape this to her." He pulled a small surveillance transmitter from his pocket and held it out to her. "Right here." He indicated a spot below and between the breasts. "She'll be wearing a lot of tight stuff . . . uh, not a *lot*, but you know what I mean."

"And where are you during all this?"

"In the wings. I think this'll be better if it's done on a woman to woman basis. It's gonna freak her out more."

"Thanks," she said, shaking her head. "You're a real sensitive guy, aren't you?"

When Rosa Losada's intercom buzzer sounded, she jumped. It wasn't that she didn't expect their arrival. She was as ready as she'd ever be. But it was just that she'd never been involved in actually shaking someone down before. Not like this.

She'd sent her roommate, Cindy, off to the movies with orders not to return until after six.

It was still early. Barely four-thirty. This was a slow night in the trade, but Sammy still had rounds to make and would have to get the girl back to Harlem in time to rope in his charges and herd them south for the evening.

When she answered the door, the Condor and a sullen Cheri stood in the hall outside.

"She's all yours," Sammy said. "I'll be waiting downstairs. Send her down when you're finished." He smiled, turned, and walked to the elevator.

Rosa gestured the girl into the apartment and closed the door.

"What the fuck's going on?" Cheri demanded. "I don't know what he told you, but . . ."

Rosa smiled. "You're just here for a little talk," she interrupted. "Come into the living room, Cheri. Make yourself comfortable."

"How do you know my name?" the girl demanded.

"I know a lot more about you than just your name," Rosa replied. "A Coke? Iced tea?"

Cheri shook her head. She was slouching spread-legged, trying to look bad-ass.

"Fine," Rosa said with a shrug. She moved to a side table, picked up an envelope, and depressed the record button of a cassette machine.

"What's that for?" Cheri asked.

"Posterity," Rosa replied. "I've got some things the Condor and I want you to see. Then we have a proposition to make."

She opened the envelope and withdrew the dozen photographs depicting Cheri engaged in the transaction of Willie Davenport's business on Forty-second Street. When she spread them on the coffee table, Cheri's jaw dropped.

"What the fu . . . ?"

"You, Cheri. Photographed while you engaged in the trafficking of controlled substances. Turned over to the cops, considering that you already have an extensive arrest record for prostitution and drug possession, I imagine that they could be pretty rough on you."

"You're a cop!" Cheri hissed. "A mother-fucking narc!"

Rosa smiled condescendingly. "I am a business woman,

dear. These photographs were taken for a purpose other than to incriminate you. You see, we need you."

"We?"

"The Condor and I. We are associates."

"I don't believe I'm hearing this bullshit. *Associates?* What kind?"

Rosa looked the girl straight in the eye.

"Willie Davenport was a piker, honey. Greedy and stupid. The Condor is an *operator*. You and me are gonna work with him, blackmailing johns. A picture with you, along with a nice little cassette of you helping him get his rocks off on his way home from work. He wouldn't want his wife getting ahold of something like that, now would he?"

Cheri's eyes narrowed. "A cassette?"

"That's right. You see, you'll be wearing a neat little bug between your tits. I'll be in a car down the block. You're gonna be the rock, and I'll be the hard place. Johnny boy finds himself pinched between them."

"What's in it for me?" Cheri asked, carefully feeling around as everything came clear. Rosa could see her confidence returning.

"Ten percent."

A look of disdain crossed the whore's face.

"You call that an offer? Ten lousy points? Why should I bother?"

"Because it's money," Rosa said. "And if you don't take it, we always have these." She picked up the sheaf of photographs and fingered them. "I didn't come here to negotiate, if that's what you're hoping."

"I don't believe you'd turn them over," Cheri said.

Rosa smiled at the challenge. "Then you don't know me, and you don't know the Condor. He's a proud man, and I'm a coldhearted bitch."

Cheri swallowed, staring at the eight-by-ten glossies. "I bet you're a cold fuck, too," she grumbled.

Rick knew that he had to get hold of himself. When he'd returned to the townhouse before dawn on Saturday, he collapsed on the sofa beneath the radiant gatefolds and slept. Awakening after sunup, he had difficulty remembering what had happened since leaving the place shortly after midnight. When it came back to him, it was like remembering a dream. Until he descended to the garage and saw the inside of the car.

There was blood everywhere. Seeing it, the memory of his frenzied rage flooded over him. She hadn't been there. He had looked everywhere. And then there was the fat one with the huge, grotesque tits. She had mocked him. His rage became a wash of crimson light.

As he ran the water hot in the laundry tub, mixing it with a strong, pine-scented cleaner, he knew that he could not use the car again. He had lost control and gotten careless. It was hard to recall what he had done with her. Dumped her someplace. Yes. But when? And where? He fought to remember.

Monday he would have to get another car.

Brennan was alone in the foundry, repairing areas of the clay damaged in transit before beginning the casting process. On the wall alongside him, four sketches, executed to scale and divided into sections by fine grid lines, supplied a detailed master from which to work. They were covered with casting notes as well, indicating where the components were to be sectioned and then brazed together; where the core pins were to be set; and where the gates, risers, and runners would be positioned. He had been attending to a slightly distorted ear when he heard footsteps behind him on the concrete.

"Hi," he said, not looking up.

"This is different," a voice returned with the hint of sarcasm. It would appear that Charlie had momentarily lost track of the most recent love of his life.

He looked over at her. She was studying the sketches.

"Charlie said that you draw better than he does. I didn't believe him. Haven't you forgotten the women with the big boobs?"

"Is superiority something someone like you is born with?" he asked, continuing to prod the clay.

"Pardon me?"

"You heard me."

"I'm not sure I understand what you're asking."

Brennan turned, pointing the dental pick he'd been using at her. "Let me put it like this. Charlie says you have talent. We all know you have money. You act like you think that's enough. How naive are you?"

She looked surprised. "I don't think you know me well enough to make that kind of observation," she said, obviously affronted.

"How well do I have to know you?" he asked. "From what I just heard, you've made up your mind about who *I* am. Why are you any different?"

"I don't do cheap commercial nudes and commissions of rich old bags."

"You never had to."

"Why don't you like me?" she demanded. "Because of Stuart?"

He shook his head. "Stuart is too pathetic to bother with. You bother me because you make dimwitted judgments of other people. Who are you? You've had a couple of academics tell you you're good. Whoop de fucking doo! Let's see you make it play in Cincinnati."

He turned and started in on the ear again. It was almost

right now. Carefully, he picked some loose clay clear of the undercut beneath the top flap.

"I was rude." Her voice came from behind him. "I shouldn't have said that about the women with the big boobs. This is a lot different. I like it."

He turned again, eyeing her.

"I'm sorry." She shrugged. "I don't know why I did that."

"Don't worry about it," he grumbled. "Are you going to draw with us tonight?"

"Charlie said it was up to you," she said.

"Why not?" he shrugged. "You're my guest."

"And she expects that I'm just going to sit here and continue to write checks that keep her in the lap of luxury?" Stuart Sprague ranted, sitting across from his wife. They were poolside at their East Hampton estate. "You gave her your permission?"

"You know I don't have any control over her, Stuart," Penny returned. "She met that awful painter and just announced that she was running off up there for the weekend."

"I won't stand for it," he seethed. "If she thinks she can rub dirt in my face like that, she's got another think coming."

"It all started when you didn't put your foot down about this art thing."

"*I* didn't? She's your goddamn daughter. I just pay the bills around here. But things are going to change. She's got a fat surprise coming. Brown and that apartment of hers are costing me thirty-five thousand a year. I'd like to see how much art she'd study if I refused to subsidize it."

Penelope Sprague frowned. "Don't you think you're being a bit harsh, Stuart? After all . . ."

"The man doesn't know his place," Sprague snarled.

"Now your goddamn daughter is spending my money spreading her legs for some Chinese freak under his roof! I'll be fucked if . . . !"

"Stuart!" The houseman was approaching with fresh drinks. Penny insisted on silence until he departed. "Please," she said once they were alone. "I understand why you're angry."

Sprague took a long pull on his gin and tonic. Standing, he stretched and eyed the sparkling aqua cool of the pool.

"She's your daughter, Penny. I want this nonsense to stop. I don't care how you have to do it, but I won't have someone taking my money and then spitting in my face."

EIGHTEEN

Dante had suggested that Rosa meet him at his place in the Village after her conversation with Cheri. Sammy and his string were due out on the street sometime after eleven and with it being a Sunday night and all, he thought it might be a perfect opportunity to try different locations for sound levels.

She arrived at the address on Perry Street at a little before eight o'clock. It was a tree-lined block of beautiful houses and antebellum tenements. Wonderful, ornate architecture that reeked of history. Dante's building was a narrow, four-story Federal with climbing vines covering half it's red brick face. She climbed the wide stoop and pressed the top buzzer. Her partner occupied the ground-floor apartment in the back of the building.

"How did it go?" Dante asked as she stepped inside.

"Okay," she replied distractedly. She was looking around. "I've always loved this neighborhood. It's got a real special feel to it."

"Yeah," Dante grunted. "Cheri, Rosa."

"Signed, sealed, and delivered. Once I finally convinced her that she didn't have to talk to her tits to make the thing work."

Dante chuckled. "She went for the blackmail story?"

"No problem. Like you said, the pictures scared the shit out of her. After that, she was like putty." She had pushed past him and was surveying the layout. It was obvious that her partner had taken some pains to straighten up. No stray dishes. No beer cans. The magazines on the coffee table were stacked in a nice, neat pile.

"Nice place," she said. "Working fireplace?"

"Yep."

She wandered through, fingering the heavy woodwork, inspecting the kitchen, and then discovering the French doors leading out back.

"You have a garden!" she yelped. ". . . and a kitty!"

Copter, sensing an opportunity to get some of the attention he incessantly craved, worked her left ankle as she stooped to stroke his head.

"He's gorgeous. What is he?"

"An Egyptian Mau. Left in my care by a neighbor who couldn't take the pressures of Gotham. He likes to be tossed in the air. Copter Cat."

Rosa had the purring animal up and wrapped in her arms. "He's cute."

"Right," Dante said, rolling his eyes. He led the way out onto the patio. "We've got a couple of hours to kill. Can I get you something to drink?"

Rosa yawned and peered at her watch. "They're late."

"Slow night," Dante replied. "There's no rush to get downtown on a Sunday."

Paychecks either spent or safely in the bank, most of the blue-collar world stayed home Sunday night and rested up for the work-week ahead. They watched television and turned in early. On a real hot night, they'd sometimes take a drive to cool off and end up looking to get their ends off as well. But tonight, just after sundown, it had rained hard for over an hour. Most of the clouds were cleared off now, but the few girls out had gotten soaked. The scene was a pretty sorry one.

It was almost midnight. With the rain, the night-life over on Times Square was surely dampened as well. But when it was dry enough for the cockroaches to crawl back out of their holes, the Condor would be there to service them. It wouldn't be good form to be there waiting. The guest of honor never came early to a party.

And then suddenly there they were. The Condor's Jag pulled to the curb at the agreed-upon location, half a block ahead of them. His girls climbed out onto the pavement. East of them on Thirty-eighth Street, Dante reached between himself and Rosa in the front seat of the 300 ZX and adjusted the volume on the receiver. The little cabin of the Nissan was flooded with the noise of giggles and foul-mouthed hooker jive.

Cheri had been told to work just this short piece of block. She was to direct her customers into the shallow, darkened driveway twenty yards diagonally across the street from them. They would be the first line of defense. As a backup, the Condor's wheels were rigged with an electronic squealer attached under the rear bumper. In the event of trouble, it could be activated from the inside of the Nissan.

Ten minutes after they'd deployed, Cheri got her first john. A blue Pinto eased up next to her, and she leaned in the window.

"Goin' out?" filled the air inside the cabin of the sports car. Dante heard Rosa take a deep breath.

"You bet, babe. How much?"

"Twenty bucks. Let's see it."

Down the street, they saw Cheri straighten and open the car's passenger door. As she was climbing in, Dante grinned and turned to Rosa.

"This is where you might pick up a tip or two. Pay attention."

"Fuck you," she grunted, waving him off. She was listening intently.

The next thing they heard was the door's loud closing *whump*.

"Down the street and into the drive on the right."

"Name's Arnie, babe. What's yours?"

"Cinderella. You're still soft."

"I thought you could help me with that."

"I ain't a sex therapist, buster. Park it. I ain't got all night."

"C'mon, babe. You ain't bein' very nice."

The clanking of a belt buckle, assorted grunts, and the tearing of a condom packet came next.

"You gotta do it with a rubber, babe?"

"How 'bout not at all, Jim?"

"It's Arnie . . ."

Rosa shifted uncomfortably in her seat.

"Nice, huh?" Dante grunted.

"God." She squirmed. "How can she do it?"

"She's a whore." Dante grinned. "It comes with the territory."

The receiver, meanwhile, was emitting a series of ungodly grunts and wet, slurping sounds. Then the guy let out a low groan, and in the dim light of the drive across the street, a rubber flew out the window and onto the pavement.

"*Gak!*" Rosa choked.

Seconds later, Cheri was out of the car and trotting back

toward the Condor's corner. In all, the transaction had taken no more than five minutes.

"Think of it," Dante said. "The poor slob probably worked two hours to make that dough. In a few seconds, a whore sucks it into the end of a rubber sock."

"Spare me the philosophy," Rosa said grimly.

They sat through a dozen more of these sordid encounters. The total of Cheri's take astounded them.

"She's made a hundred and sixty dollars in less than two hours," Rosa calculated. "That's amazing."

Dante nodded. "Free enterprise. And this is a slow night. Willie must have been pulling down an extra eight or ten a week off these girls."

Eventually the Condor herded up his chicks and drove them back to the nest. It hadn't been a particularly exciting night, but it served its purpose for a dry run. The equipment worked. The setup wasn't too bad.

"Buy you something to eat before you go home?" Dante asked Rosa. "We can hit the Market Diner up on Forty-third."

"Did I hear the magic words? You're buying?"

"Sure."

A couple of uniforms were seated in one of the booths as they entered. A Midtown North unit was parked outside in the lot. Late-night shift. You didn't get to spend it home with the wife, but it was generally the easiest duty. Drink coffee. Listen to the radio.

Joe and Rosa were halfway through a sandwich and beer when the portable radio the pair of patrolmen had propped on the table squawked out the officer in trouble code. In a flash, Dante was on his feet and hovering over it. The cops looked up in surprise.

Dante flashed his shield. "Up from the Tenth," he grunted, straining to catch the location.

"Transit cop down. Eighth Avenue and Forty-second

IND station.'' He threw a twenty onto the table and raced for the door.

Rosa was up, sandwich still clutched in her hand, and hurrying to follow Dante and the two uniforms out the door.

The 300 ZX, tires smoking, reversed out of the lot and careened wildly onto Forty-third Street. Jamming it into first gear, Dante floored it, rocketing across town to Eighth Avenue. Sirens were already wailing, and one regular department unit sat crosswise in the street a block up as they screeched to a halt at a subway entrance and jumped out of the car.

Guns drawn and gold shields hung around their necks, they rushed underground. The stench of stale urine filled their nostrils as they hugged the wall at the bottom of the stairs. Dante held a hand back, making contact with his partner, and peeered cautiously around the corner. The light was bright down there, reflecting off graffiti-covered wall tile. Down the way, a uniform was on one knee, bent over a sprawled body. He had his gun out and was looking frantically around.

''Which way?'' Dante shouted, hailing him.

The man looked up, seeing the badge and the gun. ''Up the tunnel toward Times Square.'' He pointed. ''He's gotta have an ambulance.''

''The call's out,'' Dante shouted, leading Rosa past him. ''How many are there?''

''Just two, I think. Hispanic kids. One of them's got Jack's gun.''

At the entrance to the tunnel, they vaulted the turnstiles and raced up the incline, staying as close to the walls as they could. Two-thirds of the way along, they heard two gunshots. At the top of the stairs to the Number Seven train, another cop was down, this one hit in the upper arm.

"My partner's down there." He winced, waving them on. "I think they jumped onto the tracks."

The man still had his portable radio.

"Get on that thing and tell them that they're headed for Fifth Avenue," Dante told him. "Tell them there are three of our own down there after them." Turning, he raced down the steps and on to the platform.

"We've got to go onto the tracks," he told Rosa. "If you see a train coming, hit one of those indentations in the wall. And watch out for the third rail."

Together, they leaped down into the filth below the platform and advanced into the gloom. Ahead, they could see a succession of pale light pools created by weak incandescents. There was no visible movement. Leapfrogging from shadow to shadow, each exchanging the lead position and then covering the other, they worked their way east across town. And then, about two hundred yards ahead, the report of another gunshot. This time they saw the muzzle flash in the darkness. And thirty or so yards closer to them, a gunman returned fire.

"Idiot," Dante spat.

"What's the matter?" Rosa asked.

"He's out of effective range. Now he's just confirmed his position."

Leaping up, he ran straight ahead along the near wall, sticking to the darkness. Ahead, more shots were exchanged. Stopping about fifty yards short of the action, Joe waited for Rosa. He was considering the situation. There was another platform entrance at Sixth and Forty-second. The Sixth Avenue F and D trains also intersected there. The pursuit could easily cut the gunmen off now that the wounded man had radioed their direction. So why had they slowed down and made a stand here? And then it hit him.

"We've got to get to the street," he said, searching the tunnel walls around him.

"Why?" Rosa asked.

"That guy was shooting just to pin down the pursuit. The bastards *know* they can't make it out at Sixth Avenue. They're climbing up down there."

He found what he was looking for. The rungs of a ladder imbedded in the wall of the tunnel. Grabbing hold, he began to scramble up it.

Beneath Forty-second Street, there were Con Ed power lines, telephone lines, sewage access, and God knew what else. The street itself was dotted with dozens of manhole covers providing means to reach these various utilities. And among them were emergency evacuation passages running deep underground to the subway tunnels. Dante and Rosa had a long scramble to the street. When they finally reached it, over a hundred pounds of steel disk stood in their way.

Putting a shoulder into the cover, Dante used his back and legs to push it high enough up to start it sideways. All the while, he prayed the damn thing wouldn't be hit by a car.

At that hour, traffic was extremely light. It turned out that they were almost in the gutter on the south side of the street. Dante hoisted himself into a sitting position on the edge of the hole and reached to grab Rosa's hand. A truck was parked against the curb between them and the next access hole. Pulling their guns, they hurried to it and peered around the cargo box.

Directly ahead, one man already stood on the street, and another was coming out of the hole fast.

"Hold it! Police!" Rosa shouted. Aiming her revolver in the air, she pulled the trigger. The report and jolt it gave her arms surprised her. It was the first time she had ever discharged her weapon in the line of duty.

One of the figures wheeled and fired recklessly behind him on the run. They were headed diagonally across Sixth and into Bryant Park, behind the public library. Dante and Rosa sprinted in pursuit.

The pair ahead zigged to the south side of the park, staying to the wide footpaths for speed. Halfway up Fortieth Street, they veered suddenly to the right and hit the sidewalk, making for the opposite side of the street and ahead, Fifth Avenue.

There was a lot of construction in progress along that stretch. The sidewalks were protected by scaffolding and a covered right of way. The new Republic National Bank Tower, fronting on Fifth, was entirely surrounded by such a system. On Fortieth, it zigged in and out to accommodate the work carried out behind the plywood barricade. Once the suspects reached that stretch, Dante and Rosa were going to be sitting ducks.

Dropping across the hood of a parked car to steady himself, Joe took time to lead his man, take in air, and begin to expel it slowly and evenly. Three times the PPK barked and jerked in his hands. One of the two men fleeing ahead of them crumpled to the street. Without a word, Dante was up and moving again.

Rosa couldn't believe the shot. Minutes earlier, her partner had criticized the man in the tunnel for shooting from approximately the same distance. Thirty yards. And he was right. It was considered out of effective range for a handgun.

The fugitive, still on his feet, running on pure instinct now, mistakenly failed to take advantage of the topography and merely sprinted all out for the corner. Dante, much faster than Rosa, was hot on his tail. By the time she'd reached Fifth Avenue, her partner was already approaching the opposite sidewalk. Another new building was going up there. More scaffolding and plywood barricades surrounded it. The suspect disappeared around the far corner, heading east on Thirty-ninth. Joe pulled up just a second to check the lay of the land and then charged after him.

When Rosa reached the opposite side of Fifth and Thirty-ninth, her heart was pounding like a jackhammer and the air burned in her lungs. Pure adrenaline was keeping her up now. Ahead, she searched the shadows. Joe had stopped to crouch on the sidewalk. He was sweeping his pistol back and forth in front of him. The fugitive had apparently vanished into thin air. Cautiously, she advanced, trying to see into shadows.

Out of the corner of her eye, there was a dull glint of something. Down low. Or was there? Dante was almost opposite the parked car. Streetlight on the chrome of the bumper? And then she saw it again. Minuscule movement. Dull blue gleam. Nothing more really than a differing density of shadow.

"Joe! Behind you!" she screamed.

Dante dived for the pavement, somersaulting and bringing his weapon up in the combat stance as two shots rang out from beneath the parked car. Rosa was already on one knee, two hands supporting her weapon. All the training rushed back. She prepared herself by rote. Holding it steady. Beginning the exhale, letting the air out evenly. Two muzzle flashes. Sighting on them. Squeezing the trigger. Once. The weapon jerked hard. Twice. And again. From Joe's position, his automatic also spat angrily.

The man beneath the car, caught in a withering cross fire, never stood a chance. As Rosa and Dante approached him, gasoline trickled onto his face from the ruptured tank above, mixing with the blood from his mouth and washing it away. The wide open, surprised eyes didn't blink.

NINETEEN

It was sunup before the partners finished filing reports and making their statements. In an incident involving a racial minority member being killed by a police officer, especially after the shooting of two patrolmen, the facts were carefully scrutinized. The duty captain from Midtown South who was the presiding officer raised his eyebrows at the information that neither of these partners from the Tenth were on duty. Larry Morris and Gus Lieberman eventually arrived and shut themselves in with the captain to confer on the incident.

Joe and Rosa had both turned in their guns for examination and were sitting down waiting for permission to go home when the sergeant and the inspector emerged from their huddle.

"You two just in the area to take the air?" Lieberman asked gruffly.

"It's not costing the city any money," Dante returned

defensively. "We're working on a theory. We have reason to believe our man has a type. We even think the hooker we have our eye on may have been seen talking to the guy." He told him about Brennan and the dented car.

"A little speculative, isn't it?" the inspector asked.

"It's the best thing we've got, sir."

"How about this third murder? The victim doesn't fit your type at all."

Dante shrugged. "Psychos are unpredictable."

"The sergeant here thinks you're barking up the wrong tree. He thinks the abduction of Willie Davenport proves that there's something heavy going down over there."

"We've got a pretty good ear who says different. He's right inside it. I have to believe he'd know."

"Who?" Morris asked.

"I can't tell you that, Sarge. The favor he's doing is strictly personal."

Lieberman shrugged. "I've persuaded your commander to take you off the duty roster. From now on, you work this thing full-time. As good or bad as it might be, yours is the only hunch we've got. Don't let me down."

Joe and Rosa looked at each other in surprise. They'd half expected to be pulled. Instead, Downtown was as much as giving them free rein.

"I want a report, in writing, every day," Morris said. "It doesn't matter if you have to sign your name to the bottom of a blank sixty sheet. I want it hand-delivered on my desk."

They nodded.

"And by the way. Nice work tonight. How did you know they were coming up out of the tunnel?"

Dante smiled. "Just a hunch."

Back in the Nissan, Dante drove toward the Village. Rosa had left her car parked in the yellow zone in front of the church. Traffic was already starting to pick up, morning delivery vans beginning their routes and tradesmen getting started on the day.

"I owe you one," he said. "You saved my ass back there."

"We wouldn't have been there if it weren't for you," she returned. "And if you hadn't gotten that first one, who knows what would have happened when they reached the construction site?"

He looked at her, shook his head, and smiled. "You're all right, Detective Losada. There aren't so many who've saved my butt that I'm soon to forget. I hope I never have to do the same for you."

In front of the church on West Eleventh Street, he parked the car and turned it off. "I'd offer to buy you breakfast again, but I'm afraid I'm becoming a bad influence."

"I'll accept if I can have a rain check," she said. "Right now I just want to go home and sleep. I've never shot a man before, Joe. I need to think about it."

"Don't," he advised. "I wouldn't be here right now if you hadn't." He held out his hand. Rosa looked at it, smiled, and reached to grab it. They both squeezed hard.

Rick had to have another car. Something neutral. A car that no one would take any notice of.

Years ago, as a rash young entrepreneur, he had engaged in a number of questionable business dealings. To be safe, he'd established a second identity. Searching the obituaries in the library's back issues of *The New York Times*, he found the name of a child who had died in infancy. The Hall of Records supplied him with the dead child's birth certificate. With it, he obtained social security number, driver's license, bank accounts, passport, and, eventually, credit cards. To the machine of bureaucracy, he was also known as Richard Lawrence Wakeman.

Richard Wakeman eventually purchased a condominium in Los Angeles. Officially, this was his residence. He paid taxes in California, although he was rarely home. To his neighbors he was a man who traveled quite a bit.

On Monday Rick informed his secretary that he planned a trip to the coast the following day and had her book a morning flight. At 10 A.M. Tuesday he boarded an American Airlines flight that got him into LA in time to make a Beverly Hills luncheon with several business associates. They pitched him a number of film deals, and he, in turn, inquired about a stalled real estate development down in Encinitas. Returning to his room, he checked for messages, asked not to be disturbed, and drove out to the condo in his rented Cadillac. There, he spent a relaxed afternoon dozing by the pool. The girls out there were incredible. Aspiring actresses. Airline stews. He lay in his lounge chair, watching them behind dark glasses and thinking of the girl. They had the same youthful, tanned bodies. Tight thighs and perky breasts. Before returning to Beverly Hills for dinner, he telephoned Hertz and reserved a blue Chevrolet Citation to be picked up the following afternoon at Kennedy in New York. He read the reservations clerk his American Express card number.

After six hours a night, five nights in a row, spent hunched down in the cramped cabin of the 300 ZX, they still didn't have a nibble. According to an informal tally Rosa was running, they had listened to sixty-seven blow jobs. Once the novelty wore off, it was pretty tough to take. By three A.M. Thursday, they were both ready to scream. Every sorry bastard with a hard-on and a line of shit seemed sorrier than the last.

The Condor, on the other hand, was busy having the

time of his life. It seemed that the big girl Lila had decided he was the hottest thing since Vesuvius. And on the business side, four short days of these fun and games were already solidifying more evidence for felony convictions than he might normally hope to gather in as many months. What started out as skepticism had been converted to rampant enthusiasm. He'd seen the mother lode. Once the murder thing blew over, he was going to bust the entire district of Midtown Manhattan, wholesale.

By 3:00, Dante wondered if maybe the show wasn't over for the night. Traffic had slowed to a trickle after a brief thundershower. The girls started to get distracted. Cheri, in particular, was being even less than her usual charming self.

Rosa produced sandwiches from home in an effort to stave off the acute hunger that accompanied the shifts. In the distraction of unwrapping and starting to eat them, the shiny new Chevy Citation passed almost unnoticed.

The girl turned over without tying her suit top that afternoon. She was unaware that he was on the terrace above her, watching. It was just as he had imagined. Her breasts were spectacular. Young, firm, and tight like the rest of her body. But so pearl-white, protected from the tanning sun. Eyes closed, she squirmed there on the chaise, straining to pull the fabric back around her and into place.

For Rick, the ecstasy of the moment flooded over him like a deluge of hot oil. The fire in him burned so hot now that it hurt. Retreating into the shade of his perch, he pulled his erect penis from his shorts and stroked it intently. Beads of sweat rolled down his face.

"Suck me, you bitch," he hissed under his breath. Edging forward in his chair, he could just see her there, glistening in the sun. The fire was making him crazy. As he jerked himself furiously, the sweat poured off his face in the heat.

That evening, he took a cab to the townhouse. The rented car was now parked in the garage. At his bar, he poured himself a double scotch and tried to relax. All around him, the girl hung in her myriad of inviting poses. He drifted with them, imagining himself coupled with the bodies in the pictures. The smooth, creamy buttocks. The inviting twats. The firm, ripe tits. She beamed down at him from every angle. Damn, he ached. He had seen her revealed to him now. He had found the perfect surrogate. He thought he would go insane if she weren't there tonight.

Earlier, once darkness settled, he walked out into the Chelsea night with screwdriver and pliers. He stole the plates off a Volkswagen Rabbit and exchanged them for the plates already on the rented Chevrolet.

At two-thirty the rain broke suddenly, then passed. Rick's automatic garage door opener hummed into action, revealing the rear end of the Citation. Rick backed it cautiously into the street, excitement coursing up from his stomach. His shoulders and arms trembled.

As soon as he had begun the hunt, he knew she was out there. He could almost smell her in the close confines of the car. The pretty bitch with the hard mouth and the defiance in her eyes. When he talked to her that night, he had been able to see the girl lying there in the bright sun of the terrace. Now he would have her.

The action was further uptown tonight. He last saw her on Twenty-ninth or Twenty-eighth. But tonight there were only a couple of sorry-looking junkie whores down that end of Eleventh. He drove west to the river, turned north, and moved slowly up the highway frontage.

The odd glass and concrete geometry of the new convention center ominously reflected the amber streetlight as he passed beneath it and bore right on Fortieth. Ahead, there were more of them. Half-a-dozen beckoning as he drifted slowly by. But she was not with them. He pressed on, almost tasting her in his mouth now.

He drove to Eleventh and turned right. A block down, a white Jag stood parked at the curb, facing uptown. He didn't remember having seen it before. He was drifting by and eyeing it curiously when his heart began to pound, rising up in his throat. She was there.

Swinging left abruptly, he crossed the avenue and into Thirty-eighth Street. She walked slowly his way. Her. She was coming to him. Tall. Slender. Beautiful. His mind flashed through all the girl's poses. Inviting him. Abreast of her, he stopped.

"Goin' out, honey?" she asked distractedly, leaning in the window as he ran it down.

"How about you coming in? It's cool in here, babe."

"Let's see the green, honey."

Rick displayed a large roll, peeling off a twenty and setting it on the seat beside him. She opened the door, sat, and picked it up.

The glint of the massive diamond ring tickled vague recollection. She looked closer. Silk shirt this time instead of the jacket. But same pants. And same gold bracelet and chains. The shirt was unbuttoned to the navel, exposing a thick mat of gray hair. She'd seen this guy before.

"That driveway there." She pointed, to taking control. "How are you feeling tonight?"

"I got a hot cock aching for your hot mouth, baby. It's ready to burst."

He complied with the suggestion of location. As he concentrated on guiding the car into the obscuring darkness of the drive, she reached over and touched him.

"Oooh," she crooned, caressing the heat straining against the shiny hide. "Are we ever ready."

"Not yet." he hissed. Throwing it into park, he killed the lights. "When I say so."

"Oh yeah?" she growled irritably. "You pay by the job, not by the hour."

The eyes of the man hardened.

"Wrong, baby. You should know by now that it's not right to talk back to me. You always talk back to me. All I ever wanted you to do is love me."

"You're crazy, buster." She shook her head, suddenly afraid. She had gotten them like this before. Unhinged. Once, she'd ended up in Roosevelt Hospital for a week.

Fury filled his eyes and tightened the muscles in his jaw. In a move so lightning-quick that she didn't see it coming, he had his arm around her head, yanking her hair. She grabbed frantically for the door handle. He saw her intention and moved to stop her. She bit hard into his extended arm. Gasping, he momentarily loosened his grip, wrestling with her. Reaching under the seat, his fingers wrapped around the handle of a stiletto.

She hadn't remembered to scream. Now she felt the blade pricking her ribs before she actually saw it. The heavyset old guy was quick. She'd underestimated him.

"Oh my God!" she screamed. "Get me out of here! He's got a knife!"

When the Chevy pulled up alongside Cheri, Rosa paused to elbow Joe. "Another one."

They'd watched as it pulled into the drive. Nothing unusual about the opening. They'd heard the transaction so often, with so little variation, that it had begun to have a hypnotic effect. But then something seemed a little strange. Cheri ceased to be quite so sharp-tongued. Generally, when she saw a guy was ready to pop, she'd go on in and try to get it over with as quickly as possible. This guy wasn't having any of it. And then he started babbling something about talking back.

"This one is a nut," Rosa said apprehensively. "I can feel it, Joe."

"Do you want to break it up?"

"What if this is our man?" she aked, undecided. "Nothing has really happened yet. Maybe this is just the way some guy gets . . ."

She was interrupted by a grunt, a gasp, and Cheri's bloodcurdling scream.

As the woman's terror flooded the car, Dante reflexively thumbed Sammy's alarm switch. "Call for backup," he yelled, throwing open his door and jumping into the street.

It all happened too quickly. One moment he was mesmerized by the developing tension, and in the next, all hell broke loose. Sammy was twenty-five yards up the block when the alarm's shrill scream split the night. The big man was amazingly fast, bearing down on them full-bore before Dante was even out of the car.

Cheri's terror still poured from the radio inside the Nissan. It mixed with the sudden roar of the Chevy's engine in the drive. Dante closed the distance just as its tires screamed and it began to come backward at him. He dived for the driver's door handle, jerking it as it gained momentum. To his surprise, the damn thing came open in his hand. He lost his balance. The handle slipped away, and he tumbled backward.

Sammy arrived just as he was going down and dived right into the car at the guy as he frantically tried to get his door closed. He didn't see the knife until it flashed inches in front of his eyes. There was no time to react. Almost as quickly as he reached for the man, he lurched backward, clutching at his neck. A great spurt of blood cascaded over his arm and across the chest of his white linen suit. And another.

The car was moving out now. Dante, absorbing events peripherally, leaped over the fallen Sammy and grabbed for the receding doorjamb. His fingers caught hold. He was jerked violently from his feet. The bastard was so close that he swore he could smell his aftershave. But he couldn't see him. The car swerved as he clutched at the driver's arm. The knife flashed again. A searing warmth spread from his right bicep to his cheek. Another glint of the blade, and a burning seared his clutching fingers. They became slippery. He was losing his grip. When the driver braked hard, he fell. The pavement rushed up, delivering a blow that knocked the wind out of him. As he lay writhing on the street, struggling for air, the Citation sped for the corner.

In the distance, sirens wailed, still a couple of blocks away. Rosa, revolver drawn, dropped to one knee. Taking aim at the rear window, she pulled the trigger. The explosions in her hands were remote, as if at a distance. She squeezed again and again until they stopped.

At Eleventh Avenue, the Chevrolet careened around the corner, skidding almost out of control and ignoring the signals. Rosa was back on the radio, calling in the location and direction. He was heading south at high speed.

"Chase him!" Joe gasped. "Get the bastard!"

She climbed behind the wheel of the turbocharged sports car, still in a fog. For all she knew, Joe and Sammy were dying there on the street. Setting her jaw, she shoved it into first and tromped the accelerator to the floor.

Dante tried to focus on what had happened. Sammy! Jesus! With a lurch, he was on his feet and limping toward his fallen comrade.

Blood was everywhere. The lunatic had slashed him

hard across the neck, severing his carotid artery. No more than a minute had passed, and already his friend was dying. Sammy lay there, desperately trying to hold his life in.

"Fucker got me, Joey. Got me good."

"Take it easy, partner. You're gonna be okay."

Down the street, a squad car squealed around the corner. He flagged it frantically.

"Too late, Joey," Sammy whispered, trying to smile. "Fucker was quick. I let my guard down."

The two uniforms in the patrol unit gaped at the horror confronting them as they leaped from their car.

"Get the goddamn back door open," Dante ordered. "Fast. We don't have time to wait for an ambulance."

Together with the two cops, he struggled to get Sammy into the backseat. "Saint Vincent's. Take Ninth to Fourteenth."

Rosa took the turbo hard around the corner, feeling the power under the hood shoving her back into the seat. The taillights of the Chevrolet were already just pinpricks in the gloom ahead as she accelerated after them. And then they disappeared. Either the guy had turned abruptly or gotten wise and cut them.

"Shit!" she muttered, heart racing. Grabbing the radio, she reported losing visual contact at 29th Street. "I'm moving on to the West Side Highway, south. Suggest coverage north and east." By then half the units in the city had to be converging on the far West Side. South made the most sense to her. There were the most places to turn off and try to get lost quickly. She sped along the roadway, nearly abandoned at that hour. The speedometer pushed up past ninety miles an hour. Any faster on that stretch of road, and she risked going uncontrollably airborne.

* * *

As the cruiser rocketed down Ninth Avenue, siren wailing, Sammy sighed and clutched at Dante's hand.

"Relax, little brother," he said. "Ain't no hospital gonna fix me now."

"You're gonna make it!" Dante hissed.

"Feelin' dizzy already, Joey. Damn. Mother-fucker was quick, wasn't he?" Sammy's eyes were trying to focus on Dante. "Cut you, too, didn't he? Bad?"

"I'm fine."

"Sure, you're fine. We're both just fine. . . ."

"You are, Sammy. I swear to God. Just hang on. We're almost there."

"Not close enough, partner. You take care of Rosa, Joey. She's okay. I think she's good for you."

The big hand gripped tight against his as the huge frame began to convulse.

"No!" Dante screamed. "Don't! You can't!"

By the time they reached the door to Emergency at Saint Vincent's Hospital, Sammy Scruggs was dead. The doctors and paramedics who jerked open the back door of the squad car found a tough-looking white guy cradling the giant black head in his lap. He was sobbing hysterically. There was so much blood that they could not immediately determine the extent of the carnage. It wasn't until they managed to get the grieving man into the Emergency Room that it became apparent much of the blood was his own. He had been cut badly; cheek, shoulder, upper arm, and hand. There were also three broken ribs. The man was so agitated that they had to sedate him before closing his wounds.

Out on the West Side Highway, Rosa Losada could find no sign of the killer. Other units spread out and crisscrossed the lower half of the island. They had no better luck. The dark blue Chevrolet Citation had vanished.

TWENTY

Joe Dante drifted in and out of consciousness. He remembered concerned faces, leaning to peer at him. Bright light. When he finally came to, a uniformed nurse smiled at him.

"How are you feeling?" she asked.

He groaned, trying to move.

"Easy," she said. "You're pretty banged up."

It was painful to breathe. His whole left shoulder and arm were immobilized.

"There are people here to see you," the nurse told him. Turning, she pulled open the door and nodded into the hall. His parents, Rosa, and Gus Lieberman came in.

"Sammy," he croaked. "Where's Sammy?"

"He's in another room, son," his father said. "He's going to be fine."

"He's dead," Dante whispered. "Cheri, too?"

Rosa and the inspector looked at each other.

"Concentrate on getting well," Lieberman said.

"Aw, fuck." The wounded man shook his head. "I don't believe this. I actually touched him. It's a nightmare."

"If you'll excuse us," Lieberman said to his parents. "We'll only be a minute and then he's all yours."

"We fucked it up, Gus," Dante said when his mother and father left the room.

"Did you see him? Can you make him?"

"Just the side of his head. Short gray hair and kinda jowly. Jesus, was he fast. What kind of trouble are we in?"

"Bad enough." Lieberman grunted. "Working with a wire *and* a narcotics man without authorization. They're even hotter Downtown than I am."

Dante's eyes moved to Rosa.

"Chained to a desk pending a full investigation." She nodded. "Then they'll probably suspend both of us. Or worse."

He tried to shift into a more comfortable position again and couldn't. "I got her into this," he told the inspector.

"A good man was killed, not to mention an innocent civilian. You violated the chain of command. I've just been all morning trying to pull a lot of people's fat out of the fire."

After Lieberman left, his parents came back. His mother was beside herself. Something she'd feared for forty years had finally happened. Recognizing how uncomfortable it made him feel, his father helped by keeping it brief. Dante found himself alone with Rosa.

"Well, partner," he said. "It doesn't look good."

She nodded. "Larry Morris is none too pleased. Leiberman knows about the wire and is covering it."

"He what?"

"You heard me," she said, shrugging. "As far as I can tell, it hasn't made it Downtown. If it had, I'd be in jail instead of here."

"Goddamn," he breathed.

"He knows how close we got, Joe. I'm sure he realizes you would do something like this. He assigned you."

"God, I hurt," he complained. "It's a blur, it was so fast. I heard you shooting. What happened?"

"I emptied my gun into the back of his car. Or at least in the general direction. The back window shattered, so I know I hit it. I got a plate, but it was reported stolen. I chased him, but he vanished into thin air. Great, right?"

"And the car?"

"Nothing. Half the department is out looking for it. They're checking every auto glass place in the metro area."

"Tell me about Cheri."

Rosa didn't like this. He was supposed to be resting. They'd put 212 stitches in his shoulder alone. He was down almost a quart of blood.

"Later, okay? I'll give you all the details."

"Now," he insisted.

"She died in the trauma unit five hours ago. The knife punctured her liver. They found her dumped three blocks down Eleventh Avenue. There wasn't ever any real hope."

Rick's first impulse once he dumped the body was to run and keep on running. Then he realized that he needed to get to ground as quickly as possible. The garage in his townhouse was the quickest and closest option. At that hour no one saw the car.

With trembling hands, he released the safety harness. There was blood everywhere. When he kicked her out the door, the whore still wasn't dead.

What had happened? How did they know? He understood the big black pimp. But who was the other? The white man. And who had she screamed for?

The confusion was absolute, as was the terror. His legs

trembled so much that he knew he could not stand. Not for a while. His head fell back on the rest. Chest heaving, he tried to breathe normally. The cold sweat was evaporating, giving him a chill. When his teeth began to chatter, he was not sure if it was from the cold or from relief.

Groping for the door handle, he let himself out of the car. The garage swam before his eyes the minute he stood. Clean the car, the little voice said. Bucket. Soap. Sponges. He had to get rid of the mess. Turn the car inside out if he had to. Clean every square centimeter. And then take a shower. The filth was all over him.

"Oh, baby, baby," he mumbled. Shaking his head, he ran hot water into the laundry tub. "You double-crossed me, you little bitch."

Someone had actually shot at him. Goddamn! Two bullets had hit the back window. The rear seat was full of glass. Once he made sure there was nothing of him left in it, he would have to get rid of the car. And that meant Richard Wakeman had to go with it. Resurrected so many years ago, he was dead again.

Between sobs and curses, he tried to wash out the inside of the car. With all that blood, he had no idea if a fingerprint might lurk in the hidden gore. Slowly, diluted buckets of the carnage were poured down the laundry tub drain. Truly frightened, he washed again and again, sweating in the heat. It was hours before he felt satisfied enough to go upstairs and bathe.

Friday morning broke bright and crisp over Long Island Sound. Out across the water, wisps of steam from the generating plant were torn quickly apart in the breeze. Gulls wheeled and dived for fish. Brennan had worked late setting the mold separators into the clay in preparation for starting work on his wax positives. The actual casting of such a large piece was a drawn-out and painstaking process. Next came the creation of the light plaster and fiberglass negatives into which he would pour enough wax to approximate the thickness and shape of the actual bronze components. He would begin to tackle that this afternoon.

The late hours seemed to have no particular effect on his energy level. The anticipation of the day when he could fire the furnace and pour the molten bronze never failed to charge him. This morning he was up after only five hours sleep. Slipping into swim shorts and rubber thongs, he crossed the lawn and down the flight of wooden stairs to the sand. The water was like a bathtub this time of year. He dived in and swam back and forth, parallel to the shoreline. Using a couple of trees as reference points, he did twenty laps of about seventy-five yards. He was a good swimmer. In the city, the chlorine of pools bothered him, so he ran. But water was what he'd grown up in. Rivers, inner tubes and rope swings. Now the water and the exercise gave him a feeling of invigoration. As he swam, he thought about his work. By the time he got out of the water, he knew more clearly how he'd organize his day.

Wandering back to the house, he enjoyed the solitude. Diana rode back into the city with Charlie and Jill. That was early Monday. He'd had the week to himself, splitting his time between *The Steelworkers* and the pouring of a number of figurine-sized commissions. At night he would drive his '54 Dodge pickup into Niantic for a couple of beers, or he would read.

Breakfast this morning was a leftover pork chop from last night, a couple of eggs, and a beer. Popping the cap, he turned on the radio news. Both the Mets and the Yankees had lost. Pro football season was almost on them again, and a high draft choice had been let go from the Giant's camp. The current heat wave was expected to continue unabated through the weekend.

The hard news broke with the top story of the morning. A tragedy on Manhattan's West Side. Brennan focused sharply when they mentioned Thirty-eighth between Tenth and Eleventh. That was only half a mile north of his place. A cop and a prostitute had been killed. Another detective was hospitalized in stable condition. When he heard the names Scruggs and Dante, he nearly fell off his stool reaching to turn the volume up. Sam Scruggs apparently died of knife wounds inflicted while attempting to foil the prostitute's murderer. His partner also sustained knife wounds. The assailant disappeared, and a four-state search had been launched to find a dark blue Chevrolet Citation, New York license number 6010 AWA.

"Dante!" he muttered, riveted. "Jesus."

Reaching for the phone, he placed a call to the Tenth Precinct in Manhattan and asked for Detective Losada. He was informed that the detective was on leave and couldn't be reached. He left a message asking her to get in touch with him.

Losada, he thought to himself. Dialing Manhattan information, he learned that they had no listing for a Rosa Losada. He tried the 718 area code, hoping there might be something in either Queens, Brooklyn, or Staten Island. This time he got lucky. There was a Rosa Losada listed in Brooklyn. He tried the number.

"Hello?" a voice answered cautiously.

"Rosa Losada?"

"No, she isn't here right now."

"Is there any way I can reach her?" A couple dozen reporters must have already called asking that question.

"May I ask who is calling?"

"My name is Brennan. Brian Brennan. She knows me from the investigation she's been conducting."

"Oh, yes." The woman's voice registered recognition. "She mentioned having met you."

"Listen," he said. "I'm trying to find out how Joe Dante is. Can you have her call me?"

When the woman said she would pass along his message, he left his number. Whatever the detective and his big black friend were cooking up last week, it had apparently blown up in their faces. He felt sorry for the guy. There was something about him he liked. Maybe it was the way he refused to pull punches. Brennan had seen one of the victims. Hearing about Dante being laid open by the guy made his skin crawl.

Rosa returned to see Dante again after her shift. As the one who talked Cheri into wearing the wire and working for them, she had her own baggage. At first they didn't talk much to each other. There wasn't a whole lot to say. She brought the *Post*. They printed an EXTRA to cover the story, managing to dig up some old file pictures of Joe and Sammy from their uniformed patrol days. The two of them looked young and innocent.

"How?" he asked, pushing the paper aside. "It happened so fucking fast. You think you've trained yourself for just this kind of thing. Then there you are, and it's like one of those nightmares where your feet are in cement."

She shook her head. "I don't know. It wasn't like you'd never been there before. I guess it's something that happens. You can't explain it."

"They're gonna try to fry us Downtown." He sighed. "Lieberman may be mad, but he's not going to let them have everything."

"Why not?"

"He can't. He'll sit on it. He doesn't have much choice. If something like that broke, it would be more than just a couple of cops catching the flak. The mayor would want the commissioner's head on a platter."

"They've got detectives from three precincts swarming all over it now, Joe. And I'm chained to a desk."

"We're gonna get him, Rosa. I don't care what it takes. That bastard's ours. And when we're done with him, there's not gonna be enough left over to try in court."

"They've put you on a one-month medical, Joe. I'm stuck sifting through paperwork. We're off it."

"Like hell!" he growled. "This one's personal now. He got away once. The second time I'll be ready for him."

Brennan got a call from Rosa Losada that evening. She sounded tired.

"I appreciate your getting back," he said. "I just wanted to know if there was anything I could do."

"He's going to be fine," she told him. "The cuts are pretty deep. He's lucky he can still use the fingers on his left hand."

"I suppose the fact that the killer wasn't driving a BMW or whatever sort of blows my credibility, huh?"

"Not necessarily. The woman you identified in the picture is the one who was killed.

"Please pass along my best," he said.

"I'm sure he'll appreciate it. He's pretty down right now. Sam Scruggs was his friend for a lot of years."

In the Saturday *Times*, Brennan learned that the funeral for Detective Scruggs was to be held in North Carolina, but that a memorial service would be conducted the following Tuesday at eleven o'clock on the steps of city hall. The fallen officer was to be remembered by a host of prominent religious and civil leaders. Every off-duty police officer in the five boroughs, some fifteen thousand men and women, would be honoring the hero. The exploits of the Condor, given full exposure in the media, had made the dead detective something of an instant legend.

Brian was decided to attend. He felt an odd kinship. It sprang from the impotence he'd felt that night, staring down at the mutilated body. Helpless, he could do nothing more than turn the horror of his discovery over to men like Joe Dante and his friend. They had a thankless job.

TWENTY-ONE

A sea of blue uniforms jammed the plaza in front of city hall. They were so numerous that they filled the immediate area and crowded the sidewalk. There was a mixture of sorrow and anger there. These were people who knew the risks too well. And knew that a man shouldn't have to die the way Sam Scruggs did.

First in his class at the academy after forgoing offers from a dozen eager universities. The All-City defensive lineman who had gone on to earn the gold shield in just three short years. Cited for bravery half-a-dozen times as a detective at the Fiftieth in the north Bronx. Cut down in the prime of his life. A good-humored mountain of a man rendered lifeless by a psychopath on a lonely street, where no one deserved to die. There was no justice in it.

A murmur swept the crowd like a wind as a car pulled to the curb and Inspector Gus Lieberman helped a wounded Detective Joe Dante from the backseat. Beside him, holding his elbow, stood a shapely Hispanic policewoman in dress blues. The three walked up the center steps to the erected dais and took seats in the front row.

The mayor, police commissioner, archbishop, and a number of other clergy and politicians filled the chairs beside them. Sammy's only brother and his wife sat across the aisle. It was all Dante could do to look at them.

One by one, luminaries rose to eulogize the man they'd come to remember. Words of sorrow and of indignation. Next to last, the archbishop, recently elevated to cardinal, extolled the virtues of a man who would selflessly surrender his life in the service and protection of his fellow man. That such an exemplary individual as this should fall victim only deepened the tragedy.

Finally there was only one speaker left. Sam Scruggs's former partner and best friend. A hush fell over the place as the wounded officer struggled to his feet and moved forward with painful slowness.

"Sam Scruggs was my friend," he began, his voice surprisingly strong and resonant for the condition he appeared to be in. "Somewhere in North Carolina, he has a grandmother too old and infirm to be here today. I'm sorry that she could not, because I would like to be able to look her in the eye right now and somehow try to tell her that the pain she suffers is also my pain. Not only because he was my greatest friend, and that he is dead, but because this was going to be his last hurrah. You see, we worked hand in hand for five years, completely cut off from the world. When I would wonder what I thought I was doing out there, he was the one who reminded me of what all of us here have given our lives to. What we had to wade through may have sickened his soul, but he was the kind of man who would never turn his back on duty.

"Sam Scruggs was the guy out there, working in the dark, flushing out the gun or the knife that might otherwise take you down some lonely night. We are here today because without Sammy, and other people with his sort of guts, there might be a whole lot more of these things to go to. Even if you never met him and came to love him like I did, you still loved him. You loved Sam Scruggs because he was everything a cop is supposed to be.

"Sammy wanted to go home to North Carolina and help his sick grandmother with her farm. He told me it's a place where the dirt smells beautiful after a rain. This isn't the way I wanted you to go, buddy. I'm sorry. Wherever you are, I hope God is merciful."

Brennan was waiting for the appearance of Joe Dante when he spotted Stuart Sprague with the mayor and the district attorney. It appeared that all the pillars of the community turned out in force when there was guaranteed television coverage. When the press stopped Ransome and His Honor for questions about the progress of the investigation, the tycoon stood in there tight, making sure he'd be caught by their cameras.

Dante appeared moments later, hounded by reporters. Brennan tried to get close and was buffeted about by a logjam of frantic photographers. Turning to retreat, he was spotted by Detective Losada. Surprise registered on her face.

Waving, she pointed at the car waiting on the curb. When he got close, she enlisted the aid of a mounted cop working crowd control. Together, they managed to get him through the throng and into the empty passenger seat beside the police driver.

"Who's this?" Lieberman demanded as they pulled into traffic.

"It's okay," Dante assured him.

"Why?"

"He knows the score. How're you doing, Brian?" He

reached across the seat, wincing a little with the effort. Brennan shook his hand carefully. It was the first time the detective had used his Christian name.

"Somebody want to fill me in?" Lieberman said.

"This is the man you were so worried about getting into the papers," Dante said. "Inspector Lieberman, Brian Brennan."

While Lieberman registered surprise, it was Brennan's turn to look confused.

"Worried about me? The papers?"

"Concerned citizens for the welfare and image of your father-in-law," the inspector grunted.

Brennan waited for him to continue, but there didn't seem to be anything else forthcoming. His eyes flicked to Dante.

"I understand there's some hot water. What's his status?"

"He's on medical leave."

"For how long?"

"Until Downtown says differently. You're not planning to get up on any white horses of your own, are you?"

"I'm spending the next three weeks at my place in Connecticut on the Sound. It's quiet and secluded. The phone number is unlisted, and a reporter would almost have to have a bloodhound to find the place. An injured man could enjoy unimpeded recuperation there."

"Is that an offer?" Lieberman asked.

"I could cast it in bronze if you'd like."

"Not while Sammy's killer is running around loose," Dante retorted. "There's no way I'm leaving the city."

"Downtown wants your badge, Joe." The inspector shook his head. "I'm not gonna let them have it. But don't tie one hand behind my back, huh? We've got every available man in the city working on this thing now. It's not yours anymore. Go to the beach. Get your rest. Stay outta my hair until I can get some of the ruffled feathers smoothed."

In the end it was Rosa who finally convinced him that it might be okay to lay up for a week or two.

"I'm going to be right here, Joe. There's nothing of even the slightest significance that you won't hear. I swear. I'll be on the phone to you every day. I'll even come up weekends to brief you if that's what you want."

Dante threw up his hands in surrender and almost passed out for the trouble. "Fuck!" He gasped, doubling over.

"Yeah," Lieberman grunted. "You're a real ball of fire, cowboy. Do us both a favor, huh?"

Paul Garriston and J. A. Wainwright rose as the two new arrivals were shown to their table.

"Harry." Garriston smiled, shaking hands with the district attorney. "I'm pleased you could make it. I know you're busy."

Harry Ransome pumped the offered hand enthusiastically. Stuart had asked him to join them for lunch. Such an opportunity was not to be dismissed lightly. Candidacies evolved from just such gatherings. Senator, governor; the sky was the limit.

Sprague was saying something to Wainwright about a horse they had both been involved in syndicating. Apparently, it was showing promise in its first few races. Garriston, meanwhile, was being surprisingly solicitous.

"How is Jennifer, Mr. Prosecutor?"

"Quite well," Ransome replied.

"I'm glad to hear that. Terrible, this thing about the undercover detective. A good man, I gather."

"One of the best," the D.A. assured him. "It was a real tragedy."

"Aren't you getting a little ahead of us, Paul?" Wainwright asked, overhearing them.

"Not at all." Garriston smiled. "We're all here. Sprague?"

Stuart Sprague nodded, agreeing that whatever they were about to discuss could commence any time they saw fit.

"Fine, then." Garriston continued, "We have just learned that the governor intends to run for the United States Senate next year. After careful evaluation of his candidacy, we have decided to endorse him. What we would like to have before his announcement is a handpicked successor. Someone *he* can endorse. You've been a team player, Harry. Stuart recently filled me in on how you handled my son-in-law's involvement in this prostitute thing. I appreciate it. And now I speak for these gentlemen and a dozen other civic-minded citizens in asking you to accept our support of a Harry Ransome governorship."

The district attorney was stunned. He had dreamed that this might someday come to pass. He *had* been a team player. But plenty of such men never got a shot like this. Governor of the state of New York. He turned to smile appreciatively at Stuart. There was no mistaking where this offer came from. Or, for that matter, where his career had come from.

"I'm . . . I'm overwhelmed," he stammered. "This is extremely generous."

"Nonsense," Wainwright scoffed. "You've been an excellent D.A., Ransome. Excellent exposure as well. People know you. You're synonymous with hard-nosed integrity. Law and order. Old values. The man on the street wants that nowadays. We want it."

"You're the best goddamn man for the job," Sprague threw in. "It's as simple as that. The Democrats are going to put up another pantywaist, and we'll fight them with a candidate who stands for something. The climate is very favorable."

Ransome nodded, looking around the table at the three of them.

"I'm flattered," he said. "I could never undertake something like this without your full confidence and support. I accept, and I will do everything to keep you from ever being disappointed."

"Good man," Garriston said, raising his glass. "We have already selected the public relations firm to handle the senatorial race. I trust that working in conjunction with them, we can make this a clean sweep. We'll schedule someone to see you in the next day or so. Current photographs. Updated biography. That sort of thing."

"Okay, what's up?" Diana Webster asked, sitting across from Brennan at a window table overlooking all of Manhattan. "I can smell an ulterior motive a mile upwind."

"I need some help. I'm wondering if you could spend the next couple of weeks up in Connecticut."

"And pay my rent with what?"

"I'll pay you," he said. "The detective who was wounded last week is being discharged from the hospital tomorrow morning. He's going to spend some time recuperating at Pleasure Beach."

"What? A cop?"

"You heard me. We've gotten to know each other the past couple weeks. His best friend was killed. I thought it might be a nice . . ."

"Brother." Diana snorted. "Beneath that crusty exterior beats the heart of a Mallomar. What are you now, the Good Samaritan?"

"He's a decent guy," Brennan returned. "And he's taking some heat right now. He's banged up pretty badly. I thought I might be able to use a hand."

"Why me?" she asked. "Why not hire a nurse."

"Maybe it's just an excuse to get you trapped up

there.'' He grinned. ''I don't imagine I could take the same liberties with a nurse.'' His leg rubbed hers under the table.

''Stop it,'' she snapped, reaching down to swing at him.''Two weeks is an awful long time to have to put up with you at a stretch.''

He shrugged. ''Take weekends off. And maybe I could get Charlie and your good friend Jill to come up and distract you.''

Diana frowned. ''Lay off the kid, huh? She's not really so bad. I'd feel intimidated, too, if I was shoved into a strange situation like that.''

''She's spoiled rotten.''

''But she's good, Brian. You saw her shit.''

''She'll never get anywhere with that attitude.''

''Look at you.'' She laughed. ''You're as big an asshole as they come. And Fung, for God's sake. The man sells paintings for twenty grand a crack, and he's a bona fide pervert. You ask me, Jill Warren fits right in.''

''What do you say we skip dessert, run on back to my place, and screw our brains out,'' he said with a leer.

Diana's eyes widened. ''Are you kidding? When I'm wined and dined to be primed for some bleeding-heart con job, I stay for the chocolate mousse *and* the brandy.''

TWENTY-TWO

Rick was not sure what compelled him to attend the dead detective's funeral. Curiosity most likely. The other man, the white one, had been named in the papers. As a matter of fact, the papers had made many things clear. The big black pimp hadn't really been a pimp at all. They were cops. He had killed a cop. And wounded another. Dante.

How did they know he would be there that night? It was still a mystery to him. He mulled it over and over again in his mind. Had he ever seen this Dante before? The photographs in the papers made it hard to tell. The man he'd slashed looked a lot different than the rookie patrolman in grainy black and white. Seeing him in person, pale and weak, had not made things any clearer. He had no recollection of the man.

Then something happened to confuse him further. On the sidewalk in front of the cathedral, the sculptor, Brian Brennan was ushered to the front seat of Dante's car.

What could it mean? What could the connection possibly be? Dante and this man who gave voluptuous form to inert material.

The little voice inside him was near panic now. He did not want to admit the evidence of a conspiracy against him. Always he had prevailed over the powers seeking to destroy him. But now they seemed to be gaining strength. Could they have detected his intentions? There had been no satisfaction this last time. Only agitation and terror. The surrogate had been perfect, and still communion eluded him? Could Brennan be the agent directing the forces against him. Had he discovered his secret love?

Again this week he had seen the girl sunbathing with friends. The ache he felt drove him to distraction. His mind wandered, unable to deal adequately with his business interests. At every moment he expected to hear a knock on the door and the muffled announcement that the police wanted to speak to him. The fear of it made him so nauseous that on several occasions he actually vomited.

If Brennan knew something and was leading them, he should be watched. To see where he went and who he saw. Perhaps this would lead him to the answers he sought. If he discovered a link, he could destroy it before it could work to destroy his love.

They were looking for a Chevrolet Citation. All the papers said so. The BMW would be safe if he were careful; if he did nothing to draw attention to himself. He wouldn't wear his leather and his jewelry. He would not try to be with her again. He mustn't. Not until he discovered the size of the force opposing him.

It was midnight Tuesday before the ancient Dodge pickup rolled to a stop in front of a Twenty-seventh Street loft building. The artist climbed out. He was with someone. A woman. They walked a little unsteadily, but even in the amber-hued gloom, Rick could make out the lines of her body against the thin cotton jumpsuit. The way it clung to her hips and stretched across her breasts. It made his breath catch in his throat. All the other surrogates paled by comparison. The pictures above his bar flashed through his mind's eye. A perfect match for the girl wriggling to cover her breasts on the terrace.

The bastard! Was this the connection? This Brennan conspiring to steal his love from him by somehow conjuring human flesh instead of metal. A vessel he could never resist? He seethed as he watched them climb the steps to the door of the building. Her leaning into him. His hand sliding down over the curve of her ass. Fornicator! Of course. This was the connection. The man was a sorcerer. Dante and the giant black were his demons. The thought of such evil even touching the vessel made him sweat with fury and the ache of longing. And she leaned into him willingly. She suffered his hand in pleasure. Created at the sorcerer's hand, the vessel would have to be purified before it could ever be used for his holy purpose.

When, at eight-thirty in the morning, Brennan and the vessel emerged from the building to climb back into the truck, Rick was waiting. He sat in a state of bleary-eyed exhaustion. Starting the BMW, he followed at a distance as they crossed town to the East Village. On Saint Mark's Place, he watched as the woman hopped out, waved, and entered the door of Number 62.

The bell had been ringing on and off for a good minute before Dante could struggle far enough out of his pain-killer haze to determine that it was the front door. Trying to move to answer it was another story altogether. It had to be Rosa. She was coming to help him pack and drive him to Connecticut.

"Hi," he grunted, finally making it to the door.

"You look swell," she said sarcastically. "You'd better sit down."

"I feel like I'm ninety fucking years old," he complained, easing onto the sofa. "I don't know what that shit they gave me is, but the aftereffects are almost as bad as the reason I took it."

"Relax," she said, beginning to size up the situation. "Where are your suitcases?"

"Plural?" he asked. "I've got only one. How many suitcases does a guy need when he never goes anywhere . . . except maybe to Atlantic City?"

"You spent three months last year in San Francisco."

"I traveled light."

"You're a joy first thing in the morning. Okay, where is your suitcase, singular."

"In the closet." He pointed.

"Thanks." She opened the door and dug around until she came up with an old leather Samsonite case. "Vintage," she commented. "Anything else in here you want along?"

"Skip the racket," he grunted. "Doubt if I'll be playing much tennis."

It went on like that, him being difficult and her being indulgently understanding.

"Have you eaten anything?" she asked, as she finally closed the lid and snapped it shut.

"I thought you'd never ask," he said, eyes sparkling with the knowledge of the hoops he'd just made her jump through. "I just might be able to limp around the corner and buy you breakfast. If I remember correctly, I still owe you."

She held up a hand, shaking her head. "I'd never take advantage of you in your *condition*, Detective. Please, allow me."

"I'm staying right here if I've got to listen to that crap in the car all the way to New London."

"You're in a weakened state, Dante. Be careful how you talk to me."

Sitting outdoors in a little open-air cafe on Seventh Avenue, Joe asked Rosa for an update on the case. She, unfortunately, had little or nothing to tell him.

"Nobody's been able to come up with either the car or the knife," she said. "They've got the neighborhood so heavily patrolled that the johns are staying away. It's like a detective's convention over there."

"How about that run of black BMWs and LeBarons?"

"Albany sent it down Monday. It goes on for three pages. And almost half of those are registered to corporations. Company cars. Finding out who actually drives them is something else again. And I'll bet you can guess who got the honor."

Dante sighed. It was something he'd had plenty of time to think about. Even with his initial doubts about her, he knew he had jumped too quickly on the negatives of a female partner. Beyond proving herself a damn good cop, she demonstrated a loyalty he found hard to ignore. Her troubles were a product of having agreed to play the game his way, but even now she wasn't blaming him.

"Listen," he said. "Someday I'm gonna make this up to you. How rough is Morris being on you?"

"He's angry, Joe. He resents the flak he had to take. And he doesn't mind giving me his shit work, if that's what you're asking."

He shook his head. "I've never fucked anything up so badly."

"Forget it." She smiled sadly. She knew what he had to be going through. "You took a calculated risk. If it'd worked, we'd all be heroes right now. Believe it or not, I think you've helped me see something more clearly. I really believe now that you can't win big if you don't take chances. We were *that* close."

She held up her thumb and forefinger, a quarter inch between them.

Brennan and Diana had only just arrived and finished putting away the purchases of an extensive grocery shop when Joe Dante and Rosa Losada pulled into the drive. Waving from the shade of the sprawling veranda, they hurried down the stoop to help with the bags. Or bag, as it turned out.

Dante still looked a bit under the weather, his skin color off and his movements obviously causing him pain. Rosa helped him to his feet while Brennan hefted his case.

"You haven't met Diana Webster," Brian said, introducing her.

Dante took in the tall blonde in the shorts and halter top. He recognized her from somewhere.

"You were in one of those girl bands." He grinned. "The one who wore the sequined leopard bodyskin. Dynamite act."

Diana's eyes widened in surprise. "You actually saw Queen of Beasts? Where?"

"It must have been the Mudd Club. About five years ago."

"Outrageous. How could you remember? That's amazing."

"Nope." He shook his head. "*You* were amazing. That had to be about the greatest getup I've ever seen a woman poured into."

"That's pretty hip," she said in amazement. "A cop who used to do the Mudd Club."

"You might not think it was quite so hip if I told you I was doing it as a skinhead narc."

Brennan chuckled, while Rosa rolled her eyes. "I swear," she told him. "He promised to behave himself."

"Don't worry about it," Brian said. "This ought to be great. An undercover skinhead and the original leopard woman. I don't have to worry about them getting along. This is one of six humans on the planet who remembers Queen of Beasts. How many gigs did you play, Diana? Three?"

Dante was shown to a large airy room on the ground floor. One large window and a pair of French doors opened onto a deck overlooking the sound. A fresh load of wood filled a big wicker basket next to the fireplace, and a huge four-poster bed stood directly across from it. He sat on it, testing the firmness.

"Is this going to be okay?" Brennan asked.

"Great," Dante replied. "I want you to know how much I appreciate everything you're doing."

Brennan waved him off. "Forget it."

After sitting in the sun and eating a dinner that proved Diana couldn't cook as well as she stuffed a sequined body stocking, they sat in the roomy study and had brandy. It was then that Dante realized how much Brennan drank. It wasn't that he got out of control, but for every glass he had, his host had three. Diana seemed to be aware of it. As a matter of fact, for someone with the appearance of flakiness, she didn't seem to miss much.

He yawned over his drink and looked at his watch. It was still early, but he'd run out of gas.

"Tired?" Rosa asked. "I ought to get back to the city. It's a long drive."

Joe nodded. "This was as much moving around as I've done in a week. A little bit at a time, I guess."

Pushing himself slowly out of his chair, he said good night to his hosts. Rosa joined him.

"I'd like to come up Saturday, just to look in on him."

"By all means. Why don't you come Friday and stay the weekend?"

"I'll check the duty roster," she said. "They're doing a lot of juggling with all the overtime on this thing." She looked at Joe.

"Come say good night," he said.

Dante sat on the edge of the bed. "It was nice of him to invite you like that."

"I could come Friday night," she said. "But I wanted to make sure you wouldn't rather be alone or something."

"I'd like it."

"I suppose I'd better, just to make sure you aren't being spoiled rotten."

"We're not jealous, are we?" he asked, grinning slyly.

"Of what? Someone with legs like Diana Webster waiting on you hand and foot . . . and you eating it up? Hell, no. Whatever for?"

"You are!" he said gleefully. "I knew it."

"You flatter yourself, Detective."

Almost unconsciously, they caught hands. As they realized it, their eyes met.

"I'm just so glad you're okay, Joe. I don't know what I would do if you weren't. The thought of it gives me nightmares."

Reaching up with his good hand, he brushed her cheek with his fingertips, pushing back her dark, lustrous hair. She was strong. Stronger than he'd ever imagined.

The face he had started seeing when he closed his eyes at night came toward him. His eyes were open now, asking questions and getting answers. Their lips met.

"Take care of yourself, Joseph," she said, fingers lingering on his face. "See you Friday night."

TWENTY-THREE

The game had changed. He drove through there in the light of day and saw them. Everywhere. He wondered who they thought they were fooling in their beat-up Plymouths with stubby little trunk antennas and plain black tires. Plainclothesmen. At least a dozen of them. Did they think he would be such a fool as to go back?

Rick laughed to himself, stretched out on the sofa beneath her in all her enticing invitations to love. They lay in wait for him, and she wasn't even out there anymore. She had become his enemy's whore. And in a way, this only sweetened it. The gauntlet was down. Blood had been drawn. Even in ambush, he had prevailed. The first round was his. The power of his love could overcome sorcery.

Brennan unwittingly tipped his hand in delivering her to the building on Saint Mark's Place. He had her now. He could play her like a cat might a wounded bird. Taking his time. Waiting. Delighting in it.

But first he must dispose of the car sitting in his garage. It was almost a week now since he scrubbed every inch of it in terror. It fairly glistened down there now, except for the shattered rear window glass. But he had a plan so they would not even find that. Carefully, so as not to arouse suspicion, he collected gasoline in plastic containers, one gallon at a time. There were ten of them in it now. Four in the front seat, four in the back, and two in the trunk. He had also siphoned all but a pint from the tank. Heated by the inferno raging above it, the tank would fill with the dense fumes of this remaining gasoline and explode like a bomb. Rick planned it carefully. There would surely be nothing left of a fingerprint, a speck of blood, or even a hair. They would be incinerated, the glass melted and metal twisted in the heat.

With Thursday less than an hour old, Rick climbed into the front seat of the Citation and started it. Directly across the street from the townhouse, a little park fronted on Tenth Avenue. He had only to drive quickly around the block, park in the empty space adjacent to the hydrant on Tenth, light his crude fuse, and move himself quickly back across the park to Twenty-second Street and the safety of his brownstone.

The gasoline-soaked rag lay already in place as he hastily parked and stepped out of the car to light a Lucky Strike. The fumes burned his nostrils as he leaned in the back window, laid the cigarette butt-first against the rag, and walked quickly away.

The garage door hummed closed, and he rushed upstairs to peer out past the front-room shutters. Eventually the chemically treated tobacco of the Lucky carried the cherry-red ember to another, more volitile source of combustion.

At 12:27 A.M. on Thursday, the twenty-second of August, officers Bert Orr and Donna Whelan left the River

Diner with a thermos full of fresh coffee and rolled south on Eleventh Avenue. This was their second extra shift since the Scruggs murder, and they'd had the bad luck to pull a midnight to eight. It wasn't that the duty was so bad. Both of them actually liked the easy pace of things in the wee hours. But ever since Bert was paired with a younger woman, his wife had been having fits. As long as he worked days, she was manageable. But when the rotation took him into the off-hour shifts, she became very difficult to live with. The fact that Donna was engaged to be married in six weeks didn't cut any ice with Bert's wife. Not since she'd suddenly developed herpes six months ago.

Bert must have been a carrier. He had no manifest sign of the disease. Donna swore that her boyfriend hadn't had any either.

"What do you say we ease on down to the cement plant, pull it in out of sight, and mess around a little, huh?" he asked, winking at her.

"I'm not in the mood, Bert. Let's just drive a little, okay?"

Orr smiled to himself, rolling south and blinking his headlights at a cruiser from Midtown South. Turning toward the river, he slid up around to Twelfth, rode past the convention center, and then turned left onto the West Side Highway. At the Circle Line, he guided it into the tour boat lot while Donna threw a little light around just to keep the rats honest.

"What are you doing?" Donna asked a few minutes later.

He had lulled her into a sense of false confidence, making like he was just doing his job while all the time homing in on the cement plant.

Built as a makeshift processing plant for the thousands of cubic yards of concrete the mob had coerced the city into buying for its new convention center, the riverside works were in part isolated from the flow of traffic by a wall of immense concrete blocks. When the supply of sand and gravel was low, as he had noticed it was this evening on the way into work, a car could be tucked neatly away behind them, totally obscured from the view of passing motorists.

"What's it look like I'm doing?" He grinned. "Nooky time."

"I told you . . ."

"I heard what you told me. But those were only words. Your body's saying something different, baby."

"You're impossible," she said.

"Yeah, but you like it." He switched the ignition off and unclipped his equipment belt. "I make you hot like that squirrelly fucker you're marrying never could. C'mon, baby. Loosen up." His hand was already on her blouse, unbuttoning it and sliding in, fingers working their way under her brassiere. When they found her nipple, she gave a little moan of pleasure and moved against his hand.

"Bert!"

Her voice was muffled and far away.

'Bert!"

"Wha . . . ?"

"That's us." Donna was listening to the radio. A car was reported on fire. Twenty-first and Tenth. She reached to grab the radio mike.

"Unit 6312 responding."

Bert was struggling back behind the wheel. "Goddammit!" he grumbled, pounding the door while steering the car in reverse, one-handed.

Back out on the highway, he flipped on his dome lights and siren, cutting around and back across Twenty-third. Even at a distance of two long blocks, they could see a bright orange glow dancing in the night sky. Ignoring the lights, they took the corner wide on Tenth and proceeded the two intervening blocks against the intended flow of traffic.

There, next to the little park at Twenty-second, a car was engulfed in flame. More fire than a car alone could justify.

"Torch job," Orr muttered, jerking the cruiser around to block oncoming traffic in the near lanes. He knew that if the fuel level were critical, the tank could go at any time. Already a little knot of rubberneckers stood dangerously close. Leaping from the car, he waved at them frantically.

"Get the fuck outta there!" he bellowed.

While Donna moved out into Tenth Avenue, directing the sparse traffic away from the scene, Orr gave the burning vehicle a wide berth and skirted it, running east. While moving the onlookers back to a safe distance, he could hear the distant wail of fire equipment. All he could do was keep people out of the way and sit tight.

The two fire units had just pulled on to the scene and didn't even have time to unleash a salvo from their foam cannon when the gas tank went. In a tremendous whoosh of concussed air, the rear of the car came apart, the curbside quarter panel actually bouncing off a concrete retaining wall inside the adjacent park. A bright ball of fire hurtled more than a hundred feet in the air, followed by more acrid black smoke as the remaining plastic and rubber were incinerated. Even the tires were now on fire.

A pair of fire fighters aimed the foam cannon from the top of the truck and sent a great arching geyser washing over the inferno. In another few minutes, the wreckage had been completely smothered. As it sat smoldering, the rest of the firemen went into action, dragging cushion foam into the street with their axes and hitting it with CO^2. The show was over. Residents began to straggle back into their buildings. Apparently, the car hadn't belonged to any of them.

By the time the fire department was finished with the car, nothing remained but a blackened, windowless shell sitting on bare rims. Orr approached for a firsthand look. From the shape of the body, it appeared to have been a fairly late model. But a late model *what?* was the immediate question. The rear end was either gone or so badly twisted that the identifying insignia had disappeared. The vehicle bore no plates. Same problem, more or less, with the front. With all the efforts made by manufacturers to reduce weight as of late, such things as bumpers and grilles, as well as most of the interiors, were made of plastic. These had entirely melted away. Donna joined him in staring at the thing.

"What was it?" she asked.

"Beats me," he answered. "Not our problem."

For no reason he could see, Donna began to chuckle.

"What's so funny?" he asked.

"You forgot something," she said, pointing at his crotch.

Bert Orr had been working crowd control with his fly open.

When Rosa Losada parked in front of the Tenth Friday morning, it wasn't with much enthusiasm that she looked to the shift ahead. More shit work, calling hundreds of names on a list of dead ends while Morris passed occasionally, avoiding her eyes. The rest of the guys in the squad weren't much better. Meehan and Naglack were being particularly abusive now that Dante wasn't around to back her up.

The uniformed sergeant behind the long mahogany front desk nodded as she entered. Separated as the squad of detectives was from the uniformed force, it was hard to get a read on how they were reacting to the recent events.

They tended to be a little less judgmental, she thought, if only because they were removed from the politics of the division. There was no love lost around the Tenth where Pat Meehan was concerned, and word had a way of getting around. If she had a beef with a jackass like him, she had to have something going for her.

"Morning, Rosa," the sergeant said pleasantly. "How's your partner?"

"Feeling a little better, I think," she answered. "Still not running any wind sprints."

"Give him my best."

"I will," she said. "Thanks."

Walking upstairs was like stepping into the deep freeze.

"Losada," Morris barked.

She walked to his door. "Yes, sir?"

"Burned vehicle last night on Twenty-second and Tenth. Suspicion of arson. Take a run over with the book and see if you can dig out the serial number."

Now they had her working burned cars. Great. But at least it would be a break in the monotony of the list. She went downstairs to the precinct commander's office and picked up the Passenger Vehicle Identification book. The Turbo ZX remained parked in front of the station, and she was still the only one with a set of keys. Smiling to herself, she unlocked it and slid behind the wheel. A moment later, she was squealing in reverse out into the street. At the corner, she turned left one block and then back again to drive west to Tenth Avenue.

Every automobile has a hidden manufacturer's serial number stamped somewhere on the engine block. The National Auto Theft Bureau publishes a listing of all current stolen cars and a book telling where the serial number is located on each model. Rosa already knew this before reaching the scene of the wreckage. It should be a fairly simple task. Find the model, find the number, get a little dirty in the process. Bring it back to the squad and run it through the computer. No such luck.

When she saw the thing, her heart fell. To find the model in the book, you had to *know* the model. This twisted heap of metal could have been an asteroid for all she knew. She parked, then sat and stared at it in disbelief.

Finally she decided that the only way to approach the thing was by process of elimination. Paging through, she immediately ticked off cars that were obviously too large or too small. To her surprise, this narrowed the field considerably. A phenomenal number of the cars in the book fell into the subcompact, midsized, and full-sized categories. This car, judged by the distance between its front and rear axles, was what they called a compact. In this category, there were still a large number of entries, ranging from Ford's Tempo to Honda's Accord. Wading through them all could take a week.

She noticed the data included dimensions such as wheelbase, overall height and length, number of cylinders. Maybe this was an answer. Starting the car, she drove around the neighborhood until she found a hardware store. She purchased a measuring tape.

A passing youngster on a bicycle willingly held one end of the tape while she recorded the car's various dimensions in her notebook. She thanked the boy, returned to the Nissan, and sat with the book, comparing each model to her own findings. When the numbers suddenly fell into place like a piece in the sky of a jigsaw puzzle, her heart began to race. The damn thing was a Chevrolet Citation.

Two fun-filled hours later, her blouse ruined by soot and her overall appearance resembling that of a chimney sweep, she returned to the Tenth Precinct and marched into Larry Morris's office. With a look of triumph on her face, she slapped a smudged piece of paper on his blotter.

"What's this?" he asked, looking her up and down in surprise.

"You run that serial number through NCIC, and I'll bet you a week's pay that before it was burned beyond recognition, it was dark blue."

The commander's eyes widened. He picked up the number and stared at it. "Chevy Citation?"

She nodded. "Six cylinder."

"Get on the horn to Sanitation," he told her. "I want that fucker impounded, and I want you to personally escort it to the Queens garage. I'm gonna have a forensics team waiting for it. McDermott! Ainsley!"

As Rosa moved to the phone, the two detectives appeared. Morris handed them the serial number.

"Talk to I.D. I want to know who, what, and where on this thing. It's a dark blue Chevy Citation. Follow it to the end. Now."

TWENTY-FOUR

It was one o'clock before the sanitation truck bearing its load of junk finally pulled off the Brooklyn-Queens Expressway at Fifty-second Street and entered the police department shop. Rosa was right behind them in the ZX. As soon as they stopped, she parked and hurried off to find the division's forensic men.

"That was a fucking car?" one of the two guys said. He threw his cigarette onto the ground and worked it with his heel in disgust. "Why's it always us that gets this shit, Bernie?"

"Because you're ugly, and I'm so brilliant they're criminally envious," the guy called Bernie replied. "Go ahead," he told the Sanit man operating the winch. "Might as well drop it offa there." Pulling a cigar from his pocket, he bit off the end and spat it out. "Go find that mechanic and tell him to get his fanny out here, Russ." He turned to look Rosa Losada up and down. She'd had time to wash but not to change.

"Don't tell me," he said with a grin. "You were in this thing when it burned."

Bernie and Russ, Rosa thought. Oh, brother.

The mechanic they referred to finally ambled over, a sandwich in one hand and a Diet Coke in the other. She wasn't quite sure what the low-cal drink was doing for him. He had to approach being the fattest civilian employee of the department.

"*This* is it?" he asked skeptically, emitting a small belch.

Bernie nodded. "You got it, fella. And if you don't mind, there's a rush on it."

"There's a rush on everything." The mechanic sighed. "I'll rush back here right after I rush to the can. Okay?" He set his soda on the roof of the burned shell and ambled off.

Bernie and Russ began to set up shop, erecting what amounted to a portable laboratory on a long folding table they commandeered. Bernie turned to Rosa in the middle of his preparation, the mechanic still nowhere in the picture.

"I suggest you find yourself a comfortable chair, miss. I got a feeling it's gonna be one of them nights."

Six hours later, stomach rumbling from acute hunger, Rosa watched as the mechanic removed the car's steering assembly and laid it out, piece by piece, on the floor. Inside the backseat area, Russ and Bernie were combing over every square inch of the gutted interior. Seat brackets, loose debris, and other surviving metal fittings had already been removed and examined on the folding table. It was beginning to look like the man had done a pretty thorough cleaning job before he ditched it. Either that or one hell of a job vaporizing any latent evidence.

Stretching, Rosa rose from the chair and walked toward the garage office. When she'd called in over an hour ago, they still had nothing on the car, other than that it belonged to the Hertz Corporation. Hertz was checking records. Picking up the phone, she dialed the squad number and got McDermott.

"Anything, Randy?" she asked.

"Just in," he answered. "Chevrolet Citation 1985 rented to a Richard L. Wakeman. Los Angeles, California. Picked up at Kennedy early last week and paid for with an American Express card. The sergeant has a friend at LAPD checking on the guy. We've got NCIC running him on this end. FBI, banking, motor vehicles. Everything we can think of. Ainsley and I are calling hotels and airlines."

She thanked him and returned to the activity in the garage. They had a name now. Richard Wakeman. But it didn't make sense that he'd just come in from out of town. What about the other murders? The fat whore the previous Friday night. Would a psychopath or anybody for that matter fly into New York every week to commit murder and leave? Anything was possible, but Cheri had talked to the guy midweek as well. And what about the BMW or whatever it was. He'd been seen in it over an extended period of several weeks. And it was dented. Did rental companies let out damaged luxury cars? Not likely.

She wanted to call Joe and update him, but her pals in the wrecked Citation were getting close to where there was little left to interest them. Parts and pieces were strewn everywhere. It was beginning to look like any secret the car might hold was going to be carried to the scrap yard.

"Detective." Bernie motioned to her. "Come over here a second." He had been inspecting the doorpost directly behind the driver's seat.

Rosa snapped out of her rumination and hurried over.

"Check this out." He pointed. A small, perfectly round hole had been punched into the metal.

"I passed over it twice, thinking it was a bolt hole until

I checked the opposite side over there. I just measured it. Same dimension as a thirty-eight caliber slug would make. You say you shot at this guy?"

"I emptied my gun at him."

"Then it looks like you were only about eight inches unlucky. Let's see if I'm right."

Picking up an elongated red power tool with SAWZALL emblazoned across it, he began to cut a hole in the door-frame where it met the rocker panel. It took about five minutes before he had an area large enough to fit his fist into. Dousing the cut area with cold water, he aimed the beam of his flashlight inside.

"What do we have here?" he asked, reaching in and producing a distorted little chunk of lead. It had mushroomed on impact with the post, peeling its own outer layer back like a banana. More distortion was probably attributed to the intense heat of the fire. But secreted within the protection of the heavier-structure steel, it hadn't melted.

"It's my guess,"—Bernie winked—"that there's still enough here to get a match with another bullet fired from your gun."

By the time Rosa Losada returned to the Tenth's squad room, it was almost midnight. She still hadn't eaten dinner, but she *had* accompanied Bernie and Russ to the forensics lab at the academy on East Twenty-first Street and watched as they fired her gun into the water tank. Upon comparison, the results were conclusive. The burned Chevy Citation had been used in the murder of Cheri and Sam Scruggs.

McDermott and Ainsley were still on the phones, working down hotel and motel *Yellow Page* listings for a fifty-mile radius. It was too late to phone Dante. He needed his rest. Tossing her handbag on a chair, she pulled up in front of a phone and had the two other detectives give her some of their lists.

Up early Friday morning, Brian Brennan crawled out of bed quietly to avoid disturbing Diana. She lay on his pillow, arms wrapped around it as if it might disappear if she let it go. Hair tousled and mouth slightly ajar, she was the portrait of peace. Brian was pleased with how things were going. Even though the wounded detective was from a different world, she had taken to him. Thursday afternoon the pair played backgammon in the sun. No innocent when it came to the world of fast-paced nightlife and drugs, Diana was invariably intrigued by the idea of infiltrating it to ferret out the hustlers and big-time suppliers. Dante was no idiot either. He knew what the scene was like. All he had to do was look at her to know that she took it all pretty seriously. Spiky hair, close-cropped on the sides, eccentric eye makeup, and blood-red lipstick. But there was something earthy and basically upfront about both of them. They respected each other, and the curious chemistry worked.

The sun was up bright and sharp in the sky. There was no fog on the water, and the day promised to be warm. Topping the stairs to the beach, Brennan was surprised to see the lone figure of Joe Dante struggling determinedly across the flat, wet sand below the tide line. Dante saw him as he hit the beach and waved.

"Nice day," the detective puffed, out of breath.

Brennan moved to drop in step with him. "You're not letting any grass grow under your feet," he observed.

"Can't let myself get totally out of shape just because I've got a few scratches," Dante said.

"And broken ribs?"

"Cracked," Dante corrected. "Going for a swim?"

"Gets the cobwebs out," Brennan replied.

The two men parted. Dante continued to puff slowly up

and down the beach while Brennan stroked back and forth in the water just offshore.

Forty minutes later, Brian hauled himself out of the water, pooped, to discover Dante still at it. Wandering wobbly-legged up the beach, he collapsed on his towel and lay there panting in the sun. Dante, looking pretty worked over himself, angled toward him and collapsed on one knee, wincing.

"Mind if I join you?"

"Not at all," Brennan said. Swinging around, he kicked the edge of his towel in Dante's direction. "Have a seat."

The detective joined him in staring out over the Sound past the generating plant to the horizon.

"Gotta hand it to you, Brennan," Dante said. He swallowed hard, still a little out of breath. "It's nice up here."

As if on cue, they heard a cheery voice behind them on the stairs. Turning, they watched Diana come toward them. She was dressed in a loose-fitting cotton tunic, wore no makeup, and her hair was even more disheveled than usual after the night's sleep.

"Everybody feeling all healthy?" she asked as she approached.

"Just hunky-dory," Dante said.

"How's the water?" she asked Brennan.

"Same as yesterday. Warm."

Crossing her arms over her head, she grabbed the loose fabric and pulled it over her head. Tossing it to the sand, she stood before them in a stunning black one-piece suit. French-cut up high over her hipbones, scooped to coccyx in the back, and plunging in a deep V down past her navel in the front. Only some marvel of engineering kept it all where it was supposed to be. Turning, she ran toward the water and dived in.

"Holy shit!" Dante muttered.

"And you thought the leopard sequins were wild." Brennan laughed.

"They were. But damn . . ." He shook his head.

"I've got a feeling your lady detective cuts a pretty decent figure in a bathing suit," Brian said. "I'm a student of such things."

Dante looked over at him. "And what's that supposed to mean?"

"That I'm not blind." He shrugged. "And neither, it would seem, are you."

A tiny smile flickered at the corners of Dante's mouth as he said, "I appreciate your inviting her for the weekend."

"Joe. We found it." It was Rosa on the phone and she sounded excited.

"Slow down. What? What did you find?"

"The car. The guy ditched it and burned it in Chelsea. The lab recovered one of my bullets. There's a positive match."

"Any I.D. yet?" he asked.

"Hertz rented it to a guy named Richard Wakeman. He used his American Express card. They list his residence as L.A. A friend of Morris's checked him out last night. He owns a condominium in a place called Hermosa Beach. Neighbors say he's hardly ever there."

"How about a description?"

"They're working on it. So far all we have is a heavyset man, gray hair, probably mid- to late fifties. He seems to have perpetually worn those reflective French sunglasses. McDermott, Ainsley, and I spent all last night checking every hotel in the metro area. Airlines, too. Nothing. The last activity on his credit cards was the car rental at Kennedy. He wasn't listed on any passenger manifest from L.A., and once he picked up that car, he seems to have vanished."

"How about credit card activity before that?"

"This is the strange part," she said. "There's nothing for almost two months. He bought a ladies' wristwatch from a jeweler on Rodeo Drive. Eight thousand five hundred dollars. And nothing before that for another two months. Seems strange, doesn't it?"

"One eighty-five–hundred–dollar watch," Dante mused. "Yeah, that's odd. What do this Wakeman's bank balances look like?"

"He's loaded. Fifty-thousand dollar C.D.s at three California banks. The condo is owned outright, and they say it's a beauty. Right on the beach. His credit is excellent. And get this; a judge okayed a search warrant for his place. They found seventy-eight thousand dollars in a shoe box."

After Dante thanked her for keeping him up on it and asked when she would arrive that evening, he hung up the phone and wandered out into the sunshine of the deck. Brennan had walked down to his shop after breakfast, and Diana was inside trying to work something out on the piano. From where he sat, he could hear the now-familiar melody line start, falter, stop, start again. Each time coming a little more together.

The son of a bitch had been in the city all the time. He was sure of it. Maybe he'd taken a quick trip out to L.A. to rent the car, but Wakeman wasn't his real name. He could feel that in his bones. It was something dope dealers did all the time. Put together a separate identity and establish a safe house somewhere. Salt away some bank and ready cash reserves. This Wakeman or whatever his real name was had done a first-class job of it. In New York, they could chase this shadow of a man until hell froze over. Unless he'd done something fundamentally stupid, he could simply turn his back on it all and cease to exist. Dante doubted that this one had done anything stupid.

"You slippery fuck," he muttered through his teeth.

They weren't dealing with an ordinary psychotic. This one was smart and still lucid enough to plot and counter. That almost entirely ruled out a drug-induced disorder. He was much too stable. However intense his paranoia was, it hadn't crippled him yet.

Sitting there, Dante turned his attention to his own condition. A full week had elapsed since the incident. He was on the mend. Getting out of the city might not have been such a bad idea. Out here, his mind had a little distance on things. His body was healing quickly. Already the ribs hurt only when he moved abruptly. The hand wound was completely scabbed over and was starting to itch. That was a good sign. The wound across his shoulder and upper arm was going to take a little more time. But Brennan had a doctor up here who would take the stitches out Monday. Real solid scar tissue would start forming a couple of days after that. The worst bruised soreness was gone now, and he could move without stiffness. Still, it was going to be another few weeks before he felt whole again. Sighing, he lay back in his chair and closed his eyes.

TWENTY-FIVE

All Wednesday evening he watched the building on Saint Mark's Place, until early Thursday morning. She never appeared. He watched again Thursday night and still did not see her. There were twenty apartments in the building. He read all the names on the buzzers. Which was hers? It frustrated him not to know it. By the time Thursday turned into Friday and he had still not seen her, he was beside himself. She had to be with Brennan. But there was no activity at his address either. No lights. No pickup truck. In the face of this, his loathing grew. He'd never hated a man more. A conspiracy to rob him of the one real treasure in his life had been launched against him. The desire for revenge grew in his heart.

In the very early hours of Friday morning, he returned to his townhouse. The girl still posed there before him, spreading herself, beckoning. But now her smile seemed to be mocking him. Furious, he took a felt-tipped marker to the pictures, scrawling large speech bubbles, their tails touching her lips. Into them, he put words of longing, hunger, and lust. She told him what she was dying to have him do to her. When he finished, she posed there in her multitude of aspects, describing a litany of his fiercest desires. Unzipping himself, he knelt before them and began to read her words. His excitement grew.

When Rosa arrived late Friday night, Brennan informed her that she hadn't missed much at dinner. They were drinking in the front room, a fire crackling on the hearth.

"I had a quick burger on the road," she told him. "Traffic was murder."

"You look like you need a drink. You've got some catching up to do."

"Forget about trying to catch *him*," Diana remarked. "The two of us are still within reach."

Rosa accepted a rum and tonic. "How's the patient behaving himself?" she asked, settling in.

"He took me for fifteen bucks this afternoon. Never play dollar-a-point horseshoes with a one-armed man. The sympathy factor will kill you." Diana was grinning.

"Sounds like rough duty," Rosa commented. "Sure you can handle it?"

Dante was trying to keep a sober face. "It's all bullshit. She thought she could take advantage of me."

Rosa smiled. "He looks rested enough to me," she said to Diana.

"Two days of sun have given him a glow." Diana snickered. "That and my cooking."

"*That's* what that is?" Brennan asked.

"It's not so bad." Dante shrugged. "She's getting better. Tonight it was hot."

"Screw you guys," the victim of this abuse retorted. "I know what *he* eats"—she pointed at Brennan—"a man who thinks *everything* melts at twenty-two hundred degrees. Including toasted cheese."

Brennan drained his glass and pushed himself to his feet.

"I can get this sort of abuse by opening any art magazine." He smiled good-naturedly. "Charlie and Jill are threatening to make it up early tomorrow. With the headache I figure to be nursing, I'd better hit the hay now, or the day will be shot."

Diana rose to join him. The two said their good nights and departed. Dante and Rosa sat, finishing their drinks.

"How are you making out?" Rosa asked. "Is everything okay?"

"I'm not sure I understand what makes them tick, but I like them. And the liquor's good."

"No shortage, either," she observed.

"We're all up here relaxing," he said. "I don't know how he manages it day in and out though. The man is up at the crack of dawn like it was Seven-Up he was drinking all night."

"Practice." Reaching across, she caught his good hand in hers. Their fingers intertwined.

"No second thoughts?" he asked.

She shook her head.

"Do you wonder if it could work?"

She smiled. "I think the ingredients are there. It's not like I haven't been thinking about it."

His fingers gripped tighter. The man was about to become her lover, and there was little doubt in her mind that it was what she wanted. He saw her eyes appraising him, taking in the bulk of the shoulder bandage beneath his shirt and the wrapping on his left hand.

Biting her lower lip, she suppressed a chuckle.

"This is going to be tricky." Rising, she led the way to their room.

* * *

The two detectives were relaxing in the shade of the veranda Saturday afternoon when a Mercedes 600 Limousine turned into the drive. The crazy Chinese painter and his pretty young friend were down in the studio with Brennan. The three of them were presumably drawing Diana in the buff, a notion that kicked Dante's imagination into overdrive. Not that he wasn't feeling pretty good about his own situation.

The elaborate automobile came to a halt on the gravel drive. A uniformed chauffeur climbed out from behind the wheel and opened the rear door. Two elegant, expensively attired women got out, shading their eyes against the bright light of day. One appeared to be in her early forties, the other about thirty-five. Both were tall, aristocratic, good-boned. Their hair was that color blond only a Madison Avenue salon can create.

"Where are they?" the older of the two women demanded, spotting the pair on the porch.

"I beg your pardon?" Dante asked.

"My daughter and that wretched painter. Where are they?"

"I'm not sure I like the way you're asking," Dante returned. Brennan had mentioned who Jill was. So this was Mrs. Stuart Sprague. It would appear that the big man wasn't the only one who liked to throw his weight around.

"Mrs. Sprague doesn't like to be kept waiting, buddy," the gorilla in the jacket and hat broke in. "I suggest . . ."

"I suggest you fuck off, chump!" Dante cut him off. The guy had a thick neck and hands as big as hams. The wounded detective had his PPK stuffed into the waistband of his pants at the small of his back. It was silly, up there in Connecticut, but he frankly felt naked without it.

The big guy looked surprised, like a pit bull who'd just been barked at by a toy poodle. At that moment the door to the studio down the hill opened, and Brennan stepped out. First surprise and then anger registered on his face as he strode up the path toward them.

"What the hell are you doing here?" he asked the younger of the two women.

"She's helping me find my daughter," Penny Sprague told him. "Is she down there in that . . . *barn*?"

"No one invited you here."

"No one had to," the younger woman countered. "Connecticut is a community property state, Brian. Or have you forgotten that we are still married?"

Brennan shot the woman a dirty look. Dante glanced quickly at Rosa. So this was the estranged wife. The almighty Paul Garriston's daughter.

"Goddammit, Lisa. What do you want from me?"

"Nothing, Brian. I've finally seen through you. I know all about that punk tramp."

For a second, Dante thought Brennan was going to hit her. He saw the reflex of the fist clenching and the muscles of his jaw tightening. And then, just as quickly, they relaxed.

"She doesn't measure her worth by the size of her stock portfolio. I'll bet you can't comprehend that."

It was Lisa's turn to look like she might do damage. But more immediately, Penelope Sprague had broken away from the two combatants and was heading toward the studio under a full head of steam. Brennan took off in hot pursuit, Lisa on his heels. Dante and Rosa were left to entertain the chauffeur.

Brennan had gone to the house for beer and soda. Diana, unclothed, had only recently moved from a draped pedestal to recline on the chaise. Her back started to ache after two hours of sitting in one place.

Suddenly the door flew open and an aristocratic-looking

woman with fire in her eyes stormed in on them. Brian and another woman were seconds behind her.

"I will not stand for this, young lady," the woman barked at Jill. "You are coming back with me this instant." She turned the wrath on Fung. "And you! You are disgusting. Do you have any decency? She could be your daughter!"

"I don't believe you and I have ever had that pleasure," Charlie replied, a little nonplussed.

Penelope Sprague appeared to be in imminent danger of stroke. Lisa leaped between them.

"How can you associate with an animal like this?" she snarled at Jill. "After everything your parents have done for you. I think it's scandalous!"

"Hey," Charlie said. "Look who's here. The Ice Queen."

Lisa wasn't backing off. "Him and this . . . this *whore*!" She spat the word at Diana.

Brennan had awakened with a worse headache than usual. Brandy often did that to him. It took some effort to get on top of it to the point where it no longer interfered with his functioning. Suddenly it came storming back, locking up on his back brain like the overheated brakes of a Mack truck.

"Get out!" he roared at Lisa, turning purple with rage. For a moment it looked as though he were going to swing at her. "You fucking bitch! And you want to know why I want a divorce? Because you're a walking goddamn disease! How dare you come in here like this!"

Real fear filled Lisa's eyes. She was backpedaling into the bright sunlight of the yard. Brennan was right on her, leaving Penelope Sprague alone with his guests.

Fung got a funny look on his face. He was staring hard at Penny, brow furrowed. "Wait a minute." His eyes lit up. He pointed at her. "I knew it was something, but I couldn't put my finger on it. Late 1969. I had my first really big show. At the Simon in Pasadena. There was a big opening party."

Penny's mouth opened.

"Or were you too wasted to remember?" Charlie continued. "Lots of L.A. show biz types. Rocking Randy Warren and his debutante wife. How old were you then, Mrs. Sprague? Twenty-eight? Thirty at the outside?"

Jill was looking quickly back and forth between them.

"Time can really change a person." Charlie shook his head. "Fifteen years. We were all different then, weren't we?"

"What are you talking about?" Jill asked.

"Your mother and your late father. They were an outrageous pair. You must have been only three or four then. A month after my opening, I remember reading about the crash. Rock 'n' roll superstud mixes half the drugs in the PDR and tries to fly his Ferrari across Laurel Canyon."

Penny Sprague stood rigid with wrath. "You're a bastard, mister!" She seethed.

"Straighten your halo." Charlie grunted. "You were doing such a wonderful job of fooling everyone. Including yourself."

Penny turned to her daughter. "Are you coming?" she asked. Her voice was small and tight in her throat.

"Not now." The girl shook her head. "I'm working. I'll be home tomorrow night. We can talk then."

TWENTY-SIX

The three men were talking about the upcoming political campaign. The usual breeze that prevailed far out on Long Island had died in the early morning and it was hot. Stuart Sprague and Harry Ransome had decided to forgo their tennis game. Even in such weather, the time could be used profitably. Sprague found Paul Garriston in and invited him over for a swim. With Mary gone, Garriston's Hamptons weekends were less social now. And with Lisa visiting, he welcomed the diversion. While he and his friends plotted the state's immediate future, the three women sunbathed by the pool.

Something strange had happened to Lisa since her return from her lousy husband's Connecticut place the previous night. She didn't want to talk and had gone directly to bed. But this morning she appeared poolside at Sprague's in a stunning new bathing suit. She was proud of her body, but this eclipsed anything he had ever seen her in. It was almost as if she were flaunting herself. While they were talking, she came over and rested her hand playfully on Sprague's shoulder, asking him to rub lotion on her, when one of the other women obviously could have. Sprague and Ransome ate it up. When she climbed out of the pool, nipples straining against the glistening fabric of the skimpy suit, she arched her back, tossing her head and stretching like a cat. He would not have wanted his friends to know the thoughts that he was thinking, all the while being too aware of theirs.

"That son-in-law of yours needs his head examined," Sprague joked pointedly, prying his eyes from her long enough to sip his drink.

For once Harry Ransome did not feel he was sucking up when he joined them in a nervously lewd chuckle.

By Wednesday whatever progress made in the investigation petered out in a series of dead ends. Richard Wakeman had apparently been seen briefly by the pool of his Los Angeles condominium, rented a car in New York the next morning, and vanished. Four of his West Coast neighbors gave police composite artists four entirely different facial descriptions. The only common element was the sunglasses. Apart from those, the heavy, jowly head was featureless.

Rosa's own search for the small black car proved equally frustrating. Even after following Dante's suggestion of eliminating all owners who were under fifty and not male, she was still stuck with about 40 percent of her original list. The corporations were the biggest problem. Without a positive I.D. on the make and model, she felt as if she were chasing her tail. And then some companies were holding companies for other companies. It went on and on.

* * *

"I've been wondering how in hell you do that."

Brian Brennan turned from his work to find Dante leaning against the shed door. He had been there almost a week now and looked about 80 percent better than when he arrived. His face glowed with the sun. He walked without stiffness.

"This?" he asked, pointing at his work. A slimy substance coated part of it, and thin metal fins protruded everywhere, cutting it up into sections.

"Yeah. Turning a clay positive into a bronze positive. What's that shit you're brushing on there now?"

"Silicone rubber," Brennan said. "It's a little complicated, but basically, it goes like this: These fins are called separators. Something this big is just about impossible to cast whole. So we try to break it up along natural lines. Once the component pieces are cast, you braze them back together. Follow me?"

Dante nodded, stepping closer.

"The actual casting process is called the lost wax process. That's because you make a mold of the clay positive, pour wax into it, build molds around the pieces of wax, melt the wax out into a kiln, and pour molten metal into the resulting void."

The detective was fascinated. "So why the silicone?"

"Soap and then silicone," Brennan corrected. "You want something that will flow into all the detail and undercuts. The soap is just to prevent the rubber from sticking. Once you have a coating of rubber on the thing, you back it with a mixture of plaster and fiberglass. These separator fins work to break the mold pieces up, creating the sections I was talking about."

"So after you put this rubber all over it, you put plaster on top of that?"

"Right."

"And then you pour wax into the mold. Got you."

"Just a coating of wax," Brennan said. "No more than a half inch thick. Statues are hollow inside."

"I guess I've just got to see it."

"Be my guest. It doesn't all happen overnight. Something this size will take almost two weeks to cast. But if you're still around for the hot metal, you're in for a treat. There's nothing sexier than pouring liquid bronze."

"So he says!"

They both turned to find Diana standing at the door in her bathing suit. "Watch out, Joe. He gets all mushy about molten metal."

Dante turned to Brennan. "This looks like a lot of work, and I'm feeling a little antsy sitting around all day. Could you use a hand? Uh . . . literally?" He held up his one good appendage.

Brennan shrugged. "If you really think you're feeling up to it. Sure. Why not?"

Diana wandered up and slid her arms around Brennan, leaning into him. "I knew you'd steal him from me. You're heartless."

Brennan reached a hand around behind her and slapped her ass. "Don't you have some music to work on or something?"

She pushed off, smiling at Dante. "I'll remember this, Detective."

"It's nothing personal." He grinned slyly. "Just an excuse to keep you from winning any more of your money back."

Obsessed beyond any control now, Rick watched each night. Thus far, she had failed to appear. Up and down that strange street, punks in multicolored mohawks, bleached butchered hair, and shaved heads came and went in a steady stream. But never once did the punk goddess appear.

Brennan had surely taken her away with him. He had a place somewhere on the Sound where he worked. Rick had also learned that this Dante had left town. The police department was calling it medical leave. He knew better. The sorcerer was secretly marshaling his forces for the final battle.

He saw the girl again in a bathing suit. A different one this time. She looked so glorious in it he ached to touch her. But to do so would be dangerous. Not until he won out over his enemies. By now he was certain that they had discovered his weakness. Until he could defeat them, the love itself was vulnerable. He would never risk something so precious.

So he sat in the BMW enduring the unpleasant task of waiting. He knew this was the key. The means his enemies meant to employ to bring him down. Only through her and with her in his power could he hope to turn the tables and preserve his secret. Preserve it for the moment of his ultimate glory.

Rosa Losada arrived in Pleasure Beach Friday evening to find a Joe Dante well on the road to recovery. Diana told her that since he started helping Brennan with *The Steelworkers*, he'd been like a little kid. After dinner, Joe took her by the hand and led her down to the foundry to show her what they'd been up to.

"This is a wax positive ready to have the mold built around it." He pointed at the front half of a body trunk. The thing had more than a dozen wax tubes branching off it like limbs of a tree.

"What are these?" Rosa asked.

"They're called gates," he told her. "The main uprights are risers, and the feeders are runners. When you pour the metal down into the mold, the gasses inside have to be able to escape. Otherwise, you get pockets that end up as big bubbles in the bronze. With these, the metal goes down inside, and when the thing is full, it runs back out the top."

"You sound like you're enjoying yourself."

He nodded. "It's sort of fun. You look at a monument in the park, and you never stop to think that something like this has to go into it. You take it for granted."

They walked back out into the night air. "You haven't told me what's going on with Internal Affairs yet," he said.

"It's not great news. It looks like we'll get a few month's suspension without pay. Inspector Lieberman told me today that they won't take our shields."

"Great." He grunted. "When are we supposed to hear?"

"No later than midweek. From what I understand, there's a battle going on Downtown. Your friend the inspector is putting up a stiff fight."

"How is Morris treating you?"

"Better since I found the car. But everyone's frustrated that it hasn't turned up more. They've had the whole West Side blanketed, and the guy hasn't hit again for two weeks. It's getting on everyone's nerves."

"He may be crazy, but he's not stupid," Dante said. "What happened that night had to scare the crap out of him. He's going to lay low. Maybe even abandon that area altogether. Who knows? Maybe the next time he finds himself in the mood, he'll try the Brooklyn Bridge."

"I wish something would happen soon." She sighed. "It might take a little of the heat off you and me. . . . Oh, I almost forgot to mention it. Our wonderful district attorney has decided to have his own people investigate the circumstances surrounding Sammy's death."

"He's what?"

"He's running for governor, is what he's doing. They announced it this afternoon. About half an hour later, one of his assistants called Downtown to tell them they're looking into the possibility of criminal misconduct in our handling of the investigation."

"Grandstanding fucking slime!" Dante spat. "A chicken shit like Harry Ransome thinks he can be governor?"

"He can," she said seriously. "A bunch of leading citizens headed by our host's father-in-law are bankrolling him."

Dante shook his head in disgust.

The next morning Brennan drove Diana to the train station in New London. With Rosa up for the weekend, Dante's baby-sitter figured she could slip into town for a couple of days, try out some new material she'd been working on, and give Charlie some time. To hear it from him, he desperately needed her body to finish a painting he was working on.

It was noon before she arrived at Grand Central Station, where she flagged a cab and went directly to her apartment. She undressed and took a cold shower to cool off from the sweltering heat. Then she sat down wet in front of a fan and made some phone calls.

Charlie was delighted to hear she was in town. He pressed her for a time when they could work.

"Tonight?" he asked.

"Tomorrow," she countered. "You can have me all day. I promise."

"Why not tonight?"

"I've been talking to some guys about fronting their band. They have a gig at a club downtown, and I want to catch it."

"But those things never start until late," he argued. "Just a couple of hours. I'll throw in dinner."

"Where?"

"You're a bitch," he complained. "Okay. Your choice . . . as long as it's close by."

She promised she'd be there by four o'clock. The doorbell rang. It was the lead guitarist of the new band. A guy named Tommy. For the next three hours, they sat together on her piano bench while she played and they discussed her new material. At three forty-five she left him with the assurance that she'd see him later that night and stepped into the street to flag a cab.

When she finally appeared on the front stoop, talking to the skinny guy with oily black hair and an earring, Rick was so prepared for another evening of disappointment that it was a full thirty seconds before he realized it was her. Then she moved away from the guy to step into the street, and the grace of her walk, a memory burned into his mind, triggered recognition. She moved like a jungle cat, totally confident and self-assured. A cab pulled to the curb. He started his car.

The taxi took her down to Prince Street in SoHo. She climbed out and mounted the low landing of an old manufacturing building with one of those ornate cast iron facades. There was an upscale pristine gallery on the ground floor, giant plate-glass windows fronting the street. But she was apparently headed upstairs. Pulling in next to a fire hydrant, he switched off his engine and waited.

The time ticked slowly by. On the street, well-dressed tourists wandered in and out of the gallery and past the car. They were a completely different crowd from the one in the East Village. A little older and certainly more affluent. People who embraced social convention rather than rebeled against it. Rick felt more relaxed here. It had to be one of his enemies' little touches to hide her over there, figuring that he would never suspect. But he had discovered their tactic and endured the hours of unpleasantness. In the end he would make them pay for it.

Evening arrived, and the crowds shifted from sightseeing to dining. It was a Saturday night, and many of them were now decked out in their weekend finery. First dinner and then on to explore the city's nightlife. Rick watched them, growing impatient.

The door opened at eight-fifteen, held by a strange-looking Chinese man. Recognition started Rick's blood to boil. And then confusion. *Two* women were leaving the place with him. Brennan's whore and *the girl!*

Sweat broke out on his forehead. It wasn't possible. But they were laughing together, walking west on the sidewalk with the Chinese man beside them.

"Oh, God," he moaned to himself as he started the car. He waited until they were almost a block ahead before pulling away from the curb and creeping along behind them. They walked three blocks to a French restaurant and entered. Again, he parked and waited. His mind was in turmoil now. He could not figure what this might mean. The Chinese man was obviously one of Brennan's agents. But how could the girl be a part of this?

Diana hadn't expected Jill. Charlie explained that when he finally convinced her to give him a few hours, he called the girl and told her to bring her pencils. She was at her parents' place on the Island all week, trying to mollify her mother. With some big buyout brewing in town, Stuart hadn't been around much, and together, they apparently ironed out some of their differences. Tonight she had supposedly returned to the city for a party.

Throughout the course of the evening's work and then dinner, Diana wondered if she saw Charlie already losing interest in his latest teenybopper. He seemed preoccupied and distant.

"Listen," she said. "Why don't you two come down to this club with me. Tell me what you think of the band."

"Let's!" Jill said excitedly.

Fung shook his head. "My gallery is going to kill me if I'm not ready for this show. Why don't you two go?"

Jill looked disappointed. "But we'll be out late. How am I going to get back in?"

Charlie gave her a weary smile. "Not tonight, baby, okay? I'm going to be beat. I think you should just go back uptown."

Diana ceased to wonder.

When they left the restaurant, she and Jill hopped into a cab to go to the club. Charlie waved good-bye and walked east toward home.

Diana's friends were not due onstage until after midnight. This was typical. The real crowd didn't start showing up until eleven, and it wasn't jammed for at least an hour after that. She and Jill edged their way through a crowd of supplicants, milling around the front door in hope of being chosen to go inside.

One of the two bouncers recognized the former singer for Queen of Beasts. He signaled her and her friend up the steps. Unhooking the chain across the entrance, he let them inside. Jill fumbled in her bag for money. Diana touched her arm.

"No problem. I haven't paid to get into a club in years."

"No kidding?"

Diana shrugged. "Sure. Everybody knows me." As if to prove her point, at least a dozen equally current-looking types crossed paths with her and exchanged greetings inside the first five minutes. After an unhurried drink at the downstairs bar where Diana introduced Jill to a number of aspiring rock 'n' roll players and other assorted New Wave arts types, they set off for the backstage room containing Tommy's band.

Dressed in loose-fitting black pj's, sandals, and blood-red headbands, Pol Pot and his Commie Snots were drinking, making trips in twos to the little bathroom, and loosening up. If Diana joined them, the current name would have to go, but what was a name when Diana Webster was threatening to lend her raunchy chords to the cause? They were all glad to see her, and the level of excitement in the room rose as Tommy mentioned a particular new tune she had played for him. He plucked it out on his guitar, bending the strings in a furious vibrato with his left hand. The drummer quickly picked up his lead and was pounding it out on the back of a metal folding chair. One by one, the rest of them followed the lead.

"Let's do it," the synthesizer player shouted. "You up for it?" he asked Diana.

"Yeah," Tommy said. "End of the first set. Why not?"

Diana shrugged. "Sure." She smiled. "If you want."

Jill and Diana were standing together in the audience when Tommy grabbed the mike and announced that they had a little surprise tonight. Diana Webster, former singer with Queen of Beasts and She-bang was going to do something new for them. The singer bounded on to the stage.

At four in the morning, Diana and Jill pushed through the front door and down the stairs to the street.

"That was great," Jill said, beaming. "*You* were great. Charlie told me you sang, but I had no idea."

"Glad you had fun," Diana said. "Share a cab?"

"That's okay. You're going east, and I'm headed almost straight up."

Diana shrugged, and together, they stepped into the street. One cab sat waiting for a fare.

"You take it," Jill insisted. "I'll get the next one."

TWENTY-SEVEN

At that hour the coincidence was unsettling. Just as Diana's cab pulled away, Jill recognized the next car to come up West Broadway toward her. The driver's side window came down as it slowed to a halt. The man inside was dressed in a hand-tailored summer–weight suit and tie.

"Stuart? What in . . ."

"I'm just coming up from Wall Street," Stuart Sprague said. "Had a leveraged buyout negotiation that ran all night. Give you a lift?" He gave the club she'd just emerged from a disapproving once-over. "Your mother told me you came into town for a party. Pretty strange place for a bunch of Brownies to get together. Isn't it?"

Jill shrugged uncomfortably. "We hardly ever roast marshmallows and sing the alma mater anymore." Hurrying around to the other side, she got in.

Instead of driving directly up West Broadway through to Sixth and on up, Sprague slid west to the highway.

"Where are you going?" Jill asked.

"It's faster this way," Sprague said distractedly. "Up to Tenth Avenue, then all the way up to Sixty-fifth and across the park. I do this a lot. I know."

She shook her head and kept her mouth shut. She and Stuart had always had what could be described only as a confrontational relationship. For all she knew, he was doing this just to get a rise out of her. She was determined that he wouldn't. Settling back, she stared out the window. At least he hadn't caught her with Charlie. She'd worked hard all week to get her mother back on her side.

On Tenth Avenue in the high teens, Sprague casually flipped down his visor and pushed a button on something that looked like one of those beepers doctors wear on their belts. Jill eyed it curiously.

"What's that for?" she asked.

The car slowed, Sprague downshifted and suddenly turned right on Twenty-second Street. Seconds later, he was steering toward an opening garage door.

"Hey!" Jill complained. "What's going on?"

Instead of answering, Sprague depressed the button on the little transmitter again and shut off the ignition. Behind them, the garage door was coming down.

"Stuart . . . !" Jill started, edging close to her door.

The expression on her stepfather's face had become distorted into a mask of rage.

"Shut up," he snarled.

When she opened her mouth to scream, he caught her head with a powerful hand and pushed a rubber ball between her lips. While she struggled against him, he got a piece of wide adhesive tape over her mouth. Wrapping an arm around her, he pulled the door latch, dragged her across the seat and out into the garage.

Her manic struggling excited him. It was like that first one; the one she had inspired him to seek. A surrogate for the expression of his love for the one now before him. This was never how he planned it to happen. He loved her. Worshiped her. The *ritual* of having her would have been enough for now. Enough until the time when it would be right to reveal himself. But she had shown herself unworthy of his love by visiting the demon's lair, consorting with him.

Carrying her kicking upstairs, he reached to turn on the lights in the entertainment room. Blinking, she struggled to adjust to the harsh glare.

Before her, covering the wall above an elaborate bar, hung an array of nude women in seductive poses. Each one had her face. White with terror, she fought against the gag, screaming a soundless scream.

"I am sorry, my love," he whispered in her ear. "It was never supposed to be this way." Kicking her feet out from beneath her, he shoved her onto the sofa.

Removing a bottle from the bar, he unscrewed its cap and placed his handkerchief over the mouth. Inverting it, he advanced with it held at arm's length and, avoiding her wildly swinging arms, slipped the chloroform-soaked cloth over her nose.

When she awoke, the room was dark, filled by the eerie glow of a dozen candles. Attempting to move, she found herself restrained. She moved her head, peering from side to side. She was on a bed. It was round. Her clothes had been removed. The terror in her heart built. She could not scream.

The door opened and Stuart walked in. He was dressed in a black leather costume that was at the same time absurd and sinister.

"You are awake," he observed. "Good. This is our bedroom, Jilly. You are going to love me, and we are going to live here together. I am going to make you very happy. But first, you have sinned against our love. You must beg for the forgiveness I can give.'' Moving to the edge of the bed, he sat and reached out to run his hand slowly down the length of her.

''I have watched you for years,'' he said softly. ''Nurtured you. You are so beautiful now.''

Great tears streamed down her cheeks as she watched him stand and remove the tight leather jacket. He loomed above her bare-chested, dozens of gold chains gleaming in the flickering candlelight. He shook his head, unbuckling his trousers.

''Try to be happy,'' he told her. ''No one has ever felt a love so great as the one I feel for you.'' With a wild light in his eye and trembling with excitement, he moved toward her.

On Sunday afternoon, Diana called Pleasure Beach. Rosa answered the phone and found Brennan.

''What's up?'' he asked.

''Don't hate me,'' she said. ''We did one of my new songs at a club last night, and a couple people from one of the big labels were there. They called and want us to do a demo. We're supposed to be in the studio tomorrow morning at ten o'clock. I'll come up Tuesday. I swear.''

''I think we can take care of ourselves,'' Brennan told her. ''Joe's feeling pretty good. Says the ribs aren't really bothering him anymore. And they took the dressing off his shoulder yesterday.''

''You're being too agreeable, Brennan,'' she complained.

''This is the beach.'' He grunted. ''And since when haven't I been perfectly agreeable, anyway?''

''Jesus,'' she moaned and hung up.

Rosa left for the city after an early dinner, hoping to get a jump on traffic. Dante and Brennan fired the two molds in the big kiln that morning. When the wax was completely melted out, they removed them to cool. The sculptor promised the detective that first thing the next morning, they would fire up the furnace and he would finally get a taste of pouring hot metal. In anticipation of the big day ahead, Dante turned in early.

Something went wrong. Jill had bucked against him. He was positioned above her, ready to impose his will on her, when one of the leg restraints broke. Distracted, he hadn't seen her knee coming up until it was too late. The pain of impact was so excruciating that he vomited and began to pass out. In a burst of rage as he collapsed, he struck out at her with all his might.

When he came to, the pain was incredible, throbbing through him. His testicles felt as though they had been crushed. Cradling himself, he rolled over and fell off the bed.

The bitch lay trussed and quiet. It was almost as if she were asleep. But her color was odd. And a great blue welt spread across the bridge of her nose. Gasping, Rick knelt upright and reached to touch her. She did not move. The fact that she was dead crept slowly across his consciousness. That naked form, scratched and smeared with blood, embodied his rejected love.

"Why?!" his tortured mind screamed. He crawled back onto the bed with her and lay there sobbing.

They had stolen it. The sorcerer had taken it. He must have. Otherwise, she would never have rejected him.

Until the run rose high in the Sunday morning sky, Rick sat confused with the body of his Jilly, the love stolen from her.

When late afternoon came, Stuart Sprague dressed in his suit and tie. The sheets on the bed had been changed, and he had washed her and layed her out naturally on the bed.

Penelope would be returning soon from the Island. Examining his face in the mirror, he tightened the Windsor knot and walked from the room, turning out the light.

At eight-thirty Sunday evening, the chauffeur dropped Penny Sprague in front of her Park Avenue building. It was a long drive in, and she was tired. Generally, she had Stuart to talk to during these trips, but this new deal prevented him from coming out. Fortunately, Paul Garriston had been available for mixed doubles.

She found Stuart in his den, tie loosened at the neck and his shoes off, watching television. He looked up as she bussed him on the cheek.

"I thought you said Jill was coming in for a party," he said absently.

"You haven't seen her?"

"Haven't been home much. Meeting didn't break up until late last night. She wasn't here when I got up this morning."

Penny dismissed it. Her daughter assured her that the fascination for the Chinese painter was a thing of the past, describing the relationship as being an opportunity to get some advice on her work and little more. She asked Sprague if she could get him a drink.

Rosa Losada arrived at the Tenth Monday morning to be summoned into the squad commander's office. Morris sat solemnly behind his desk. Inspector Lieberman was there with him.

"I'm sorry, Rosa." Lieberman shook his head. "The commissioner has ordered you a thirty-day suspension without pay. Effective immediately. When you return from it, you're being reassigned to a different command."

"What about Joe?" Rosa asked. She had expected the suspension. The transfer was a surprise.

"He stays on the payroll until the doctor pronounces him fit for duty. Then he does his time. Six months."

"Good God." Rosa winced. "Transferred as well?"

The inspector nodded. Rosa left to clean out her locker. Gathering her things together, she made several trips downstairs to the trunk of her car without bothering to stop by Larry Morris's office. There was apparently no love lost on his end, and she wasn't going to give him the satisfaction of gloating over her departure. It hadn't been a pleasant two weeks.

She was surprised to find Lieberman waiting for her on the sidewalk.

"Got a minute?" he asked.

"As soon as I dump this junk," she said, referring to the load in her arms. Walking to her car, she fumbled with her keys, looking for the one to the trunk. Lieberman was beside her.

"Give me those," he said. Opening the trunk, he watched as she dumped her belongings in a heap.

"Mad?" he asked, slamming the lid and handing the keys back to her.

"I don't know what I am." She shook her head. "It took me a long time to be accepted here. Now I've got to go through it all over again."

"I thought I knew Larry Morris better than that," he said. "We go back a long way. But he got his fanny singed this time."

"I'm not saying I blame him," she said evenly. "I'm just thinking about my own situation. And Dante's."

"Don't worry about Joe Dante." Lieberman smiled. "He just might be the best undercover operative this city's ever produced. The people Downtown know that. They may think assigning him to this was a mistake, but they aren't going to let him go to waste because of it. They also know you people came within a hair's breadth of catching the bastard. Your partner's gonna get an academy job. It's already in the works."

Rosa's eyes widened in surprise.

"So it don't *all* stink" the inspector said, eyes twinkling. "You got any special squad you been thinking you'd like to work with?"

Rosa remembered Dante telling her that the Sixth was just a couple blocks walk from his place. It seemed like that might come in handy. And it was a bigger squad, headed up by a lieutenant. The chances of fitting in there would be better than in another small squad assignment.

"Greenwich Village would be nice," she told him.

The first batch of bronze had nearly reached the critical pouring temperature of 2,280 degrees Fahrenheit when Rosa's call came. Dante took it in the back of the shed.

"Fuck them!" he sneered when he heard of the suspension. "Candy-ass bastards."

"I talked to Inspector Lieberman, Joe. He's getting you an academy job."

"He's what?"

"You heard me. And he asked me what my choice of assignment would be. Don't hate me. I picked the Sixth."

Dante's grin spread from ear to ear. "Listen," he said. "If you're on forced vacation, there's no reason you can't come back up here."

"I suppose not," she agreed. "I've got some things to do, but I could come up Wednesday morning."

After hanging up, Dante shook his head. Assignment to the academy. Rosa at the Sixth. Six months suspension was a real bitch, but as far as she was concerned, the shit had just missed the fan.

Brennan was giving him the thumbs up when he returned to the pouring area. The pyrometer read a couple of degrees over the desired mark. In addition to the asbestos aprons they both wore, Brennan handed him gloves to put on. Then, having lowered his protective goggles, he began to haul on the chain to the hoist, slowly lifting the crucible out of the furance.

The whole vessel glowed a bright, pinkish white and radiated amazingly intense heat. Dante felt it pulse at him in waves as just the merest breeze intensified it. The mold was set upright in a large sand pit. When the crucible was hauled high enough in the air to clear it, Brennan gently tugged it along its I-beam track to the pour location.

''Hold it steady right there,'' he told Dante, handing him the guideline.

With a long steel pole, he hooked the bottom of the crucible and began to slowly upend it. A cascade of brilliant, molten metal spilled in a rivulet past the lip of the spout and down into the orifice of the mold.

Dante watched in utter fascination. Brennan was right. It was primal. The move out of the stone age. The march toward civilization.

He continued to stare, riveted, as one by one the gates filled and overflowed, tiny cherry-red ribbons of metal streaming down the sides of the mold to pool and cool in the sand. Brennan eased the crucible upright again.

TWENTY-EIGHT

They were in the shed. The first pouring of the day had cooled. Brennan broke most of the mold material away to reveal a blackened positive with bits of plaster clinging to it. The runners and risers were now blackened bronze as well.

"What do you do with those?" Dante asked, pointing.

"Cut them off and grind them flat," Brennan said. "Same with these brass pins that hold the core in place." He indicated the arms, which were still full of the plaster, sand, and fiberglass mixture. "Then we have to chip all of that out of there. Otherwise it can take moisture and act as a corrosive."

"How about the rest of this? It's covered with crud."

"There's less glamour to the profession than meets the eye." Brennan grinned. "Hard work gets that off. Scraping. Light acid washes. Buffing. Finally polishing, and once it's all assembled, application of patina."

"Of what?"

"Patina. Bronze rusts, just like all other metals. The Statue of Liberty turning green. That's oxidation. A patina is a chemical way of influencing the direction of oxidation. It speeds up the process and helps the metal create its own protective film. Depending on what you want, bronze is usually treated with solutions of things like copper nitrate, copper sulfate, nitric acid. Each one has different properties, affecting the color."

Dante shook his head. Who knew?

Brennan lowered his goggles and proceeded to fire up a curious-looking tool with a dozen or so agitated metal rods. Together with the compressor that powered it, the thing made a thunderous racket. Touched to the surface of the work, it made bits and pieces of plaster disintegrate in puffs of dust.

The noise was so intense that they did not hear the arrival of a car in the drive. Or the entrance of an irate Penelope Sprague. She tapped Brennan vigorously on the shoulder. He switched the machine off.

"Where is she?" the woman demanded.

Brennan, disoriented, lifted his goggles. "Pardon me?"

"I'm furious, Brennan. Where the hell is my daughter?!"

"Jill?" he asked. "I have no idea."

Her jaw tightened. "Don't bullshit me, mister! You and your . . ."

"Hold it!" Dante commanded, cutting her off in a manner only a cop assumes. "Your daughter isn't here. She hasn't been here for over a week."

"Who the hell are you?" she demanded, a little less sure of herself.

"I'm a police officer, ma'am. I assure you that there is no reason we wouldn't tell you where Jill is if we knew. What is the problem?"

Some of the wind came out of Penny's sails. Confused now, she shook her head in frustration.

"She left our place out on Long Island Saturday morning. She was supposed to be coming into the city for a party. But there wasn't any party, and she hasn't been home."

"Have you filed a missing person report?"

"They won't let me for forty-eight hours. That miserable painter and Brennan's model friend saw her late Saturday night."

"Charlie and Diana saw her?" Brennan broke in.

Penny nodded. "She went to a disco with the Webster woman. They apparently left together at four Sunday morning and took separate cabs."

"Diana saw the cab she got into?" Dante pressed.

Penny shook her head. "She says she left first."

"There's probably some explanation," Dante said reassuringly. "Maybe she went back into the club and met somebody. It happens."

The distraught woman shrugged helplessly. "I was sure she was here," she said. "Now I don't know what to think."

When they walked her out into the sunlight, a shiny black 733i BMW replaced her former conveyance. She must have been pretty upset to drive herself up there. Brennan got a funny look on his face as he approached it to open the door for her.

"What kind of a car is this?" he asked her.

"A BMW. It's Stuart's fun car. He has the chauffeur this afternoon."

Brennan shut her in, still staring at the car distractedly. Penny regained her composure. In a reflection of her impeccable breeding, she apologized stiffly for disturbing them.

As the car pulled around the drive and headed back up the hill to the road, Brennan gasped.

"That's it! The fucking car!"

"What?" Dante asked.

"Look at the door," Brennan pointed excitedly. "The dent. The missing chrome. And see that little lip across the back? I forgot about that. It's the same goddamn car!"

Dante turned to Brennan and was staring at him intently. "That little lip is called a spoiler," he said slowly. "Are you sure about this?"

"Absolutely," Brennan said. "It's the same car I saw the tall blonde leaning into. There couldn't be two dents like that. What did she say it was? A BMW. That's not all that common, right?"

Dante was staring up the hill and frowning, deep in thought.

"This is insane," he muttered. "Do you have any idea of what you're telling me?"

"Stuart Sprague."

"It fits." Dante shook his head in disbelief. "All that money out in L.A. The condominium paid for in cash. The way he disappeared the minute he hit New York. He was here all the fucking time." Dante turned and started walking slowly toward the house. Brennan fell in step beside him.

"What do you do now?" the sculptor asked.

"Good question. Do you realize what it is we're dealing with here? The man is the district attorney's financial backer in a run for governor. He has dinner at Gracie Mansion! You don't just walk up to a guy like that and arrest him as a suspected murderer. Not without concrete proof."

"What do you mean? You've got to catch him in the act?"

"Just about. Or come across something just as good.

Holy shit! Do you know what the big boys Downtown would say if I called right now and told them I have reason to believe our man is Stuart Sprague? They'd send over somebody with a straight jacket."

"So what do you do?" Brennan asked.

Dante's eyes were smoldering now. He turned to stare his host in the eye. "Just like you said. Catch the motherfucker in the act. I've got to get ahold of Rosa, and then I'm gonna need a ride to the train station."

Dante said no more to Rosa than that she should meet him on the northeast corner of Sixty-ninth and Park Avenue in four hours. The two-hour-and-forty-minute train ride got him to Penn Station at quarter past five. He took a cab directly to Sprague's building and strolled down the ramp into the parking garage.

An attendant was sitting back in a folding chair, feet up on a metal desk and watching a miniature television. Local news by the sound of it.

"Hey!" he said sharply, looking up. "You ain't supposed to be down here."

Dante opened his wallet and showed him his shield. "Name's Dante," he said. "I've got some questions about a BMW seven thirty-three i. Black. You have one here belonging to a Mr. Stuart Sprague, right?"

The man eyed him cautiously. Rich people didn't like questions being asked about them. They paid him to park cars and keep his mouth shut.

"A car fitting the description was involved in a hit and run," Dante told him. "We don't have a plate, so we're following up on any vehicles that model and color. It's routine."

The attendant didn't exactly relax, but the explanation seemed to make divulging information easier.

"It's over there." He pointed. "Against the wall."

"Can I see it?"

"Help yourself. It's unlocked." The man eyed the nasty-looking scab across Dante's left hand.

"Lawn mower," the detective said, smiling. "Real stupid." He strolled over to the BMW and approached the passenger door. The dent was there all right, just as Brennan had first described it. The small strip of chrome running the length of the car had popped off the door on impact. He reached for the handle and opened the door.

Inside, the leather and carpets were clean as a whistle. Stem to stern. Maybe too clean. The faint odor of a cleaning agent, like pine oil, lingered. Leaning across the gearshift, he lifted the foot mat on the driver's side. There wasn't even the most remote trace of dirt. That seemed unusual. Even vacuuming generally missed something. This job had been done by someone who was interested in being more than simply thorough. Paranoid was more like it.

"Who cleans that car, anyway?" Dante asked the attendant conversationally upon his return. "I wish I could get the place that does my car to do work like that."

"Dunno," the man replied. "We jest park 'em unless they ask different."

"Nasty dent there in the right door," the detective observed. "New?"

"Maybe six weeks." He shrugged. "Man uses it pretty often. Ain't been time to get it into the shop, I guess. What time of day did you say this here accident happened?"

"I didn't," Dante returned. "When does Mr. Sprague generally use the car?"

"He has the limo during the day. This one he drives at night. Must have a girlfriend or somethin'." The man gave Dante a knowing wink. "Sometimes he stays out all night."

"Hmmm," Dante mused. "The car we're looking for was involved in the accident at noon last Wednesday."

"It weren't this one then. It was parked right there every day last week."

Dante thanked him for his time. "I'm sure a man in Mr. Sprague's position doesn't need to be bothered with a visit like this," he said. "Let's just keep it between you and me . . ."

"Dillingham. Walter."

"Thanks, Walter." He held out his hand.

To that point Dante was entertaining vague misgivings about something as wild as Stuart Sprague being his man. Brennan was an observant guy. He kept telling himself on the train that even if it had been his car and Cheri had indeed talked to him, there was room for mistaken assumption. He had to allow that. So Stuart Sprague liked to get his knob sucked occasionally. It wasn't a felony.

The odor of pine oil cemented his thinking. That and the pristine condition of the car's interior.

When he emerged from the basement garage, Dante found Rosa waiting for him at the curb in her Toyota Supra.

"What's going on?" she asked as he climbed in. "You're supposed to be resting."

She'd never seen this particular look he had in his eyes as he turned to her.

"We found the car," he told her. "It's right downstairs in that garage."

"What? How?"

"Jill Sprague is missing, and her mother arrived in it this afternoon, looking for her."

Rosa shook her head, confused.

"Brennan recognized it. I just checked it out. It belongs to Stuart Sprague."

"Oh my God." The implication of what he had said struck her like a fist. "It can't possibly . . ." Her voice drifted off.

"Why not? Leading citizens can't be psychopathic killers? The car reeks of disinfectant, Rosa. There isn't a gnat turd in it. Not a speck."

Rosa was staring at him. "This isn't just one of your hunches, is it?"

"I had a lot of time to think on the train. One thing I didn't want to think about occurred to me. What did every one of his victims but the fat whore have in common?"

"They were a type," Rosa said.

"Penny Sprague was looking for Jill. She said she didn't come home from a club she and Diana went to Saturday night."

Rosa's eyes widened. She shook her head.

"No."

"Like I said. It's not something you want to think about. But we've already established from the modus that our killer is a real sicko. A dozen years ago Stuart Sprague marries a woman with a pretty little girl. Her own father is dead, and he raises her as the apple of his eye. You get where this leads? It's sick, too."

"We don't have anything solid."

"That's right. Which means that we have to catch him with his hand in the cookie jar. Suspension or not, it's up to us. The honchos Downtown would laugh in our faces."

"I think we should tell someone, Joe. Gus Lieberman. He'll at least listen. It's crazy to try to do something like this without backup."

Dante shook his head vehemently. "This one is all mine." His voice was strangely altered.

Rosa, startled, looked sharply at him.

"Joe. Please. You can't turn this thing into a personal vendetta."

"The hell I can't," he said, voice tight. "The son of a bitch killed my best friend. Fuck the department. This guy is mine. I'm gonna personally dispatch him to hell."

She touched his arm. "That's just what I'm afraid of. That you won't be able to stop yourself."

"Why should I? There'd be one less scum bucket. He slit Sammy's throat. I watched him bleed to death in my arms!"

Rosa shook her head. "I know what happened, Joe. But if you shoot a man in cold blood, how are you any better than he is? You're denying the whole process of law."

Dante pounded his armrest. "I don't care anymore! Goddamn the law! Stuart Sprague pleads insanity, and he's back on the street in five years because some namby-pamby psychiatrist says he's cured. No way. I'm going to flush this turd!"

TWENTY-NINE

Rick had to see the other one now. Brennan's whore. Somehow, the sorcerer had stolen his love. Now this one must hold it. They had taken it from him in his hour of revelation, endowing this other with it. Their powers were greater than he had anticipated. He won the first round. They, the second. The former embodiment of his love had been stripped of it and sent as a decoy. He fell for it. But she was no longer at their disposal. Only the true vessel remained.

Did they think he did not suspect her? That he could not feel the power of his love pulsating within her? They were fools. While they sat laughing at their cleverness, he stood closer now than ever before. Tonight. He would follow her. At the correct moment, he would reveal his love to her. She would recognize him as the one who had given her everything. She would worship him for it . . . loving him like the old Jill couldn't once Brennan had torn out her soul.

God, she was beautiful. The body was so magnificent that he knew the sorcerer himself must have conjured it. He licked his lips at the thought of stealing her back from him.

At six-fifteen he left his Park Avenue penthouse, descended to the garage, and climbed behind the wheel of the BMW. First, he would go to his house in Chelsea. There he would meditate on his hate for the forces conspiring against him and dress for battle.

Dante and Rosa had been waiting for about thirty minutes when Stuart Sprague emerged from the garage behind the wheel of the 733i. Rosa started her car and slid it into drive. The car ahead moved south down Park Avenue through moderate traffic. At the Helmsley Building, it was forced by road construction to detour to Vanderbilt Avenue and around Grand Central Station. Continuing downtown to Twenty-third Street, it turned right and drove across town to Ninth Avenue.

"Jesus," Dante muttered. "Don't tell me this bastard's been operating right in our own backyard."

They followed their quarry down Ninth to Twenty-first and around the block.

"I don't believe it." Rosa pointed. "That's where we found the car. Right there." They glided slowly past the shallow park fronting Twenty-second and Tenth. Ahead, the BMW turned into Twenty-second and slowed to enter a garage as an automatic opener made way.

"Bingo," Dante said. "How convenient. No wonder he got in and out of the neighborhood so easily. He's got his own fortress of solitude around the corner."

She looked empty there now, bearing no resemblance to the living fire he had watched sunbathe on the lower terrace. The power that could awaken frenzied craving in him no longer dwelt there. She was only a shell. Empty of the love Brennan stripped from her. But Brennan was an overconfident fool. He let the new vessel out of his sight. Rick, the blessed prick, had sniffed her out.

It was a night to war against the elements conspiring against him. After this night, nothing would oppose him. The sorcerer was a clown to think he might. In exchange, he would forfeit his life.

The dressing for battle and conquest became a ritual. The tight black leather trousers and jacket. The many strands of heavy gold chain. The rings. The boots. The bracelet. The tightness of the hide made him ultraaware of his body. Every square inch of the tension that throbbed within him.

Until tonight he employed only the five-inch commando knife as backup and had needed to use it only once. He felt most comfortable with a blade. It was the weapon of his youth on the streets of the Lower East Side. He learned the subtle nuances of knife fighting while still a teenager. His continued existence, with barely a scratch on him, attested to his proficiency.

But with age had come bigger fish. Now next to the knife in his dresser drawer lay a 9-mm Browning automatic. It was only the latest of many guns Rick had owned. Picking it up, he cradled it gently, rubbing the blued barrel with the tips of his fingers. He went downstairs to the entertainment room sofa and coffee table, where he took the weapon apart, cleaned each piece thoroughly, oiled it lightly, and reassembled it. Slapping a full clip into the butt, he chambered the first round, flicked on the safety, and slid it into the band of his trousers.

On the street, Dante and Rosa waited patiently.

"I've got to get in there," he said, craning his neck to

stare up at the brownstone and the two adjacent buildings. "There isn't any doubt now. It's him."

"Do you think you *could* get in?" Rosa asked.

"What are you thinking?"

"After he leaves, we split up. I follow him and you break in here. Could you do it?"

"I'll get in." He nodded. "Where's the tire iron in this thing?"

Rosa pulled the key out of the ignition and handed him the key to the trunk. "It's under the deck mat."

Dante hopped out, located Toyota's version of a tire iron in the spare well, and returned to the passenger seat.

"Whatever happened to the good old Ford design?" he asked, examining the thing with disdain. "Look at this piece of shit."

"Will it work?"

"I don't know what kind of security he's got. If I'm gonna have any luck, it'll probably be on the roof."

"Be careful, Joe. You aren't exactly healthy yet."

"I'm okay." He waved her off. "Let's talk about how we'll keep in touch. If I had my message retriever, you could call my machine. . . ."

"Wait a minute!" Rosa started digging in her purse. "I've got mine." She produced a little black plastic beeper. "Here. I'll call and leave my whereabouts every time I move. I'll try to leave the number of a phone booth."

Dante took the instrument, got a few quick operational tips, and slipped it into his shirt pocket.

"Do you have your gun?" Rosa asked.

"Right here," he said, touching his ankle.

"Be careful, Joe. And keep an ear out. If he doubles back for some reason, I'll honk three times."

The garage door came open. The backup lights of the BMW lit as the car rolled slowly into the street.

"Off you go," Dante said, popping his door and slipping out to crouch next to the empty seat. "Be careful. And keep in touch." As he eased the door shut, the black performance coupe roared off down the street.

Rosa sped off in pursuit of Stuart Sprague. He was headed back across town, but this time, instead of turning north, he cut south on Broadway. Traffic was too heavy to risk losing him. She stayed close, assuming that he had no reason to suspect the Supra. At Eighth Street, he turned east and proceeded past Third Avenue to where Eighth became Saint Mark's Place. Between Second and First Avenues, he slowed as if looking for a place to park. A car swung away from the curb, and he moved to take its place. Rosa rolled past as if she, too, were looking for a place and pulled in next to a fire plug. She waited for Sprague to get out of his car. He didn't.

Saint Mark's Place rang a bell for some reason. For the life of her, she couldn't make the connection. Something she had heard recently? Maybe it was Dante. The Blade used to work this part of town pretty heavily. It was where the wildest of the night crowd lived.

Adjusting her rearview mirror for the optimum coverage of Sprague's location, she sat back and waited.

Rick also waited, unaware that just four cars up, a police officer had him under surveillance. It was 7:10 and still light out. Jilly's address book had given him a name. Diana Webster. It was the only one on Saint Mark's Place. The evening before, he'd returned to find it on the bell. Number seven. Diana. He liked that. Goddess of the hunt. He would wait until it was dark to make his move.

Brennan had chosen the place to hide her well. Here in a neighborhood peopled with the flotsam and jetsam of American youth. Scum. Trash. He never realized what a concentration of them existed in the city. His city. And them, seeking to destroy the very fabric of his society. Shaved heads, mohawks, chains, corpselike makeup. Rude, obnoxious, and obviously high on drugs. He was repulsed by them. The sorcerer would have guessed that. He had even disguised her as one of them.

Across town, Joe Dante assessed the brownstone on Twenty-second Street. Heavy shutters hid the interior from the street. The windows were barred below the third floor. The front door was a substantial oak panel. There were three cylinders that he could see. Who knew what else could be securing it from the inside?

Next door, an apartment building stood approximately the same height as the one he was attempting to enter. He approached the entrance and went through the sure-fire button-pushing routine. In another moment he was inside the place and hurrying up the stairs as fast as his tender ribs would allow. The door to the roof was easy enough to get out of, but to his dismay, Sprague's roof was a potentially painful seven feet below the one he stood on.

"Damn," he muttered, throwing the tire iron down first. Sitting on the parapet wall, he dangled his feet to shorten the distance, took a deep breath, and shoved off. His impact was reasonable within the constraints of what he expected. The wind was knocked out of him as he hit, trying to roll onto his good shoulder. The cracked ribs protested with a sharp, knifelike thrust to the solar plexus. Gasping in pain, he lay on his back and assessed the damage.

To his surprise, the shoulder wound remained undisturbed. It throbbed some, but he could live with that. Slowly, he attempted to find his feet.

Sprague's roof access was one of those springloaded fire doors controlled by latches from the inside. It took him ten minutes of sweating labor to pry the thing far enough apart to where he could slip the iron in and trigger the mechanism. Even with all the racket he was making, no one from either adjoining building bothered to check it out. By then, if he'd had any doubts, he was sure that the place was unoccupied.

Climbing down a steel ladder with aching ribs was a tiring chore. The first thing to hit him when he touched bottom was a peculiar odor. Not very pleasant, like slightly ripe garbage but different.

The place was dark as a tomb. The miniflash on his key ring fought back the gloom as he inched along a short hall to the top of the stair landing. The tire iron, he realized, was gripped defensively in his left hand. Slowly, he began to descend.

The first real occupied level of the house presented a carpeted hallway fronting opposing panel doors. All were closed. Before exploring them individually, Dante thought he better make a sweep of the whole house. As quickly as his stiffening joints allowed, he worked down the remaining two levels to the floor above the garage. The flashlight found the wall switch at the bottom of the landing. He reached to flip it on.

THIRTY

It was her. Rick sat bolt upright in the seat and stared hard through the windscreen. She had a yellow nylon duffle in her hand and she was leaving. His mind raced. The plan would have to change. He would have to adapt it to this new situation. The bearer of the soul was moving. He could see it in her. It glowed, infusing the body of the vessel with intense life-force. The spring of her step and bounce of her breasts made his hands tremble on the steering wheel. Starting his car, he prepared to follow her as she turned at the bottom of the steps to walk east toward First Avenue.

The sight confronting Joe Dante as his eyes adjusted to the light shocked him more violently than anything had in sixteen years of the job. Even the life of a skinhead dope fiend failed to prepare him for the lair of Stuart Sprague. The *scope* of the sickness was what hit him like a hammer.

The room was a large kitchen-bar-den area. Very contemporary stuff and obviously designed for the culinary entertainer so prevalent in current Manhattan social circles. Restaurant range, commercial upright refrigerator, copper cookware hanging from ceiling racks. Large-screen video rig and a stereo rack on one wall. But any normalcy, if you could choose to call it that, stopped there. The walls were literally papered with *Playboy* and *Penthouse* gatefolds. This in itself would have been queer enough had not each and every model had the same smiling face pasted over it. And the graffiti. Words scrawled inside bizarre speech bubbles protruded from every mouth. Reading them, he felt suddenly nauseous. The face was Jill's.

"Holy fucking shit!" he whispered aloud. There it was, the link he hadn't anticipated.

Brennan has stolen my love for you and locked it away in the imposter. You can never have what is rightfully yours until he dies.

Turning on more lights, he began to search the place in earnest. The piles of hard-core porn. Vials of love oils. Battery-operated devices. Restraints. The huge video porn library alone made his skin crawl.

The next level seemed almost insanity-free as he explored a living room full of leather furniture, walnut tables, and chrome lamps. Off of it ran a short hall, leading to two doors. The first revealed a marble powder room, very elegantly appointed. He closed the door and tried the second.

The sight of a woman asleep in the bed of the master suite nearly stopped his heart. Until he inhaled and realized that this was where the peculiar odor had emanated from. It wasn't really bad yet. The air-conditioning hummed, and the room was like a refrigerator. Switching on the lights, he gagged.

The unclad body laid out in repose on the bed was Jill's.

Face badly bruised and torso scratched, she had obviously been washed and carefully arranged. Her hair was combed, her hands folded on her abdomen. Gutted candles sat on every available surface.

Trying to contain the urge to vomit, Dante approached the huge circular bed. The sheets had apparently been changed. There were no signs of struggle and no coagulated blood. From the wound on her face, it appeared that her nose was broken. The cause of death could not be immediately determined. Drugs. Snapped spinal cord. Suffocation. All were possibilities. If she had been gagged and her nose broken, drowning would be the most reasonable guess.

He remembered Jill in her bathing suit on the beach. She *had* been beautiful. And young. Dante felt the thickness in his throat and the tears of rage sting his eyes. He moved to the telephone. A series of clicks on Rosa's machine were followed by a short, frantic message.

"Joe! It's eight-thirteen and I'm on the Eighth Avenue side of Penn Station. It's Diana, Joe. He watched her buy a ticket to New London. I don't have Brian's number on me. I'll wait. Hurry!"

He glanced at his watch. Eight-fifteen. She'd just called. Disconnecting, he hurried downstairs to the front door and began frantically throwing dead bolts. When he reached Tenth Avenue, there were no available cabs in sight. Across the street, at a deli, a pair of them sat idle, their drivers on break. Dante ran to the first, jerking open the rear door. The sandwich-munching driver spun in his seat.

"Get the fuck outta there! I'm on my dinner."

"Police," Dante spat. He shoved his shield in the cabbie's face. "Drive this thing to Penn Station as fast as you can. Now!"

"Wait a fuckin' min . . ."

"Now!" Dante growled. "Lives hang in the balance, buddy. Screw your dinner. Get it in gear."

The cabbie scowled, dropped his sandwich into a brown sack, and started the car. He gave Dante his money's worth. With the detective hanging out the window of the Checker, waving his arms and screaming at other motorists, he employed the avenue curb to curb. At Thirty-fourth Street they turned right to race the two blocks across town, twice employing the oncoming traffic lane. At the light on Eighth Avenue, Dante spotted Rosa waiting diagonally across the street, threw the guy a twenty, and hoofed it, dodging traffic, to reach her.

"Let's go!" he shouted, jumping into the Toyota. "He's after both of them!"

"Who?" Rosa asked, pulling into traffic.

"Brennan, too. Something about him stealing Jill's soul or something."

"What?"

"I found her in there. She's dead. And this guy's as cracked as they come. Real sick shit. We've gotta call up there and warn them. The local cops, too."

Rosa nodded. "I'm almost out of gas. There's a Hess station on Tenth around Forty-fifth. You call, and we'll get on the West Side Highway from there."

Frantically punching his credit card numbers into the pay phone, Dante waited as the phone in Pleasure Beach rang over and over again with no answer. He cursed, hung up, and punched Area Code 203 Information. A minute later, he was dialing the Connecticut State Police.

"Detective Joe Dante, NYPD," he informed the trooper who answered. "We have reason to believe that a man driving a black 733i BMW, license number 6010 AWA, may make an attempt on the lives of two people at 482 New Shore Road. That's on the coast east of Niantic."

"Can you hold?" the man asked. "I want to switch you directly to the resident trooper down there, Detective."

In another thirty seconds, Dante was speaking directly to the man in the field.

"Yeah, New York. What's all this about?"

"There's a guy named Brennan at 482 New Shore Road. We know him to be material to homicides down here. Indirectly. There is strong reason to believe the killer is on his way up there now, after him and a woman guest. It's a big white house down the hill toward the beach. I've tried to raise him with no luck."

He repeated his description of the car and told the trooper that he and his partner were on their way. Running to join his partner, he leaped in.

Out on the open road, Rosa drove north, reaching speeds of eighty and ninety miles an hour. At the George Washington Bridge–Cross Bronx Expressway interchange, they bore East on I-95.

"What was it like in there?" Rosa asked.

Dante shook his head. "You read about it, but . . . this guy really *is* nuts. Maybe it's just a hyperparanoid state of schizophrenia, I don't know. But sweet mother! The place is done over like some porn-crazed satanist's love nest. I found Jill on this big round bed in the master bedroom. It wasn't pretty. She went hard."

"Oh, God." Rosa shook her head.

"There's a sort of swinger's den downstairs. A couple hundred video porn cassettes. All kinds of sex boutique crap. And the walls were papered with magazine foldouts. Every one of them had Jill's face pasted over it. That's why he killed all those whores. They were accessible, and she wasn't."

Fortunately, the Monday night traffic was light. It was dark now as Rosa pushed the Supra along at the top end, weaving in and out of slower cars. Twice, she took to the shoulder when all three lanes were blocked. Dante was amazed at her aggressiveness behind the wheel.

"What's this stuff about Brian and Jill's souls?" Rosa asked.

Dante shook his head. "He had that kind of cartoon speech drawn on some of the centerfolds. Real disgusting shit. Part of it is about Brennan's stealing her soul or something. I can't figure it, but maybe it has something to do with the fight they had last month. Either that or her staying at his place with Charlie Fung."

"It doesn't make much sense," Rosa said.

"The man is deranged," Dante told her. "It doesn't matter if it makes sense to us. It does to him."

Rosa swallowed hard, concentrating on the Interstate ahead.

"He's got a twenty-minute head start, Joe. And we bought gas. Make it thirty."

"We should make up something here," he contended. "Maybe ten, fifteen minutes. And the troopers ought to be there by now."

THIRTY-ONE

Diana phoned in the early afternoon to tell Brennan she would be on a later train, arriving in New London at ten thirty-two. The recording session was dragging on. She didn't anticipate wrapping it up until after six. Even if they were that lucky, there was no way she could make it home, change, and be on the six-fifteen.

At eight o'clock, Brennan drove into New London to do some grocery shopping, have dinner, and meet Diana at the train station. Eating alone never bothered him. Tonight he ate a steak rare and polished off a bottle of Mondavi Cabernet. Drinking alone didn't bother him much either. On this night he was fairly up. The casting was going extremely well.

He sat sipping from his glass and considering the day's events. Killing whores. That would be just like Stuart. He detested the little people of the world. They were to be habitually exploited. It wouldn't take much of a mental leap from that to murder.

The train from New York was a couple of minutes early. By the time Brennan steered the pickup into the station parking lot, Diana was already waiting with her bags at the curb.

"You look beat," he observed as she climbed in.

"Let's just say that it wasn't one of the smoother sessions that I've been party to."

"A late-night swim, a drink, and bed." He smiled. "We have the place all to ourselves. Hungry?"

She shook her head. "Had sandwiches at the studio. What do you mean about being alone? Where's Joe?"

"He ran off to the city this afternoon." Brennan proceeded to relate the news of Penny Sprague's visit and the suspect car.

"Stuart Sprague?" Diana exclaimed. "Unbelievable! The mother called me about Jill this morning. I feel bad about taking the first cab the other morning."

"How did she know how to get ahold of you?"

"Charlie. He told her he'd left her with me."

"It's strange." Brennan nodded thoughtfully. "Frankly, she seemed too uptight to be the type who lets herself get picked up."

Diana rolled her eyes. "Come on. She *was* screwing Charlie Fung."

"With motive," Brian said. "I never said her mother hadn't taught her something about getting what she wanted. Charlie's big. He's connected to the scene. It'll make a great 'What I Did with My Summer Vacation' essay back at Brown."

"I don't think they do that sort of thing in college."

"You know what I mean. Impress her little prepster friends."

"Maybe," Diana conceded. "All I'm saying is that she appears to have a libido. All twenty-year-old Ivy Leaguers aren't Barbie dolls."

Brennan grunted something about how they could have fooled him. Dropping down off of the Interstate, he rolled coastward toward New Shore Road. It was a nice night, perfect for a quick dip. The moon was full just a couple of days back. Now it hung low and huge in the night sky. On the water, it would be spectacular. Diana was known to respond favorably to the wonders of nature and a little wine. He was looking forward to it.

The woman was going to New London by train. Once she bought the ticket, confirming her destination, Rick climbed back into the car and drove to intercept her at the other end. His radar detector allowed him to make excellent time, arriving ten minutes before the train from New York. It was a couple of minutes early. When she appeared on the sidewalk outside, searching up and down expectantly, he knew he was in luck.

For a moment he contemplated picking her off right there, telling her that Brennan had sent him to get her. But now that he was this close, his thinking changed. Now the sorcerer could conveniently witness the destruction of his treachery. With the two of them together, his triumph could be all the greater. More complete. The idea so excited him that he began to smile in satisfaction. Already the sight of her stimulated him, causing the impending satisfaction to build against the tight, polished hide. He would follow them to this place and take them at his leisure.

The disgusting, ancient pickup truck driven by his nemesis arrived. The woman climbed into it. He followed at a safe distance. The territory was unfamiliar.

He knew to be cautious, respecting his adversary's advantage. He soon discovered that his caution was not unwarranted. On a coastal road dotted with substantial homes and Brennan's truck several hundred yards ahead, he rounded a corner to discover a pair of State Police cars in the road. Thinking quickly, he slid into the first available drive and killed his lights. Avoiding the brake pedal and the taillights it would trigger, he rolled slowly off the drive and into a clump of low bushes. He removed the 9-mm from the glove box and slipped it into his pants. Then he climbed quietly from the car.

The two State Police cruisers parked outside his drive caught Brennan by surprise. Slowing, he leaned his head out the car window.

"What's up?"

The shorter of the two, a stocky man with heavy eyebrows, stepped up to the cab. "Resident Trooper Art Liggett," he said. "Your name Brennan?"

"That's right. Is there a problem?"

"We got a call from a Detective Dante. NYPD. He believes you to be in some sort of danger. You and the lady. Something about a murder suspect. He contacted us a little more than two hours ago and said he was on his way up here."

"*We're* in danger?" Brennan asked in disbelief.

"That's right. Some guy driving a black BMW. You folks go on down. We're going to sit tight here until we can find out what this is all about. Is this driveway your only access?"

Brian nodded.

"How about the beach?"

"It's possible, I guess. You'd have to know which stairs are mine. Hell, until Dante gets here, we'll sit on the deck and watch them. Anyone comes along, we'll raise hell. You're only fifty yards away, right?"

The trooper nodded. In the background, the radios of the two cars warbled and spat static into the otherwise quiet night. Brennan turned to look apprehensively at Diana, worked the steering column shift into compound low, and eased slowly by them.

"Sprague? Here? I don't believe it," Diana said. "Why?"

"I don't know," Brennan said. "It's odd. But Dante isn't the sort to go off half-cocked. If he thinks there's a problem, there's a problem."

They parked and got out of the truck, Brennan carrying his groceries and Diana her duffle.

"Look at that moon," he grumbled. "What a waste. I was going to ply you with wine and get you to do unspeakable acts beneath it."

"The wine sounds good." She sighed. "Right about now, I could use a drink."

Art Liggett and his fellow trooper Jack Lipinski didn't quite know what to make of the situation. You always had to suspect that the big city hotshots were passing along a little hysteria just to see the bumpkins jump. But then again, if it was real New York trouble, the prospect of having to deal with it didn't please them. They'd both been hauled away from their dinners for this one. Jack's wife was eight months pregnant and touchy as hell lately. This was just the sort of thing that set her off. Liggett knew all of this well enough. His own wife hadn't been exactly thrilled to death to see him leave half a T-bone and his creamed cauliflower untouched. She worked all day in the administration office over at the high school in Niantic. That and the cooking left her pretty bushed. She liked to be appreciated for the effort.

"I think I'll wander up here a piece." He pointed east on the road. "You get the radio?"

"Sure," Lipinski replied. "I wish this guy would get here. The whole thing sounds crazy to me."

"The whole of New York's crazy," Liggett said, ambling off into the dark.

* * *

Rick had not been able to get close enough to pick up Brennan's conversation with the police. But whatever it was, a brief exchange was not enough to send them on their way. Once Brennan proceeded down his drive, more words were exchanged between the cops themselves. ". . . New York . . ." drifted to him. They were waiting for someone. And then one of the two started in his direction, walking along the shoulder of the road. With his flashlight, he searched the line of the hedge fronting Brennan's property.

What about New York? Rick wondered. If they were waiting for someone, the situation could get untenable. He hadn't counted on the police, but right now there were only two of them. The odds were still in his favor. He had the element of surprise. Who knew how long it would last. He had to act swiftly.

Slipping back into the shadows, he let the trooper pass. Short and heavy-shouldered, he might present a problem in getting the commando knife to the heart on the first thrust. Rick selected the second-best option. From his position, he set himself and waited for the trooper to turn. Knife held in his palm, fingers wrapped lightly around the hilt, he waited until the man was directly adjacent before sliding noiselessly out and upright. One powerful hand clamped quickly over the man's mouth, while the tip of the knife, positioned between the two tendons at the back of his neck, slid quickly upward with a vicious twist. The dying trooper convulsed heavily against him for fifteen seconds. It was all he could do to hang on and prevent him from making some sound. When the convulsion subsided, he let him slide to the ground, then picked up his hat and flashlight.

Jack Lipinski watched as Art Liggett returned from his stroll. The flashlight still played along the hedge. Thorough guy, though how a murderer was going to crawl through the bushes with them right there was a mystery to him. Still, the other man was making a job of it, staying close, stopping to probe here and there. Ten yards away, he suddenly turned and trained his torch directly into Lipinski's eyes.

"Hey!" Jack protested, putting his hands up.

While the officer was fending off the brilliant glare, Rick hurried three quick paces forward, aimed the Browning at the man's face at point-blank range, and pulled the trigger. In an ear-splitting crack, half his skull exploded.

Sitting in the moonlight, glass of Bordeaux in hand, Diana turned sharply at the loud report. "What was that?"

"Don't know," Brennan said. As usual, he was already a glass ahead of her and pulling away fast. "Probably kids lighting firecrackers. After the noise they made on Fourth of July, you'd think they'd have run out by now."

Diana rose from her chair and walked to where she had a view of the road. A shadowy figure under the hood of Brennan's truck caught her attention.

"Brian. Someone's out there," she said quietly.

Catching the edge in her voice, he moved to join her just in time to see the hood lowered quietly and a figure melt into the shadows of the veranda.

"Jesus!" He gulped. "Inside. Quick."

Once in the house, they bolted the back door.

"Oh God, Brian," Diana exclaimed. "What about the front?"

"I'll check it," he said. "Get on the phone and call the police. Tell them there's something wrong." He moved off, wishing he hadn't had so much to drink. His mind was foggy, slowing him down. He thought desperately about their options. Sprague just disabled the truck. If that explosion was a shot, then he had killed one of the troopers and had a gun. They were at a hopeless disadvantage.

There was the beach but where once they reached it? Swim?

"The phone's dead," Diana's voice came from behind him.

Rick watched from behind the dining room door, already inside, as the pathetic conjurer absorbed the news of his isolation. He had just locked the front door to no avail. Fool. She stood beside him, his gorgeous Jilly. Even in terror she was excruciatingly perfect in every way. He would savor this moment forever. Unzipping himself, he stood exposed. His love for her. His power to please her. With his power, he would rid her of her sin. Break the spell of the sorcerer. Purify her. They would know happiness.

THIRTY-TWO

As Rosa rounded the last turn before Brennan's driveway, her headlights picked up the form of a man lying outstretched on the shoulder of New Shore Road. Ahead, two State Police cruisers were parked at the gate, doors open and interior lights on.

"Pull up here," Dante directed. He hopped out as she slowed to a stop, then approached the inert body. On his knees, he examined him. A trooper. Weaponless, hatless, and dead.

"He's here," Dante said, looking up at his partner. "Pithed this poor bastard like a laboratory frog."

Rosa continued in the car while Dante hurried ahead on foot. Between the two state cars, Joe found the second of Sprague's victims. This time there was nothing he could do about controlling his stomach. The hot, harsh-tasting stuff of horror erupted in a spasm of nausea. As Rosa rushed up, he flung out his good arm, tackling her.

"Don't." He shook his head, choking. "Get on the radio. Tell them their two men are down and that we're going in. Meet me by Brian's truck over there." He pointed at the pickup parked in the drive above the foundry outbuilding. "I'm gonna look around."

Cautiously, Dante slid into the shadows and worked his way downhill. The maniac had done a skillful job on the two troopers. Sammy's death and his own condition were further testimony to his proficiency. Letting the man get the drop on him now would be stupid. His ears strained for every sound, each footfall's thunderous crunch in the gravel. His eyes probed the gloom. He was thankful for the moonlight. The big house was bathed in pale luminescence. Lights were on in several rooms downstairs. Beyond the house, the foundry lay in shadow. Up on the road, he could hear the squawk of the two-way radio as Rosa reported their situation. Putting one foot in front of the other, he approached the house.

Light in the wooden-paneled foyer came from a single overhead chandelier. Soft and yellow. Beyond it, the dining room lay in darkness. One of the narrow double doors stood just half an inch ajar. From behind it, he could watch her in the sorcerer's arms. Breasts straining against the thin white cotton blouse. Long, finely shaped legs set off by navy-blue shorts. A hot, flushed sweat of desire broke out under the tight leather, lubricating and sensitizing every inch of his body. He fondled himself, throbbing in anticipation. He wanted to be absolutely keyed for the moment, every fiber of flesh and synapse of thought straining with the eagerness to wield the power. It had been so long in coming; so much treachery to battle, so much waiting to endure. He was ready now. She stood before him. The triumph of his love and defeat of his enemy were at hand.

Rick kicked open the door, brandishing the automatic, and stood before them in all his avenging glory. Black leather from open jacket to boots. Feet planted apart. Gold and diamonds flashing around his neck and fists. His chest hair was matted with blood, as if he had been drinking the stuff. The black of the leather and the red of death.

Diana screamed.

"Here I am, fool!" Rick snarled at Brennan. "I cannot tell you how much I am going to enjoy this."

"Jesus Christ, Stuart!" Brennan retorted. "You can't be ser . . ."

"Rick!" Sprague roared. "*Her* rightful master!"

Diana turned a ghostly pale, leaning heavily on Brennan.

"Oh, no," Rick said, leering. "You are mine. This pig has stolen what I alone can possess. His defeat is at hand."

"Listen, Stuart," Brennan started, trying to keep his voice steady. In fact, he was seizing up; the functions of rational thought shutting down. There was nothing rational about this. "I don't know why . . ."

Rick tensed with unbridled fury, raised the gun, and fired. Brennan was thrown away from Diana with the impact. The bullet caught him in the thigh and spun him into the stair banister behind. The shot, aimed at his crotch, missed by centimeters.

"Brian!" Diana screamed, throwing herself over him.

"Get up!" Sprague raged. He grabbed her by the hair and dragged her to her knees. "I am the one you love! Rick! Look at my love, bitch!" Gripping her hair furiously, he held her head inches away from him. Diana shut her eyes tightly, tears streaming from beneath closed lids. "Look!" he ranted. "*You-will-have-me!*"

Outside the house, Dante was about two-thirds of the way down the drive when he was brought up short by Diana's scream. Rosa was still on the radio. Diana must have seen Sprague, who could be inside by now. The fresh vision of the trooper with his brains all over the road pushed him to abandon caution. Ribs protesting the breathless exertion, he raced to the edge of the house. Panting, he leaned against the shingled exterior and chambered a round into his weapon. Easing the spare clip from his back pocket to just inside his waistband, he stood and listened. The night was filled with the summer sounds of crickets and the clanking of sailboat rigging on the breeze from the Sound. The adrenaline was pumping now; his entire body quivered slightly with the high. He worked to control his respiration, pushing it in and out in long, regular breaths.

The agitation of a muffled male voice came to him. Enraged shouting, breaking off abruptly. And then a shot, splitting the air around him. Instinctively, Dante dived onto his belly, grunting with the pain of impact. As he lay trying to sort out what had quickly become critical circumstances, Diana's next scream came shrill and clear.

"Brian!"

Out of the corner of his eye, he saw Rosa crouching low and coming quickly down the drive. Digging into his pocket, he extracted his key ring and signaled her with the miniflash.

Rosa was able to contact the State Police office thirty miles west on the Interstate. They were trying to raise any available units in the area. She had recradled the microphone and was in the midst of checking her revolver when the report of a gunshot came from the house. Her first thought was of her partner as she leaped from the seat of the cruiser and started down the driveway. Dante, spotting her, blinked to her from his position in the grass alongside the house.

"Brennan's hit," he hissed as she scrambled up to lie

beside him. "We've got to figure a way in there that won't make Diana next. Quick."

Rosa nodded. "He has to know that the State Police maintain contact with their men in the field."

Dante lay still a moment, thumb and forefinger squeezing the bridge of his nose, grimacing.

"We've got to make a perimeter check. Anything. An open window." He pointed toward the veranda side of the house. "I'll go this way and meet you around back."

When Brennan first hit the floor, Diana screaming hysterically above him, the sensation in his groin was just a dull warmth. It was as though his feet had been jerked from beneath him, toppling him backward. Now, lying there, he felt the wine he had drunk work with the stupor of shock to carry him along above what was becoming an agonizing burn. It was as though a hot ember sat on his inner thigh, searing his flesh. His body screamed out. Drifting on a roller coaster of muddled consciousness, his mind was somehow aloof.

The monster he knew as Stuart Sprague had Diana by the hair. With vicious pelvic thrusts, he was pushing himself in her face. In his fury, he jerked her head from side to side by the hair. Her body moved under his hand as if she were a stuffed toy.

Brian's mind struggled to make him move. To come to her aid. What came instead was a low, anguished groan. His groping hand slid in something wet and sticky. He worked to focus on it. He was wallowing in a pool of his own blood.

Joe Dante worked his way along the foundation past the front of the house. The big window angling southeast toward the Sound was a solid pane. The veranda was too chancy. Moving quickly past the stoop, he could see shadows beyond the faceted glass of the front door. Slipping around to the deck, he surveyed the shingles where Brennan had recently been at work scraping peeling paint and resealing. Just past the rail of the deck, a ladder lay alongside the wall. The balcony off Brennan's bedroom was bathed in moonlight. A screen door was closed against bugs, but the glass door beyond appeared to be ajar. It was his best shot. He scrambled on to find Rosa.

Diana, pushed to the limit of her mind's ability to process terror, withdrew inside herself. Deathly pale and eyes squeezed shut, she ceased to shed tears. She shut down. Sprague, unable to get the reaction he sought, was losing his erection. The excitement lay in feeling the trembling intensity of her fear. His power fed on it.

Brennan watched as the frenzied lunatic suddenly released her hair and backhanded her hard across the face.

"Cunt!" he bellowed. "Bitch! Whore!"

Diana, hitting the floor, curled into the fetal position. Blood streamed from a cut where his rings had torn her cheek. Sprague dropped to one knee beside her and grabbed the front of her blouse. He was wilting quickly now and frantic to restore the tension his power needed to prevail. With a jerk, he tore the light, blood-spattered cotton. Buttons popped.

Moving in the opposite direction around the house, Rosa came across a pair of big cellar doors. A cord of new firewood, dumped in a heap about ten feet away, seemed to be in the process of making its way below ground. The doors were not locked.

Dante found her examining the entrance to the basement.

"There's a ladder," he said. "Brennan's been working on the house. I can get onto his balcony."

"This is open," she told him. "Do you know where the basement stairs are, inside?"

"The kitchen," he said. "Just left of the refrigerator. I saw shadows inside the front door. I think they're in the entry hall. The stairs lead right down into it. And the dining room doors."

"I can get there through the kitchen," she said.

"All we have to worry about is cross fire," Dante said. He grabbed the handle and helped her with the storm door. It came up with a nasty grinding sound. They both froze an instant, holding their breaths. But from inside, they heard a sudden thump on the floor and a string of violent expletives.

"Set your watch," Dante told her, aiming his little light in a tight pool on the ground. He slipped his wrist into it and punched a button, stopping the sweep second hand. Rosa moved hers beside it.

"Three minutes," he told her. When her sweep hand crossed the top of the dial, he restarted his own. "Whoever gets the drop on him has to shoot to kill," he said. "Don't hesitate." Touching her reassuringly on the arm, he hurried off.

It was pitch-dark down there. Rosa picked her way carefully to avoid running into something and raising the alarm. Slowly, her eyes began to adjust. From the open door, moonlight filtered down, giving shape to larger objects. It smelled of mildew. Above her, the floor creaked. Scuffling movement was transmitted downward like the brushing on the head of a snare drum. Time became distended. How much had passed? She searched for the foot of the stairs, eager to gain the well-lit kitchen. Her groping hand finally fell on the newel post. Setting a foot firmly on the first tread, she slid her hand up the banister.

Brennan was lingering on the edge of passing out for good. The loss of blood was making him light-headed. On the floor just feet away, Sprague, with his considerable upper-body strength, pried Diana's arms from her breasts and planted a knee on her abdomen. Grunting and sweating profusely, he swung himself into a sitting position above her and reached into his boot.

The day had been long and much too arduous for a man recuperating from Joe Dante's kind of wounds. Even with the daily hiking up and down the beach, he lacked anything approaching normal stamina. He felt the fatigue deep in his bones. Moving the extension ladder into position, straining to prevent it from banging against the house, was an act of sheer will. He was drenched in sweat and breathing hard. He checked to insure it was firmly planted, then scrambled upward. Sammy, the dead troopers, Jill, the whores, and the screams of anguish from inside drove him now. These, and pure hatred.

Eight people murdered in cold blood. Due process had nothing to do with how he felt. There was only one process.

At the lip of the balcony's shingled balustrade, he caught hold, thought through the pain of his aching ribs, and scrambled over. Unwilling to risk the telltale squeak of the screen door hinges, he opened his penknife and ripped a large hole in the mesh. In another few seconds, he was inside and moving across the master bedroom.

THIRTY-THREE

The blade of Rick's knife glittered in his hand. All over his body, muscles trembled, releasing and contracting. The heat at the base of his skull was white-hot. It flowed downward, directing the responses of his heart, his lungs, his belly, and his power. Burning clear down his spine, it throbbed.

Ungrateful bitch! He alone had made her who she was.

She refused his offering. He would break the spell. Purify her. Teach her to obey him. He stared at the distorted reflection of himself in the blade, thighs tensing against her flanks. She sensed the moment, eyes coming open to stare. They fixed on the blade. She would see her reflection as he saw his. They were together in the knife. Beneath him, he felt her body go hard in terror. The memory of the other times, of her fighting against him, flooded back. He began to grin. Ecstasy.

* * *

When she reached the kitchen, Rosa checked her watch. Two minutes and five seconds had elapsed. An eternity. Moving quickly, she crossed to the dining room and peered in through a small pane in the swinging door. The doors into the foyer stood open. She could make out Brian lying sprawled on the parquet at the foot of the stairs. There was a lot of blood on the floor and smeared across the wainscoting. The muddled shadows of movement played across the walls. Sprague had to be around the corner, just out of sight.

Applying slow, even pressure to the swinging door, she inched it open. The center of the room ahead was occupied by a clean-lined, Chippendale mahogany table and chairs. A large silver candelabra stood undisturbed amid them. But across the polished floor in front of the door, she could see large drips of blood already drying. Easing into the room, she hugged the walls, circling toward the foyer. Grunts and scrapings on the floor just beyond the door came to her. She listened hard for any noise from above. Nothing. She could only assume that Joe had made it in. Otherwise, she was on her own. Crouching in position just behind the doorjamb, she slowly eased back the hammer on her revolver and watched the sweep hand on her watch. Twenty seconds.

Brennan watched mesmerized from his fog. Far off in some detached place, he knew things were happening very quickly. But there on the floor, time stood still. As if in slow motion, Sprague planted the fist holding the knife. He steadied himself with it on the floor as he pushed himself prone onto Diana. Her eyes were open now, following his as he lowered to press against her. With the elbow of his gun hand supporting him, he slowly pulled the knife in toward her. When the point of it pricked her side, she finally decided to fight for her life.

* * *

Dante reached his position of attack with nearly a minute to spare. Crouching there, he strained to hear what was going on directly below. A man's heavy breathing and strained grunts carried up the stairwell. The adrenaline began to flow with purpose again, lifting him to a level of hyperalertness. Crouching, he shifted the automatic to his left hand, opening and closing the right to increase circulation and burn off tension. Every fiber of his body focused on the seconds ahead. He picked his stair treads, deciding which foot to launch from. Mentally, he tracked his sweep of the target area. As the second hand moved toward the final quarter minute, he took a long breath and exhaled. In the middle of it, Diana let go with a bloodcurdling scream.

Rosa reacted instinctively. Jumping the timetable by ten seconds, she launched herself into the doorway, gun coming around. Sprague was on top of a half-naked Diana, riding his wave of domination as she fought his knife. Startled, the killer rolled to his left, bringing his pistol up as he moved. Rosa wasted a precious half second steadying herself, drawing a bead. As the revolver jerked in her hand, she was lifted off her feet and slammed back into the doorjamb, mouth opening in surprise. She thought frantically that she should have better control of her weapon. The floor came up at her, knocking the wind from her lungs.

Dante made it to the turn in the stairs in time to see Sprague roll and fire. Rosa, already through the door, took a balancing step while she found the target and aimed. Both guns went off, Sprague beating her to the mark. Her shot went wide, missing his head by inches. She took his slug down low in the right hip. Hurled backward, she bounced off the doorway and went down.

All this was absorbed peripherally. Dante was planting and swinging the Walther into line with the target. He squeezed the trigger and the gun jerked in his hands. The bullet took Sprague in the right shoulder, too high to do much damage. Bringing his weapon quickly back into line, he fired again. The second shot seemed to hit the man square in the chest. But already Sprague was scrambling for cover. Jerking as the shots hit him, he continued his progress almost unimpeded. Dante fired a third time, and this shot smashed into the woodwork as Sprague disappeared down the far hall.

"Rosa!" Dante yelled, hurrying across the blood-spattered foyer. Gore was everywhere.

"Get him, Joe!" Rosa gasped through clenched teeth. "I'll be okay."

Dante moved out in pursuit, staying low and hugging the wall of the hall leading back to the big guest bedroom and deck beyond.

Wounded and moving on instinct and adrenaline now, Rick stumbled down the hall to a room with a large four-poster bed. Beyond it, he could see the moonlight streaming in through a pair of locked French doors. Lowering a shoulder, he hurled himself across the room, covering his face with his arm as he launched through the glass. Tripping as he emerged on the other side, he fell and cut himself on the scattered shards.

"Keep moving," the little voice urged. The hot flush of dominance and desire had become icy, and the cold was turning the sweat clammy inside the leather. It mixed with the warmth of his own blood. A dark, purplish hole was bored in his breastbone. He clamped a hand over it as he struggled to his feet, across the deck, and down onto the lawn. There was a squat, low building ahead. Using the shadows, he might make it there and hide. He was taking huge gulps of air to get enough oxygen.

The moon reached its zenith. Slowly approaching the end of the hall, Dante heard the shattering of glass beyond. Sprague had broken out. When he reached the bedroom, he hurried to the French doors. A light breeze billowed the curtains. Bits of broken glass lay scattered across the hardwood floor and onto the oriental rug. Peering out over the deck, he saw the shadowy figure of Sprague hobbling across the lawn toward the foundry. Steadying himself, he took aim. In the dark, at that distance, it wasn't much of a bet. He fired. Sprague stumbled, rolled as he went down, and was just as quickly on his feet again. This time he was limping as he closed on the shed door.

"Goddamn, you bastard!" Dante seethed in disbelief. This wasn't possible. He'd hit him three times. Once with a shot he couldn't hope to better. And still, the son of a bitch was on his feet.

As Sprague reached the shed, Dante moved out across the deck, crouching to present a low profile. Brennan's pickup sat parked about fifty feet away, uphill and about the same distance from the foundry. From behind it, he could cover the outbuilding's only two entrances and one window. Sprague had run into a trap.

Leaping onto the lawn, Dante raced for it.

From the safety of his new cover, crouched behind the big mullioned window, Rick surveyed the moonlit landscape. A figure was jumping from the deck and running for the old pickup truck. Breaking out a pane with his gun butt, he drew bead and squeezed off two rounds. The figure continued moving to the cover of the truck.

Rick lowered the Browning in disgust and began to survey the damage. His right calf felt as though it were on fire. The boot was warm and close as his blood filled it. His shoulder was bad but still did not prevent him from using the gun. The worst was the wound in his chest. He could feel the ache deep in there, making it difficult to breathe. If he were to escape, he would have to finish this pursuing demon soon. Dante. The name tasted of bile in his mouth as he tried to tongue around it. They met again.

The forces were stronger now. Ever since he was a boy, he had felt them. Battled them. His life had been a war against them. To prevail. To feel the heat of love. To master weakness and beauty. Yes, the forces were stronger than ever. But he would win. Even now.

THIRTY-FOUR

Between the deck and the truck, bullets scattered gravel in front of and behind the sprinting detective. Two quick reports followed on their heels. Slumping to the drive behind the Dodge, Dante winced in agony, the ribs screaming at him now. He knew that with all this activity, he might have refractured a bone not completely knit. Not good. A cleanly broken rib could puncture and collapse a lung. He lay there, trying to catch his breath. Another bullet thudded into the bed of the truck.

It was at least a minute before Dante shoved himself upright and peered around the rear bumper to survey the building. Built from rough cedar planking and battens, it was a low, simple affair. Between the main double doors and the back door serving as separate entrance to the drawing studio, a covered tank ran beneath the big window. Its roof was waist-high, just below the sill, and covered with wooden shingles. The tank held propane for the kiln and the bronze furnace.

"All right, scum ball," Dante whispered. "It's just you and me now."

Scrambling back along the side of the truck, he opened the door and tilted the seat forward. It was too much to hope for a gas can. But an empty beer bottle . . . anything. Instead, he found oily rags, a can of multigrade, a towing chain, jumper cables, road flares. No empty bottles or cans.

His mind worked back to the flares. They weren't the Molotov cocktail of his dreams, but they just might work.

Pushing the seat back, he slid beneath the dash and groped for the ignition wires. Tearing them loose, he bared the ends with his teeth and twisted them together. Key circumvented, he depressed the button on the floorboard, pumping the gas pedal with his other hand. As soon as the started motor ground over, the windshield exploded above him. His efforts proved to be of little avail. The engine failed to so much as cough.

Of course. A smart assailant would have disabled any means of escape before mounting his attack. Dante pounded his fist on the drive train hump, cursing under his breath. Slowly, he slid back out onto the drive.

Brennan's property ran on a steep incline down the drive to the house and then leveled out more or less as it approached the bluff to the sea. Dante surveyed the topography and wondered. Would it roll that far? Or at least far enough? Reaching back into the cab, he cranked hard on the steering wheel, lining up the front tires. Inch at a time, they came around.

With the hand brake off, Dante leaned a shoulder into the doorpost. Pushing, he got it to move far enough to necessitate moving his back foot forward. And again. Slowly, the old Dodge picked up momentum.

* * *

Inside the foundry, Rick finished a survey of his surroundings and came up empty when he noticed the truck starting to roll toward him.

What was he doing?

He had to stop it. With the Browning now shaking in his unsteady hand, he took aim at the tires. The first shot hit metal, the sizzle of its ricochet audible to him. He fired again, unsure of the bullet's effect. Aiming a third time, he pulled the trigger. Nothing. Thinking the gun had misfired, he pulled the trigger a fourth time.

It was out of ammunition.

He watched as the truck continued to roll toward him on the moonlit drive. But . . . the old junker was slowing down. He'd done it! The left front tire was going flat.

Dante was lying flat in the bed of the truck when it began to list slowly toward the driver's side and stop. After two shots, the gunfire stopped. The calm was eerie. Inching up, he took a peek.

The gas tank lay dead ahead, perhaps twenty feet away. He could make out a darkened recess beneath its belly. It presented no more than six or eight inches of clearance from the ground. Tearing at the first flare, he removed the striker cap and worked it against the body as if lighting a giant match. On the third try, it caught.

Twenty feet. He measured off the trajectory in his mind. Gripping the cylinder down low, he took a deep breath and let fly. Without looking to see where it landed, he lit another. Before throwing it, he peeked again. Not bad. It lay almost directly beneath the tank, just a little short. Increasing his thrust, he heaved again. This time he hit the mark. The flare rolled deep under the tank, dead center. In succession, the other two flares followed it.

How long it would take for the heat to reach the critical point was anyone's guess. But twenty feet was too close. Scrambling, he bailed out over the tailgate and crawled away in the truck's direct line of cover. No more shots were fired. Out of range, he lay on the lawn, too exhausted now to move. In the far distance, he thought he could barely make out the wail of sirens. Inside the house, Rosa was down. God knew what had happened to Diana and how badly Brennan was wounded. Minutes ticked by. He stared at the moon.

Rick crouched huddled beside the sill of the window. Blood flowed freely from his wounds now. He was feeling giddy; the breath rattled in his chest. He coughed, and blood bubbled from his mouth. It was getting increasingly hard to pull air into his lungs. His right leg and arm were both numb.

Dante had thrown flares beneath the window. Why? He could not even see them from where he crouched. Just the top of a narrow little shingled roof. The smoke from them curled up through the broken window and burned the inside of his nose. He was racked with a great, gurgling cough. Outside, the red glare lit the landscape.

Dante was still staring at the moon when the tank disintegrated in one instantaneous whoosh of fire. The concussion blew the foundry off its concrete slab foundation. Everything in the path of the giant fireball incinerated. The sirens were much closer now. The detective struggled to his feet, squinted hard at the inferno, and moved toward the house.

God, he ached. Every breath was difficult to pull now. His eyes were barely able to focus on his surroundings. Tired. All he wanted was to shut his eyes. To sleep. A delirium swept over him. He giggled. Who was more insane? A guy like Stuart Sprague or people like him and Rosa? It was like trying to hold back the sea. A Dutch boy, with his finger in the dike. Extending an index finger, he poked at the air ahead of him and crumpled to the drive.

THIRTY-FIVE

A bright light bit through his eyelids. Opening them, he tried to focus. The vague shape of someone in white stood at his feet, arms outstretched. The image hardened. A nurse, matronly, maybe late forties, was raising the shade. Brilliant sunlight flooded into the room. A pastel, peach-colored room.

Joe Dante tried to say something. The inside of his mouth was dry and cottony. It came out as a rasping croak. The nurse turned and smiled.

"Good afternoon. I thought you were going to sleep the whole day away."

Dante tried again. "Where am I?"

"Lawrence Memorial Hospital. New London."

He tried to sit up, groaned, and collapsed back on the pillow.

"Careful," the nurse warned. "You've refractured three ribs and had some internal bleeding. Do you feel up to a couple of visitors?"

"My partner," he asked. "How is she?"

The nurse smiled and opened the odor. "He's awake, Inspector."

Gus Lieberman ambled into the room. He dragged a chair to the side of the bed and sat.

"Rosa, Gus. How is she?"

The inspector looked long and hard at him, shaking his head. A smile began to curl the corners of his mouth.

"She lost some blood and will have a nice scar, but she's fine, hotshot. You sure got a knack for sniffing out the shit in this world, Detective."

"I got him, Gus. Blew his ass all over Long Island Sound. Stuart Sprague. You believe it?"

Lieberman nodded. "I do now. You broke every rule in the book doing it, Joe. Now they're out there making you a hero. The Webster broad says he was a quarter inch from running that pig sticker right through her when you blew him halfway down the hall."

"You gave me a job to do," Dante said. "Now I want you to get me a wheelchair. Last time I saw a certain lady cop, she was having trouble with her wristwatch."

It wasn't until that evening that an insistent Joe Dante was wheeled down two corridors and into Rosa Losada's room. He found her sitting upright in bed, watching a detective show on television. Her hand went to her hair, and she colored self-consciously.

"I must look awful," she said.

"You look beautiful," he said. "You're alive."

She reached for the remote control and switched off the televison. "They almost lost Brian last night. He came just minutes away from bleeding to death."

"I heard. I guess they've got him in intensive care. Diana's okay though. Came to see me about an hour ago."

"Me, too."

An uneasy silence ensued. Dante finally broke it, clearing his throat.

"Gus says I'm being assigned to the academy for awhile, as soon as I do my six months."

"How do you feel about it?" Rosa asked.

He shrugged. "Might be best, for awhile. It's good duty. The only question I have is how long I'll be able to stand it before I'm bored crapless." Looking hard at her, he got fidgety all of a sudden. "I've, uh, been thinking," he said. "If you're pulling an assignment to the Sixth, it's sort of crazy to commute all the way from Brooklyn when . . ." he stopped, unable to complete the sentence.

"When you live just two blocks away?" she asked. "I don't know, Joe. I'll have to think about it." She couldn't suppress the grin spreading across her face.

Dante decided to risk breathing again. "You know," he said, looking out her window at the bright summer day, "somewhere during the time I was out, I had this weird dream. I was back in uniform, walking the streets. It was that stretch of Forty-second between Times Square and Eighth."

Rosa nodded. "Midtown South."

"Yeah. It has to be. And there was this tide of whores, pimps, and pushers. I'd chase one off, turn around, and there'd be two in their place. They were *multiplying*. I started feeling like I was suffocating. It was the same sensation I had last night, before I passed out in Brennan's driveway."

He stopped to stare back out the window.

"Jesus. It isn't just the Tenth or the Twenty-fifth. It's the whole goddamn job that's crazy. Midtown South. That's weird. I wonder why there."

Shrugging, Rosa reached to touch his arm. "Maybe because Midtown South is the whole job in a nutshell."

He shook his head. "What are we doing, Rosa? Does anyone actually think we can win out there?"

She thought a moment. "No," she replied. "We just help even the odds a little."

Dante turned from the window to smile at her. It all hurt. Turning. Smiling. Thinking about the dream. Midtown South. Evening the odds. He made a mental note to call his neighbor and ask her to feed the cat.

ABOUT THE AUTHOR

MIDTOWN SOUTH is Christopher Newman's first novel. He lives in New York City.